The Three Baers

Book One

Baer Truth

By

Jocie McKade

Dedication

A dream can't come true without inspiration. This book is the culmination of many beautiful souls who have blessed my life.

To my mom – her love of books began my journey.

To my amazing husband. You listened to a lot of truly awful plots, ate a lot of frozen micro-waved dinners, and smiled at all the right places. Thanks for holding my hand on the journey.

To my beautiful daughters. You patiently waited while I excitedly finished a sentence, and nodded that you liked it, even if you didn't. You brought me brownies when I received rejections, and you cheered when I was accepted. Thank you for believing in me.

To my big sis. The stories began long ago, the words tangled throughout life, the plot continues. I only hope Hollywood thinks this book should be a movie too!

To my readers.......without you there are literally no words. Thank you.

Also by Jocie McKade

Heart River Inn
A romantic comedy

High Frequency
Book One - Between the Lines Humorous Mystery

Low Voltage
Book Two - Between the Lines Humorous Mystery

Roped In
Short Story

Time Out of Darkness
Anthology

Granite Rose
Historical

The Three Bears Trilogy
Romantic comedy series

Baer Truth
Baer Necessities
Baer Facts

Chapter One

Her teeth chattered, her feet were numb, and her hair was a stiff halo of frozen spikes. She shivered as she stared into the window of the cozy cafe. Lace curtains outlined the large window, with *McIvey's Cafe* painted in a happy, red semi-circle of block letters on the glass. The aroma of hot coffee lingered in the cold Wyoming air.

Abby's stomach growled. How many times had she taken a meal for granted? How she longed to walk inside, order eggs, and toast slathered with jelly, and sip on a cup of hot black coffee. She didn't have enough for a glass of water, let alone a meal.

It was mid-day and only two well-used pickup trucks sat parked in the snow-covered lot. Abby struggled to keep her hand from trembling as she reached for the door handle. The cold was easy; humbling herself for a meal wasn't.

Abby squinted back tears, peering through the door. Inside was a long counter with a green melamine countertop. The barstool seats matched the bar top's green color. The floor was black and white checkered linoleum with the black tiles looking closer to gray from years of mopping. Eight booths ringed the edge of the room with six tables scattered in the middle. What the place lacked in fashionable décor, it made up for in warmth. Only two men were inside, a customer and the cook.

Abby knew all about being humbled. She had begged her mother not to leave. She had begged the mortgage company for one more month -- hell, she'd practically told the man she'd sleep with him to save her grandmother's house. She'd literally gotten on her knees with the cold-hearted bastard at the cemetery. The only place she hadn't been humbled was in Billy's huge RV -- the one place she refused to be.

Now, here she was, about to humble herself for a meal.

Her feet ached. Not only were they freezing, but she'd picked yesterday to wear her only pair of designer stilettos. The gorgeous orange heels made her outfit rock, but they definitely had not been made for walking miles in the snow.

Yesterday, she had been heading for bigger things; today she was frozen, broke, and hungry, stranded in some backcountry town in the middle of nowhere. What was the worst that could happen? Before she let her mind wander to those crappy places, she took in a deep breath of frigid air and pushed open the door. The door was hard and heavy, just like her heart had become.

Conversation between the two men at the counter stopped instantly, as they both stared at her. Their eyes passed over her like cold water. In this cafe, in this state, she was an outsider -- punk rocker scum in the middle of conservative family values, and she didn't look very family friendly. She was the girl these people warned their kids about. If only she wasn't so desperate, so hungry.

The customer slowly sat his coffee cup down, completely missing the saucer.

"Ma'am?" The man behind the counter wiped his hands on a dishtowel, standing up straight and giving her a long, hard look.

She couldn't stop shaking. Her teeth chattered and her bare hands were a vibrant red and looked frost-bitten.

"Can I help you?" The man behind the counter had a gentle voice. He was tall and slender, with a military buzz-cut that middle age had streaked silver. Jade-green eyes twinkled at her behind a scrutinizing squint. A white apron clung around his neck and waist and a blue flannel shirt poked out from underneath.

So far, they hadn't called for the townspeople with pitchforks. She might have a chance. Plastering a smile on her frozen face, she walked toward the counter, her orange stilettos clicking with each step. Both men cocked their heads to one side, looking down at those shoes as if they'd never seen such things before.

If her feet weren't so damn frozen, she would have added a strut. Since she couldn't feel much of anything from her ankles down though, she hobbled on the slabs of frozen toes and sat stiffly on a barstool. "I have a little -- uh -- problem." She couldn't back down now -- she didn't have a choice. She sniffled a bit for effect then blurted everything out at once. "Look mister, I've just walked here from the Dermont County line and I don't have a dime to my name." Another sniffle came on cue, although her uncontrollable shivering was real.

The men gave her and her orange heels another shocked look. A hard shiver nearly shook her off the barstool. Abby wrapped her arms around herself, trying to warm up. "If you'd let me wash dishes or sweep up for a meal I'd be very grateful."

"Here, lady, I'll buy you dinner," the customer offered, angling his body to one side and pulling his wallet out of a back pocket.

"I can work." She still had some pride left. She might be broke, but as long as she could work, Abby Clark wasn't about to take a handout. "Would you be willing to let me do that?" she asked the man behind the counter. The warm air in the café brought back a little feeling to her face and her eyes began to water.

He smiled, holding out a hand. "I'm George McIvey, owner of this cafe. What might your name be?"

"My name is Abby Clark." She returned his handshake and he winced. Abby pulled away, tucking her hands inside her thin jacket.

George poured a cup of coffee for himself and then sat a cup in front of her. "Don't suppose you can cook?"

"Actually, I'm a very good cook." She forced a smile through frozen lips. A shiver lingered as she remembered making her grandmother pancakes smothered with blueberries. Then the steam and aroma from the cup captured her attention.

"Well, Abby Clark, if you'll cook today for the dinner crowd, you're welcome to a meal or two." He pushed the cup toward her, and winked. "And if you're as good a cook as you say, you might just have yourself a job."

"Thank you Mr. McIvey." She fought to keep her teeth from chattering.

"Just call me George and don't thank me. You haven't seen the dinner crowd yet." He and the customer at the counter both laughed. "There's a bathroom in the back. Get yourself dried off and warmed up. I'll fix you some eggs and toast. You'll find an apron in the storeroom and if you'll look around, there are probably some dry socks and--" he gave her orange stilettos another glance-- "a sensible pair of boots."

She smiled, rose slowly from the stool, and walked, stiff-legged, into the back room.

"Was her hair purple?" Abby heard the man snicker as she left the room. "Did you see that her vest was held together with safety pins? Pitiful, just pitiful. Where you reckon she came from?"

She stood in the doorway just out of their sight, listening. Plucking at a safety pin, she looked down at her ratty clothes. *Damn,* she thought, *it's a wonder they even let me in the door.*

"That county line is a good hour walk from here. The lady's got some brass balls to walk that far in this cold." George's grill sizzled. "Imagine walking that far in those go-to-hell heels and not a coat or gloves to be seen."

The bathroom was sparse, but clean. She found a brush and managed to tuck her hair into a makeshift ponytail. Washing her face, she stared at her reflection. "You've done it this time Abby. Some day you'll learn to just shut up and check your temper." Yesterday wasn't that day, and today she was paying for it all.

Sitting in the corner of the storage room was the pair of cowboy boots he'd told her about. Pulling the stiletto heels off was damn painful. Her feet were numb from cold, swollen from walking, and wet from the snow. She dried the shoes with a paper towel, setting them carefully out of view.

Surprisingly, the boots fit pretty well even over her cold feet. She tucked in her tangerine orange blouse, straightened her shoulders, sucked up what pride she had left, and walked back into the café.

"Well, you look much better all dried off," George commented. "You want your eggs over-medium? That's how I fix them, over-medium."

"Any way will be just fine."

He sat the plate of eggs, bacon, and toast in front of her. She pushed the bacon off to the side, and dug in to the toast and eggs.

"The bacon not to your liking?"

"I'm sure they're fine. I just don't eat meat," she mumbled between bites.

George's left eyebrow raised high above his eye. "You're kidding?"

"You one of them vegetarians?" The customer stared at her like a prize zoo exhibit.

She nodded, downing the cup of coffee and devouring what was, without a doubt, the best meal of her entire life.

Abby had seen their looks many times. No one believed you could live life without a slab of meat a day. Now here she was in the middle of cattle country, professing her vegetarianism. Some day she'd just learn to say she had freakin' allergies.

"Well, George, I'd best be getting home before Betty has my hide."

"Careful out there, Henry. Those roads are getting slippery."

Henry popped a bright red ball cap on his head. The tall, black letters read *Childers Farm Implements*. Then he pulled on a heavy canvas jacket, threw some change down on the counter, and tipped the brim of his cap toward Abby. "Good luck to you, miss."

Abby gave him a slight smile. He pulled up the collar of his jacket, bracing against the onslaught of cold wind.

"Well," George said and yawned, then scraped the grease off his grill, "you all done eating?"

She nodded that she was but kept drinking the coffee.

"You want another cup?"

"No," Abby answered, not wanting to push George's generosity.

George looked at the clock on the wall. "It's four-thirty." Abby followed his gaze to an old, aluminum clock shaped like a diner car. The face was cracked and the aluminum dulled from years of greasy residue on its surface. It hung slightly crooked on the wall. From the look of the fixtures, McIvey's Café had probably been around since the 1950's. What it lacked in fashionable décor, it made up for in warmth. There were checkered curtains in the windows and bright blue tablecloths on the small tables. Pretty blue and white silk flowers filled small glass vases on the tables, and jars of candy lined the counter where the cash register stood.

"It's Friday and the boys will be straggling in by about five-thirty." George popped a toothpick out of the dispenser, chewing it from one side his mouth to the other. "Let me show you around the kitchen, so you'll know where everything is when all hell breaks loose."

Slowly, Abby set the coffee cup down.

He chuckled. "Don't fret. The boys are just an assortment of cowhands and ranch boys. Most of them ain't married. There ain't a lot of women out here, you know." He gave her a long look, then cleared his throat. "So they come here for supper, at least on Friday and Saturday nights. There'll be about twenty to thirty of them. If it's been a hard week, like this one with the snow and all, well there's liable to be sixty straggling in through the evening. Mrs. McIvey should be in shortly. I'll help you cook and wait tables, and she'll be running the cash register."

He threw the toothpick into the trash. "I hope you're as good as say you are. Because there's a lot of cooking to do and the boys around here, they like meat. Will that be a problem for you?"

"I worked my way through college as a short order cook. Just because I'm a vegetarian doesn't mean the whole world is. It's been a few years, but I think I can handle it." She forced a smile, praying she could.

He chuckled again. "These cowboys are a lot different than those college boys."

The back door opened in a rush. A woman in beige canvas bibs, overcoat, and knee-high green boots stomped inside.

"Well, Mrs. McIvey, I'm glad the cold didn't keep you home." George's eyes lit up at the sight of her. His shoulders straightened and a smile stretched wide across his face as hurried toward her.

"Since when has the cold, the heat, or a plague of grasshoppers kept me from getting to work?" She shook her head, frowning at him.

He lifted the coat from her shoulders, and hung it on a hook near the back door. "We had a heck of a grasshopper blight just two years ago," George explained, then stepped back and introduced them. "This is my wife, Maragret McIvey."

The woman took in a long, deep breath, looking at Abby like she was a wet, lost puppy.

"Just Margaret, dear. He just likes to hear his last name. He's done it for years. I swear I don't understand why. It sounds like some drunk Irishman mumbling." Unfastening her bibs, she pulled them off and handed them to George.

Margaret McIvey was a pretty woman, solidly built. Short, brown, curly hair framed her face. Her eyes were bright green and surrounded by feathery laugh lines. As she pulled her jean legs down over her boots, she glanced curiously at Abby. Fortunately, her smile seemed to be kind.

"Seems Abby needed a meal and she's willing to cook." George winked at Margaret. "What do you think?"

"Any way I can get you out of this kitchen so the customers don't threaten to sue us, I'm all for it. Did you show her around the kitchen yet? You know them boys are going to be showing up soon." She didn't wait for him to answer. "Come on, Abby, let me show you around."

The *boys* had begun arriving, and they had arrived hungry. She'd never seen so many cowboys in her life. Actually, she'd never seen a real cowboy before. She felt like she'd fallen into a bad rerun of Bonanza. They smelled like horses, looked like canvas-wrapped hotdogs, and ate like Marines.

Cooking over the grill, Abby was as hot tonight as she'd been cold last night. The grill had been at full capacity since five o'clock. It had been a long time since she'd cooked this much food, and she fumbled on occasion.

A customer yelled across the counter, "Dang, George, did Margaret finally buy you a cookbook?"

"You're doing a good job, honey." Margaret smiled as she picked up another order. "They're asking for seconds. That ain't never happened in this restaurant before." She laughed, carrying the plates out of the kitchen.

Abby nodded. It had been a long time since she'd received a compliment of any kind.

"All right, Mrs. McIvey, that's enough out of you." George snapped a towel at Margaret's behind as she walked through the opening in the counter.

Abby set two more steaming plates on the serving shelf that divided the kitchen from the dining room. She took in a deep, tired breath, as twelve more men walked in the door. Three men sat at the counter while the rest of the customers huddled in booths, eating and having conversations. There weren't any women in the diner -- they were all probably back at the ranch, stuck behind one those massive snowdrifts. It was nearly eight o'clock at night and the café was still full.

"Well, good evening, Joe." George poured a steamy cup of coffee for a man who'd just sat at the counter. "You don't look very happy tonight."

"I'm a long way from happy. Some son-of-a-bitch trashed my cattle barn."

Abby's heart jumped. She jerked her head back inside the small serving window. Leaning against the window frame, she sneaked a peek out at the man. His black hat sat back off his forehead. He threw his leather gloves onto the counter.

"What happened?" George added a napkin and tableware set beside the coffee cup.

"I was grabbing some hay from my barn down by Larken Ridge. It's a mess. It looks like a wild cow spent the night in the place. A dozen hay bales are on the floor split open, and the barn door was left open so another dozen bales got wet from last night's snow." He cautiously sipped the hot coffee. "If I catch the squatter, I'll string him up."

Abby swallowed hard, pulling back inside the safety of the kitchen. She dinged the bell to signal for Margaret to pick up.

"Anything stolen?" George asked, as Abby strained to listen.

"No. This is really good coffee. Did you make this?"

"George, more coffee over here, and can I get another meatloaf special?"

"I'm coming, I'm coming." He shook his head and walked through the swinging door into the kitchen. "Abby, honey, you want a job?"

She stopped in mid-burger flip. "I need one, Mr. McIvey." She never thought she'd be so grateful to be slinging beef, of all things. All she could see were those big, brown eyes, long eyelashes, soft fur, and endearing moos of cows. She took in a deep breath as the patty seared on the grill. Choices couldn't always be made by your conscience -- sometimes they were made from sheer desperation.

"It's yours. I need more coffee." He handed her an empty coffeepot and grabbed the full pot off the burner, taking it into the dining room.

The burger hit the grill and sizzled. It felt good not to be completely desperate. Damn Billy Butcher, she'd make it in spite of him. Abby peered through the small serving window, smiling at the cowboys as they quietly and happily ate. Her eyes landed on the cowboy named Joe. The very *angry* cowboy. Denim-blue eyes froze on her as he glared at her over the rim of his coffee cup.

One thing Abby Clark had never been able to do was lie without being caught. If she stayed in the kitchen, maybe he wouldn't suspect she was the one who'd been in his barn. Her face always gave her away. Guilt would cover her face like a shadow. As a kid, her grandmother would always spot any lie she told, "I see it in your eyes Abby, you just can't hide a lie."

She made up more plates of meatloaf specials. Would he really be that upset? She'd only slept in there trying to stay warm in the horrible cold. She certainly hadn't "trashed" his barn. Where did he get off with that comment? Then again, she couldn't remember if she had closed the barn door when she left.

Abby rang the bell and allowed herself another quick look. The pissed off cowboy was a handsome man, with thick black hair and wide shoulders. He stared up at the window, a harsh, glowering stare that intimidated the hell out of her. She eased back into the protection of the kitchen.

"All right, George, who are you holding hostage in the kitchen?" A tall, geeky cowboy whipped open the kitchen door. "Howdy, I'm Fred Gillis."

Abby jumped at his sudden entrance. Fred was tall with a long nose and wide mouth that smiled into a crooked kind of grin. His chin jutted out just a bit farther than it should, and his Adam's apple looked like it was going to bust right through his skin.

"Fred." She nodded, pulling a stack of plates off the shelf above the grill.

"Dang, I've never seen a lady with purple hair before." He propped the kitchen door open with a cowboy-booted foot. "Are you the cook?"

"Yes." She pulled a roast out of the oven.

He waited for her to set the hot pan on the counter. Then he grabbed her oven-mitted hand and yanked her out of the kitchen into the dining room.

"This is the cook!" he yelled across the room. All heads rose and all eating stopped as they stared at her. She waved an oven-mitted hand, trying to break loose from Fred's grip. It was obvious this crowd didn't get many punk-rocker types in this town. The wide eyes, the gasps, and the dropped forks on plates were nothing compared to the whispering.

"Keep this one, George." Fred gave her a good, solid pat on the back. Losing her balance, she stumbled forward and the oven mitt flew off her hand. It sailed like a finely balanced, balsa wood model plane over the counter, smacking Joe Baer across the face, and crash landing in his steaming hot cup of coffee.

The hot brew shot straight up with the fury of Old Faithful, spewing the cowboy with a caffeine shower from neck to crotch. Joe slid backward on the barstool as it cascaded toward his crotch. His butt slid too far, sending him completely off the stool, crashing with a thud on the floor.

Laughter and snorts filled the café. Joe inhaled sharply and cussed under his breath. With a hard jerk, Abby pulled away from Fred, fleeing into the kitchen before her face betrayed her.

The evening droned on. Slap a burger on the grill, slice the roast, make a sandwich, fry the bacon -- all became automatic rituals.

Abby poured herself a glass of water after she'd finished the last order, glancing out the window into the diner. Joe and his angry stare had left. Two men remained in a booth talking quietly over coffee. Margaret and George were at the far end of the counter in deep conversation. Every once in awhile, they glanced toward the kitchen. Did she still have a job? While she was grateful for their compassion, it was humbling to be on the receiving end of such graciousness. Abby pulled up the apron hem, wiping the sweat from her face.

"Abby?" Margaret walked into the kitchen and hesitated. "Abby? Do you have a place to stay tonight?"

A tight knot of desperation lodged in Abby's throat. "Well, actually, no, I don't."

"What happened?" Margaret poured herself a cup of coffee, looking at Abby with a mix of pity and compassion.

Damn how she hated to be looked at with such pity, like a charity case. Abby filled her glass with more water, pulled the grease-stained apron off, and leaned against the counter. She was, dear heaven, she was a charity case.

"I'm a back-up singer for a rock band." Abby sipped on the water. Her recent past wasn't very attractive. She had ended up at a place she never dreamed she would. Her grandmother would have been ashamed of what Abby had become. She pushed the tears back. "At least I was until yesterday. We were heading for Los Angeles, playing gigs between Chicago and L.A. Well, Billy Butcher, the asshole lead singer of this band, decided I was not just his backup singer, but his property."

Margaret's eyes softened with compassion. She must have heard a few sob stories before.

"I decided he didn't pay me enough to tumble in his bed," Abby continued. "So, I kicked him in the fucking balls. He had his bodyguards drag me screaming off the damn bus and throw me onto the highway. My clothes, my purse, hell, Margaret everything I own is still on that bus. The only thing I have is my driver's license and a security pass to get into the concert hall." She put the glass into the dishwasher and sighed heavily. "I guess I should have picked a better place to fight back. I just want to thank you and Mr. McIvey for letting me have a hot meal."

"You more than earned your meal, dear." Margaret stared into the depths of her coffee, and cleared her throat. "If I could give you a friendly piece of advice, lighten up on the cussing. Folks around here don't particularly like it, especially coming from a lady." She glanced over the rim of the cup at Abby. "I can't believe he dumped you way out here."

Hanging out in bars, stadiums and with road crews night after night, Abby had somewhat numbed herself to the use of curse words. They had become a part of her vocabulary. She would never have used language like that in front of her grandmother. A wave of sadness curled in the pit of her stomach.

"Just where is 'out here', anyway?" Abby smiled, changing the subject. "I know I'm in Wyoming, but would you mind telling me where in Wyoming?"

Margaret laughed. "If you'll look out in the corner of the cafe you'll see the official post office logo. We are the post office for Sentinel, Wyoming. The closest town of any size is Lander, about twenty miles east."

She pulled a wooden folding chair from against the far wall, handed it to Abby, and grabbed one for herself. "I think you need to sit for awhile. You've been on your feet all night. We're pretty far off the beaten path. Why was a tour bus on this back road?"

Abby relaxed against the chair. "We were scheduled to do a concert in Jackson Hole. We'd just finished one in Laramie. I think the driver got lost."

"With the snow out here, it is pretty easy to miss your turn." Margaret pulled her boots off and wiggled her toes. "We can't offer you much. As George told you, the cooking job is yours. It's not the best, but the back room has a cot in it, a toilet, a shower, and it's warm. You are welcome to it."

Abby swallowed hard. There were actually people like this left in the world? In the clubs, crappy bars, and back road stadiums, she hadn't met any. Without Margaret and George's kindness, she had no idea where she'd be tonight. "I don't want to impose. I can try to find a room."

Margaret's brown eyes bored into her. "Where? There isn't a hotel within forty miles and you said yourself you don't have a dime. How do you think you're going to get a room? I've been down and out myself. Take the cot, work awhile, and make enough to get you where you're going. Besides, if tonight didn't show how hard you're going to work at this job, it should have. The boys will be in for breakfast starting at five in the morning." She looked at her watch.

"Five A.M.?" Abby hadn't been up that early in -- well -- she couldn't remember when.

"These are ranchers and cowboys, honey. They don't sleep late." She stood, folding the chair and leaning it against the wall.

"I'll see if I can find you some clothes and a decent pair of shoes. January in Wyoming will freeze the hairs on your fanny while you're walking if you aren't careful."

Two kind people in the middle of nowhere had given her food, a job, and a safe place to sleep. Two people who knew nothing about her. It was the first time Abby had felt lucky in a very long time.

"Let me show you where the cot and some supplies are."

Abby followed Margaret into the small back room. Shelves of canned goods, flour, sugar, napkins, and other food lined the shelves. Margaret pushed open a door. She pulled on a chain hanging from a single light bulb in the center of the ceiling.

"This is the bathroom. It isn't fancy, but it's clean and has hot water."

Abby thought it looked dreamy after spending a night in a hay barn. A barn that, unfortunately, belonged to a man who didn't seem to possess much compassion.

A dull yellow light bounced off tired melamine wallboard -- white with specks of glitter in it, circa 1970. A pedestal sink with a cold faucet and a hot faucet sat beside a vintage toilet. A white vinyl shower curtain circled a small corner shower.

Reaching into a closet, Margaret handed Abby a couple of wool blankets. "The cot is right back here." She led Abby to a small alcove with an old Army cot. "Again, it's not pretty, but it's warm and safe. There are towels in that cabinet and more blankets if you get cold." She gave Abby a gentle pat on the shoulder.

George walked into the storage room. "I've locked up, Mrs. McIvey." He winked at his wife. "Well, Abby you did a fine job. You didn't lie, you can cook." He smiled. "Are you going to stay in the back room and cook for us in the morning?"

"Yes. Thank you both, very much." Abby looked at the floor. "I don't know where I'd be tonight if you two hadn't taken me in."

"Things happen for reasons we can't possibly understand." Margaret blinked back tears. "Now, get some sleep. Breakfast is early in these parts."

"Just make sure you turn the lights out." George pulled on his coat and handed Margaret her bibs. With practiced hands, Margaret had the bibs on and snapped tight in a matter of seconds. George slid the coat on her shoulders. "We'll see you in the morning."

They walked to their pickup truck. A mist of steam curled around their heads from the heat of their combined breath. He opened the door for Margaret and carefully flipped the door lock down before he shut it. Would Abby ever know what that kind of caring from a man felt like?

Making her way to the cot, Abby sat carefully in the center of it. A wiggle or two proved it quite sturdy. She sniffed her shirtsleeve. The smell of burned animal flesh sent a wave of nausea into her throat.

She ripped off the crappy vest she had been forced to wear as part of Billy Butcher's band, Butcher's Massacre. With a paper towel, she wiped the now dry mud from her orange stilettos. They were her lucky shoes -- at least they had been until today. Her grandmother had helped her pick them out on a very rare day of shopping. Abby had worn them to an audition for a Los Angeles recording studio when they'd ask her to come. Then, her mother had shown up and screwed up Abby's life again.

Carefully, she put the shoes on a shelf. They'd bring her luck again -- she knew they would. Her grandmother had told her so, "like Dorothy in the Wizard of Oz."

Abby pulled the blankets over her. She stared up at the ceiling as the warmth of tears rushed down her cheeks.

Chapter Two

Over a week had passed and Abby was cooking with a rhythm. The *boys* were now lining up to get a plate of her cooking. Margaret had scrounged up four or five pairs of jeans, a couple of shirts, a worn but warm and comfortable flannel coat, and some boots that were, as she put it, "not designed by a sadistic man."

Fred Gillis ate at McIvey's every day, and today was no exception. "Abby, darling, can I have some more gravy and biscuits?" He smiled broadly and winked.

"Me too, Abby," Rodney added.

These boys, she had discovered, could eat a lot, and all of their meals had to contain beef. Working at the restaurant was like feeding a small army. If she hadn't hated the smell of fried cow flesh before, she certainly did now.

Almost daily, Abby got a proposal of marriage. Most were tongue-in-cheek proposals after a compliment of her cooking ability. Although a few of them seemed very sincere.

Saving every dime she had earned plus tips, she'd managed to hoard away a tidy little sum. In a few weeks, she would have enough to buy a bus ticket to Los Angeles. Her heart instantly began to pound at the thought of an audition -- they terrified her. Did other singers think they were having damn a heart attack every time they walked onstage?

A singing job would pay her good money. It would get her back to Indiana, back to make things right for Granny Martin -- better late than never. She swallowed hard, forcing back the grief. It had only been two months since she'd lost her grandmother, her only real mother. Now wasn't the time. Later, she promised herself, later there would be time for the pain.

Margaret was busy on the cash register, so Abby slid the second plate of biscuits and gravy in front of Fred.

The door opened, bringing in frigid air. Abby winced as the glowering cowboy from last week stomped the snow off his feet. He sat at an empty barstool beside Fred.

"Hey, Joe."

"Fred." He pushed the hat back on his head and stared at Abby. "May I get a cup of coffee?"

Joe Baer was flushed from the cold. He laid his cowboy hat on the counter. His neatly trimmed mustache sparkled from the mist of ice that clung to it. Fine sprays of lines outlined denim-blue eyes that bored into her.

Abby nodded, grabbing a cup and saucer from under the counter. Her hand trembled and the cup crashed against the linoleum, followed by the saucer. "Damn," she muttered, trying to pick up the pieces.

"Are you all right, Abby?" Fred asked, peering across the counter.

"Fine." She swept up the pieces and then filled a fresh cup with coffee. She set it in front of Joe. "Would you like something to eat?" she asked, unable to look him in the eye.

Creases had worn slick in the sleeves of his denim coat. His hands were large and callused. Joe was a ruggedly handsome man. Abby shook her head. She'd just gotten rid of one crazy male, she didn't need another one. Although Joe was certainly easy on the eyes. No. She wasn't about to be attracted to a man just because of his handsome face.

"Nope." Joe leaned his elbows on the counter, watching her.

"So Fred, did you get over to Riverton and pick up that gasket for the pump?" he asked.

"I'll get there first thing in the morning," Fred promised between bites. "I will." He gulped the last morsel, dropped a twenty on the counter, and nearly ran out the door.

"I thought you might like this back," Joe said as Abby came out of the kitchen. He lifted his hand off the counter, revealing a small copper hummingbird earring. "I should make you go over and rake up my barn."

"I don't know what you're talking about. That's not mine."

"You were wearing the match to this the first night you worked here." His eyes were as cold as the snow and ice outside. "I found it when I was cleaning up my wreck of a barn."

Abby took in a deep breath. Maybe if she told the truth, the man wouldn't be so angry. Maybe he would be as compassionate as the McIveys. "Look, I was freezing and desperate. Your barn saved my life that night."

"What were you doing out on that back road by yourself?"

She reached for the earring. His hand covered it again.

"It's a long, boring story. Can I have my earring?"

"Sure, when you fork over fifty-five dollars for damages."

"Fifty-five damn dollars? I only opened one bale of hay. The others were fine. That couldn't be worth over five bucks." The man was an arrogant jerk.

"Fifty-five dollars and the earring is yours." He put on his hat, adjusted it to one side, cupped the erring in his large hand, gave her a curt nod, and walked to the front door.

Abby threw his half-full coffee cup across the room. The cup shattered against the doorframe narrowly missing his head.

"That'll be fifty-seven dollars. You'll need to pay the McIveys two dollars for the cup." Joe gently closed the door behind him.

Abby stormed out of the diner right behind him. The ill-tempered cowboy might scare cowboys like Fred Gillis, but he didn't scare her. "Fifty-five dollars for one freakin' bale of hay? Was it grown by virgin haymakers?" she shouted across the parking lot.

A thick blanket of slushy snow covered the parking lot. She practically ice-skated to his truck. Snow stuck in large dollops on her hair, and the frigid air wrapped around her body like a frozen bath towel. Abby didn't care. Her face burned with anger. She wasn't about to let the damn cocky cowboy just have his say and walk out.

Joe pulled open the truck door, turning slowly toward her.

Abby hadn't realized just how big a man he was until she stood beside him. Joe Baer was nearly a head taller and twice as wide at the shoulders. Those blue eyes stared down at her in a cold, calm, frozen glare. She'd come this far. She wasn't backing down now.

"One bale? I found five bales opened, and you left the barn door open. The snow that night ruined another five or six bales. What, did you do have a party in there?"

"Party, my ass. I was freezing to death."

"Quite a potty mouth you've got." Blue eyes squinted down at her. "Potty mouth, dressed like a trollop with chains, pins and orange hair, has no regard for a man's barn. City girls. You can spot them a mile off." He snorted.

"Whoa, a trollop?" Did he actually call her that? Angry words choked in her throat. How dare this overbearing cowboy call her names? "You don't know anything about me. That's a pretty fast judgment to make based on what a person's wearing." She folded her arms across her chest.

His eyes raked her up and down. "Yeap, faster. I'm judging that you talk faster, walk faster, and do a whole lot of other things faster."

"That's very true, hick-boy. We city girls do a whole lot of things faster. Mostly we think faster. Let me tell you, I think you're a money grubbing, insulting, backwoods hick who hasn't grown up enough to get over playing cowboy and wouldn't know what to do with the likes of a real city*woman.*" All Abby wanted at this moment was Margaret's huge frying pan. How badly she wanted to slam it into the side of his head.

A dark crimson rose slowly up his face, highlighting those denim-blue eyes.

"Lady, I'd know exactly what to do with the likes of you. I'd blister your fanny and wash your mouth out with soap."

"Good solution, hick boy, just slug it once, hell that'll fix anything." Her voice picked up a country twang.

"I didn't say slug you. I said blister your fanny. There's a difference."

"Really? Slugging in the mouth or slugging on the ass, it's still slugging. Or aren't you fast enough to figure that out?" She reached into her jeans pocket. "Here's five bucks for your bale of hay."

"Add fifty bucks for the labor I had to pay to clean up the barn floor."

"That's the highest priced labor I've ever seen," she snapped back at him.

"Would you rather I call the sheriff and report you as a vandal?" He leaned against the truck seat, crossing one long leg over the other, smugly folding his arms across his chest.

"If you're that hard up, here's your money." Abby pulled the money from her pocket, reaching toward the small pocket on the chest of his jacket. Her worn boots were no match for the icy parking lot.

Two steps toward Joe and her foot slipped. Her left knee crunched against the running board of truck and her right knee crunched into his groin. Her flailing hand caught his coat pocket, ripping it off in one quick motion.

Joe's head snapped backward from the sudden impact to his groin. His head slammed into the steering wheel, smacking the truck horn. The horn didn't stop screeching when Joe's head came back up.

Abby pulled herself off his chest and out of the truck. Her knee hurt like hell. She leaned against the fender.

The horn was loud, very loud, like a hoarse goose -- and it didn't stop.

Joe limped to the front of the truck, and raised the hood. The horn was still blaring, the snow was falling heavier, and George and Margaret were staring out the café window.

With an angry yank, Joe pulled a wire that stopped the horn. Peering at her from under the safety of the hood, he shook his head. "My barn, my nuts, my truck -- are you planning on wrecking anything else in my life?" He slammed the hood down. Globs of snow plopped onto the parking lot. He pulled the earring from his pants pocket and let it fall onto the snow-crusted truck hood. Abby yanked it off the hood and stomped into the restaurant. His truck started and he drove away.

No, Joe wasn't like the McIveys. He didn't have any compassion. Abby grabbed a towel and wiped the snow from her face and hair.

Margaret walked up behind her. "I see you've met Joe Baer."

"Damn hostile man." Abby wiped harder.

"He's losing his ranch. A couple of months ago, there was a strange incident with the Childers family. Well, it was with the daughter, Kelly Childers. No one but Joe knows for sure what happened, but he's been a mighty angry man ever since." Margaret helped Abby take dirty dishes into the kitchen. "I guess losing a home that's been in your family for generations will do that to you."

Abby nearly dropped the plates, as memories flooded into her mind. She knew very well what it did to you.

"Margaret?" A deep male voice shouted form the dining room of the café. "Margaret McIvey, are you in here?"

"I'm here." She handed Abby the last of the plates and wiped her hands on a towel when the kitchen door swung open.

A tall, broad built man in beige canvas outerwear filled the doorway. Gray hair peeked from under a knit stocking cap, and warm, brown eyes squinted tight as he smiled. "Lordy, it's hot in here." He unzipped his oat. Underneath, he wore a leather vest that strained across his chest.

"You've got too many clothes on, Mike." Margaret chuckled as she leaned against the kitchen counter.

"A man can never wear too many clothes in a Wyoming winter. That is especially true if you don't have woman to warm you up." He winked, and Margaret rolled her eyes.

"Is this lady the cook I've been hearing so much about?" He smiled broadly at Abby.

"This would be--" Margaret stopped in mid-sentence. "Don't you even think about doing what I think you're about to do." She wagged an accusing finger at him, her other hand on her hip.

A wide grin spread across his face as he extended his hand to Abby. "My name is Mike Reynolds. I'm the ranch foreman at the Hidden Rock."

"*Mike*." Margaret walked threateningly toward him.

He backed up a few steps. "Settle down, Margaret."

"I'll never speak to you again," she threatened.

"Hallelujah." He jumped away from her playful slap. "Come on, you know I'm desperate."

Abby looked from one to the other, not quite sure what was happening. Mike Connor was the epitome of every movie cowboy she had ever seen. A tall, well built man in his early fifties, with naughty brown eyes that twinkled, and a squinty, half-sarcastic, half-humorous grin.

"The fellows have been talking about your cooking up at the ranch. It seems they can't work fast enough in order to get down here for a meal." His eyebrows rose, taking a good long look at Abby. "I see it ain't just for the cooking that they are coming here." He laughed.

"Thank you, Mr. Reynolds." Abby liked his face. It was lived in. He smelled of fresh earth and snow, with a hint of Old Spice.

"I'd like to offer you a job as cook up at the ranch."

Abby looked at Margaret. Her arms were folded across her chest and she gave Mike a hard, penetrating glare.

"I could pay you fifteen hundred a month and the job includes a small cottage. I'm afraid there aren't any other benefits like insurance and stuff." Mike twisted his hat around in his hands.

Abby's heart jumped at the thought of a cottage. Her own place. How wonderful would that be? She would be out of the storeroom. But she owed so much to Margaret and George. Abby glanced at Margaret. Her expression was softening, but she wouldn't look at Abby.

"There are twenty full-time cowboys, and at calving season there'd be about five more. They're a bit rowdy, but good, decent guys."

"Well, it's a good offer, but I'm not sure." No matter how much she wanted to run out the door to the cottage, she wasn't about to leave the McIveys shorthanded. They'd given her a job and a place to stay when everyone else had abandoned her. They'd taken her in, fed her, and kept her from dying in the cold. "I'll talk it over with Margaret and let you know."

"Sure. Sure. I'll be back tomorrow night to get your answer." He zipped up his coat, gave Margaret another little wink, and left.

Margaret leaned against the counter, staring at Abby with one eyebrow raised.

"I won't leave, Margaret."

"Why not? I would. It's a good job and the boys at the Hidden Rock are a good bunch. They'll give you no problems. I can't pay you nearly what he can and our store room isn't any place to live."

"I don't want to leave you without somebody."

"Honey, we didn't have anybody when you showed up." Margaret pushed the door shut on the dishwasher, set the controls, and turned it on. "Look, you needed a hand and we could do a little bit. Take the money you make and go to Los Angeles like you set out to do. On what we can pay you it'll take forever." Tears started to mist in her eyes.

Margaret wrapped her arms tightly around Abby. "Darn, I will miss you though. You remind me a whole lot of my daughter."

The two women held onto to each other for long moments. George walked in the kitchen. Abby felt Margaret's hand flip, waving him away. The door swung quietly shut as he left.

"Take the job, Abby and get on with your life." Margaret pulled back and kissed Abby's forehead. "Hey, George and I are driving into Riverton tonight for a little fun. Will you join us?"

"I don't think so." After her experiences with Billy Butcher and playing bars, she wasn't sure she ever wanted to see another one.

"Come on, you need to get out of here for awhile. Besides, the Swinging Huskers are appearing tonight. Now you don't want miss those Wyoming treasures, do you?"

"The Swinging Huskers?" What the hell was a husker?

"They're a local band, and they're actually pretty good." Margaret hung up her apron, switching off the dining room light. "George did you lock up?"

"I sure did." George danced his way into the kitchen. "Are you ready to two-step, baby?"

"Sure, when you learn how, old man."

He picked Margaret up off her feet and swung her around.

"Come on, Abby." Margaret held the back door open, smiling. Abby took a deep breath, pulled the flannel coat off its peg, and jumped into the truck with them.

Chapter Three

A massive metal pole barn in the middle of a dark field was The Sagebrush Bar and Music House. The parking lot was full when they arrived, forcing George to park the pickup truck out in the snow beyond the gravel.

Abby heard the twang of country guitars before she even opened the truck door. Inside, there wasn't an empty corner. The crowd was a blur of cowboy boots, blue jeans, and flannel shirts mixed with long skirts and turquoise jewelry. George waved to somebody at a table, making motions to ask if there were seats available. Fred Gillis waved back. The three made their way through the crush of people.

A large rhinestone-emblazoned banner with the Swinging Huskers on it hung over a stage at the far end of the huge barn. A massive, black, rectangular bar took up the center of the room. Abby counted six bartenders working behind it. Round tables with square legs and plywood tops were scattered along the sides of the barn, and a large plywood dance floor filled the area right in front of the stage. The dance floor was so packed, people were hardly moving, much less dancing.

"I'll get us a couple more chairs," Fred said. He left and came back with three well-used folding chairs.

"Thanks, Fred." George held one out for Margaret.

Fred handed one to Abby

Rodney Burris appeared, carrying four beers in his hands. He gave a whoop when he saw the McIveys. A gorgeous red-haired woman with the biggest breasts Abby had ever seen strutted behind him. "Hey, I didn't know we had more folks coming," Rodney said. "I'll grab a few more beers. Tessa, you want to come with me?" He turned, smiling down at her breasts.

"No, I'm tired, Rodney. You go get them. I'm going to sit for a spell." She planted a kiss on his nose, then sat next to Abby. Her perfume was nice and smelled expensive.

Rodney walked to the bar, and Abby nearly laughed aloud. It was the first time she actually understood what the word *saunter* meant. Rodney was the picture of a bow-legged cowboy.

"Are you the Abby that cooks down at McIvey's?" Tessa asked, slipping a hand down the collar of her purple satin western shirt and pulling up a wayward bra strap.

"Yes."

"Good to meet you. I'm Tessa Springer. Rodney's done nothing but brag about your cooking. I was almost jealous, except he never said a word about your looks -- only your cooking." She grinned. "Not meaning you're not pretty or anything, but you know, I am a jealous girlfriend."

Margaret looked at Abby and rolled her eyes. George just tapped his toe to the music. Abby admired a man who knew when to keep his mouth shut.

"I've been going with Rodney on and off for two years," she added with a bit of firmness that told Abby Rodney was her man. Her voice was as gorgeous as her face, thick with a southern twang. Tessa had dark red hair that tumbled in long waves down her back. She was petite, except for those breasts. Her cowboy boots matched her shirt. Abby never realized cowboy boots came in purple. Tessa wore tight fitting blue jeans that couldn't have been larger than a size two.

"He's a good man." Tessa sipped on her beer, leaving red residue from her lipstick around the top.

"Any marriage plans?" Abby tried to think of something that would put her mind at ease. Rodney Burris was definitely not on her list of marriage choices.

The way her life was going, marriage wasn't ever going to be an option. Who would want her? A second rate back-up singer with no money, no home, and no family. She took a drink of beer, and winced as it hit her tongue.

Tessa scooted her chair closer. "I want to get married. He doesn't."

"He wants to get married," George interrupted, turning to grin at them. "You've seen the way the man eats, Abby. He just wants a wife who can cook, and Tessa can't boil water." He laughed. Margaret smacked his shoulder and sent him a look that told him to shut up.

"If she married Rodney and cooked for him, old Rodney would be dead inside of a week," Fred chimed in, smacking the top of the table and howling with laughter.

Tessa's face grew red. She stared at the tabletop and her smile disappeared.

Abby leaned close to her so no one else could hear. "You know, cooking isn't that hard. I could teach you how to cook."

"Really?" Tessa beamed, her green eyes shining in the strobe lights.

"Yes."

Tessa wrote her phone number on a napkin and handed it to Abby. "Call me, we'll work something out. If you're sure?" Her eyes pleaded.

After cooking meals at the café, there wasn't anything else to do except watch it snow. There was a lot of it to watch. It hadn't stopped snowing she she'd arrived in Wyoming. It was starting to feel like she'd landed in the Arctic. Teaching Tessa to cook would be a welcome break in the monotony. "I'm very sure."

Rodney returned with the beers and Abby handed him some money. He made a face at her. "Later tonight, when I'm all out of cash, then you can buy, honey." She wasn't sure if he was being a gentleman buying her a drink or if he just thought of her as a charity case. She plunked two dollars on the table. Beer she could buy -- it was a life she was having trouble getting.

Abby listened to the music. Margaret was right -- The Swinging Huskers were a really good band. All she'd heard for months was punk rock, hard rock, and what she liked to call *screeching* rock. The easy country lyrics and soft guitar were a welcome change. The room applauded loudly as the song ended.

"We're going to take a break," the lead singer announced, his voice vibrating against the metal walls of the pole barn. "You all get prepared. You know what happens in the next set, don't you?"

The crowd whistled and cheered.

"We are going to have our own talent show, right here at The Sagebrush Bar and Music House," he shouted. "Tonight's winner will take home two hundred bucks." The drummer chimed in with a few beats. "So be thinking about what you want to sing. And it has to be something the band knows."

Margaret turned to Abby. "There you go, Abby. Get up there and win that two hundred dollars."

Abby coughed, nearly choking on the small sip of beer she'd taken, "are you fuc -- nuts?" She caught her tongue. "It's a country band, Margaret. I sing rock and roll, punk." She shook her head quickly, stage fright ripping at her stomach.

"Not if you want to win a talent night in Wyoming you don't. Rock, country -- it's all music. That's some quick cash. It'd be a big help, wouldn't it?" Margaret pushed her chair close to Abby.

"I don't know, Margaret." Her heart slammed into her throat.

"Well then, maybe you aren't a singer. Maybe you really don't want to get out of here." Margaret chugged the beer, motioning to George to go get her a refill. He obliged.

"I didn't lie to you." A stab of pain raced through Abby's stomach. Margaret and George were two people she'd never lie to. In a few shorts weeks they'd become like family to her.

"I know you didn't lie." Margaret grabbed Abby's hands and squeezed. "You just need to get your butt up there, open up a little, and take few chances. Otherwise, you're gonna be stuck here for the rest of your life." A faraway looked crossed her face.

"Is that something you know about?" Abby asked.

Margaret slowly pulled her hands back. "Yes, it is." She smiled, taking a long look across the room at George standing by the bar. "Don't get me wrong, I love him like a hunger. But there was a time when all I wanted was to see the world. I don't regret marrying and staying here, at least not too often. Just once in awhile I wonder, you know?"

Abby knew. "You've got to know at least one country song."

"You sing, Abby?" Fred asked.

"I sing a little, Fred." Again, Abby's heart revved like a racecar engine.

"Well, I'll go sign you up." Fred bolted from the table before Abby could utter one word of protest.

She pushed the beer away. It had been well over two years since she'd sung the lead with a band. Before singing with Billy, she'd worked at a local advertising firm singing jingles and then for another rock band as back up. She wasn't sure if she had the talent to sing lead.

She looked at Margaret who just nodded to her. If she couldn't sing here, she'd never be able to audition in Los Angeles. If she couldn't audition there, everything she'd ever wanted, both for her and for her grandmother would be lost.

She wanted to take a long drink of beer for courage, but just couldn't do it. If she smoked she would have had a pack, but she was too wimpy to inhale. Drugs were as easy as candy to come by in Billy Butcher's world, but after spending a few nights in the emergency room with band members, she didn't have the courage to do them either. How was she going to get the guts to do this? Bile began rising in her stomach. Abby swallowed it down.

The band returned to the stage. "Well, it looks like we've got us about six contestants tonight, folks. I need Johnny Rodriguez on the stage. Where are you Johnny?"

A dark skinned man dressed completely in black leather hopped onto the stage. "I'm Mike, nice to meet you."

"I want to sing a song for my lady." Johnny was smiling from ear to ear, tucking his thumbs into the top of his leather jeans. The smile never left his face. His Hispanic accent was very thick. "Her name is Maria and she is standing right there in the front."

A lovely, dark haired woman waved and smiled.

"I want to sing Yellow Rose of Texas, you know it?" He turned toward the band. They all nodded that they did.

"All right, one, two." The band and Johnny began.

Johnny was handsome, but he could not sing, and the audience wasn't kind. Boos and hisses filled the air. Johnny had apparently drunk enough beers to get him up on stage, but had not drunk enough to make him get him down off the stage. He flipped the audience his middle finger and kept on singing, making the audience laugh. A few couples even started dancing. Finally, it was over.

"Abby if you're going to teach me to cook--" Tessa leaned into Abby, speaking in a whisper-- "then I should teach you how to lookhot. Come with me." She held out her hand.

Abby followed her into the ladies bathroom. Several women were smoking, and a few were applying makeup. Most of them were trashing the men at the bar.

"I don't mean to be forward but if you go up on that stage with that hair in that ridiculous ponytail and no makeup, well you are going to look just pathetic."

While Abby never thought of herself as a very pretty girl, she didn't consider herself in the realm of *pathetic*. Had she fallen that far in the months since her grandmother died? She'd never partied hard like the rest of the band, spending most of her nights alone in a hotel room. Maybe life on the road had taken a toll.

Tessa kept talking about what she was going to do, what she wanted to do, and what she thought Abby should do to look better. Abby chuckled at her accent as she listened to her talk, and talk, and talk.

"Tessa, where are you from?" she asked when Tessa stopped just long enough to take a breath.

"Why, I'm from Texas, honey, didn't you know?" She smiled, fluffing her teased hair, stealing a glance to her breasts. "We like everything bigger in Texas."

They both laughed. It had been a long time since Abby laughed with a girlfriend. She had forgotten just how good it felt.

"You're really cute, but with a little makeup, I'd think you could look just gorgeous." Without further comment, Tessa pulled the rubber band from Abby's hair, giving a little squeal as the purple streaks burst forth. "Oh, my. Why on earth would you do something like this?" She ran her hand through the colorful strands.

Abby shrugged.

"Hmm. Would it be all right with you if I just trimmed a little of this color off?"

"What? Cut my hair here? Now?" Sheer terror ripped through Abby's chest. She swirled around and looked at her reflection. Her hair had grown and the blonde roots were looking pretty shabby next to the clumps of purple.

"Sure, honey." Tessa reached into her bag and pulled out an assortment of scissors that would have made airport security pass out. She brushed Abby's hair straight down her back, flipping it around with expert hands. Abby closed her eyes tight. After a few snips, Tessa giggled. Cold chills ran down Abby's arms.

"Wow, it looks real pretty with that weird color out of it." Tessa reached down into the depths of the largest purse Abby had ever seen. "I should have -- yes, I do." Tessa applied a coat of foundation, then blush, then eye shadow. It seemed the entire contents of her makeup bag went onto Abby's face.

She turned Abby toward the mirror. "What do you think?"

Abby nearly screamed, not recognizing her own reflection. Her cheeks were a soft peach, her lips were copper with a bit of shine, and liner outlined her eyes, which were dabbed with a soft brown shadow. It had been a long time since Abby had felt pretty. A long time since anyone had told her she was pretty. Is this what pretty felt like?

"I used to do facials at Marco's in Dallas." Tessa smiled. "You've got a light complexion and natural blonde hair, so you don't want to use anything too dark. But I did give you a little extra since you'll be on stage under the lights. In another couple of weeks, the rest of those awful colors will be grown out. I'll cut it again if you like."

"Thank you." Abby flipped her hair back. She took in a deep breath. "I hope I can do this." The crowd had booed Johnny, after all. What would she do if they booed her? Run? She didn't think her legs would work.

"You'll be fine honey. They might be a little mean to the cowboys that sing, but when a lady gets onstage they are pretty polite." She applied lipstick to her own lips, zipping her bag shut. "Come on, get out there, and win that money. Hell, we can get real drunk on two hundred bucks."

They laughed, leaving the bathroom. In spite of everything, these people liked her and cared about her. She felt like Cinderella tonight.

They'd no sooner reached the table than her name was announced from the stage.

"Go get 'em girl," Margaret shouted. George gave her a wink and a thumbs up.

Abby swallowed hard. The bar seemed exceptionally quiet as she walked toward the stage. Her heart beat like thunder and her legs were rubbery. Fred stood right beside her. He squeezed her hand and led her up the steps of the stage. Abby blindly followed him. He leaned down and gave her a sweet kiss on the forehead, then practically pushed her to center stage.

*****

Joe Baer set his beer down on the bar. The name sounded familiar, but this woman couldn't be the same one he'd had a fight with at McIveys, could it? Abby Clark walked to the stage. What had she done to herself? She sure did look pretty. Joe sighed. Damn beer, drinking enough of it could make anybody look good.

Besides, women were horrible creatures. All women, especially this one -- the city girl with the potty mouth. Abby's purple hair was gone, as were the ratty, punk clothes, replaced by a soft flannel shirt and jeans. She actually looked nice.

Joe smirked and took another chug of beer. Women, they were all the same. Take your heart or your money and leave you destitute. Ben Childers had gotten what he wanted, what he had been trying to get for years, all because Joe had been a sucker for a desperate, pretty face. No woman would ever do that to him again.

He was losing everything that ever mattered to him -- everything -- because of a desperate, pretty face that hid a worthless soul. He nodded to the bartender for another beer.

"Hello, honey." The bandleader smiled and led Abby to center stage. She looked scared to death. "Wow, she's a pretty one," he remarked.

The cowboys hooted and hollered.

"Look it there, she blushes! I haven't seen a lady do that in awhile."

Joe grunted. The woman could put on a good show. How the hell did she go from looking like a punk rock prostitute to being a blushing innocent thing in flannel? Women were experts at changing into whatever they needed to be to get whatever they wanted. Did he think she was going to be the exception?

"Do you have a song, Abby?" the bandleader asked.

"Yes."

He waited, holding the microphone in front of her.

"Do you want to tell me what that song might be?"

"Tears, by Winslow Dodge."

He glanced back at the band. "You want a particular key?"

Her hand shook and she swallowed hard.

"Whatever it's written in."

The music began, but nothing came out of her mouth. The band began again, her words started as a whisper, then suddenly turned into the most mesmerizing, beautiful voice Joe had ever heard. He choked on his beer, wiping splatters off his chin. Abby Clark looked utterly angelic standing on the stage. Bathed in a soft spotlight, her eyes closed and she totally transfixed the room. The crowd was completely charmed by her. By end of the first chorus, the bar was silent and Joe watched the band members struggle to play while listening to the angelic voice that came out of the flannel-shirted woman. She had a voice that curled around your soul. Joe couldn't pull his eyes off her.

A flash of copper earring sparkled and a wave of guilt poured over him.

No, damn it. No woman was ever going to make him feel guilty again, and certainly not the foul-mouthed, plain looking, city girl standing on the stage.

Chapter Four

Abby started to speak, but nothing came out. She cleared her throat, glancing across the audience. There were a lot of people standing in front of that stage. The crowd felt smothering. Her heart slammed into her ribs and her breath didn't want to fill her lungs. She prayed she didn't pass out, or forget how to sing, or pee down her leg.

Sweat burst out in her armpits and she was grateful for the dark flannel shirt. Trying hard to control her breathing, she stared at the bandleader. He smiled, and gave her a reassuring nod.

The band began the song. Abby opened her mouth and nothing, not a sound came out. Her throat felt constricted, her mouth dry.

The band stopped.

Abby took in a large gulp of air, and nodded for them to start again. She closed her eyes, pretending she was singing in the living room of her grandmother's Victorian house. Granny Martin was smiling in the rocker, tapping her toe with Sunny the cat curled in her lap. Suddenly Abby's voice sprang forth like a geyser.

The song ended and Abby didn't hear a sound. Her heart raced so furiously she thought she would pass out. Did she seriously think she had the cords to sing lead? Billy had told her she wasn't good enough. She should have listened.

As she started to bolt from the stage in utter humiliation, one man started to clap. Then several others joined in until the entire room was on their feet. A few stood on tabletops, applauding with gusto, whistling and stomping their feet.

The bandleader pulled off his Stetson and bowed. The audience screamed for her to do another song. She shook her head no, nearly running into the next contestant. The cowboy put his hand up when called to the stage, then nodded toward her and began clapping. Was he clapping for her?

"Well then, I'd say we have our winner." The crowd cheered even louder than before. "Come on back here and get your money, Abby." She was ushered back to the stage by the cowboy.

The bandleader handed her an envelope. "You were fabulous, darlin'."

This is what a crowd cheering just for you, for your voice felt like? It felt like at least for that one instant, Abby was special. Goosebumps covered her arms, tears pooled in her eyes, and she wished her grandmother could see her. The Sagebrush Bar was small, no one outside of this Wyoming county knew it existed, but right now, right here, she was a superstar. How many times had she played this kind of night over in her dreams? Even when Billy told her she didn't have the talent to sing lead, a small part of her kept believing.

"Thank you," she whispered, bowing slightly to the audience. Clutching the envelope with all her strength, she wound her way through the crowd back to Margaret.

Margaret threw her arms around her neck and danced in a circle with her. "You were amazing," Margaret whispered in her ear. She pulled back, staring in her face. "When you said you were a singer, I had no idea you could sing like that! And you told me you didn't know any country songs." She laughed.

"It's the only one I knew," Abby said. She turned to Fred who had followed her back to the table. "Thanks for signing me up. I never would have done it otherwise."

Fred smiled, dipping the corner of his cowboy hat in a salute to her.

Margaret squeezed her hands. "Take the money and the job Mike offered you, and get to where somebody can hear you sing."

Several people came to the table complimenting her. For this one brief moment, Abby Clark felt like Cinderella -- a happy Cinderella, in a mythical place called Wyoming. She smiled, not wanting the moment to ever end.

Handing Fred some money, she asked him buy a round for everyone at the table. Abby made her way through the crowd to the ladies' room, taking compliments along the way. She needed a cold splash of water, fast. With her heart racing, and the heat of the stage lights, she didn't want to end such a fantastic night by passing out.

She held the wet paper towel to the back of her neck, smiling at her reflection. She could still sing. Maybe in Los Angeles, she had a chance. A chance to build a life. A chance to fix the past.

A chance was all she needed

Abby fluffed her hair, straightened the collar on her flannel shirt, and swung the door open, ready to take on the world.

"It's good to know you can do something besides vandalize a cattle barn." The deep, male voice startled her from behind.

She turned and stared into chest, lots of wide, muscular, male chest.

Joe Baer stood close to her shoulder. Very close. Abby looked up into those denim-blue eyes. They seemed kinder tonight. It was probably the beer. He wore a neat pair of black jeans, a black, western cut shirt with small roses embroidered on the front shoulders, and his ever-present black cowboy hat.

"You got your money, Mr. Baer. Why don't you drop the subject?" Abby tried to walk around him. Another confrontation she didn't want -- not tonight. He stepped in her way.

"That was business. I just wanted to tell you that you sing very nice." He tipped his hat slightly. "And to apologize for calling you a trollop." Joe walked across the room and leaned against the bar, not giving her a second look.

Why had the cowboy made a point to compliment her and to apologize? Until now, he'd been nothing but rude and insulting. Now he was suddenly being nice, why? It was too bad he was such an ass, because he was a darn good-looking man. His hair was soft and wavy, the ends just touching his shirt collar. The western-cut shirt did little to hide the corded muscles in his arms. Joe Baer was tough, rugged, and masculine. Why were all the good-looking ones either taken or jerks?

Margaret and George weren't at the table. She searched the dance floor -- no luck there, either. Tessa and Rodney were dancing, which looked more like vertical love-making. A tinge of jealousy tweaked her heart.

Abby sat the table, giving the bar and Joe Baer a sideways glance. He watched the band, sipping on a beer. The man looked very alone, almost sad, until a gorgeous blonde woman walked beside him. She was the type of woman who looked like she could perk up any man, but Joe's face showed disgust and anger.

The woman ran a finger along his jaw line, slid the beer from his hand, and took a drink. Laying cash on the bar, Joe tried to get up, but the women stopped him, pushing her very sexy body tight against him.

She began talking, and Joe suddenly backed off the barstool and walked around the bar. The woman stormed in front of him, slapping him harshly across the face. He said nothing, just stared at her.

The blonde stomped her foot and put her hands on her hips. Just as she raised her hand to slap him again, his hand came up like a lightning strike. Joe grabbed her hand and easily forced it down onto the bar. The woman's face went crimson. She screamed something that made those sitting closest to them turn and stare. Then she stormed away.

Abby had to give the cowboy credit; he kept his temper in check with the woman. Men in the backstage road crews she'd traveled with would have slapped her back, hard.

"Come on, honey," Tessa shouted next to the table, trying to yank Abby to the dance floor. "Everybody has to dance to this one. Sitting it out is just un-American." Tessa's voice was louder than the band. "God Bless Texas."

Abby shook her head. The crowd was doing a nearly perfect line dance and she had two-left feet.

She jumped onto a table, singing at the top of her lungs. Rodney laughed, his hands caressing Tessa's thighs. The song turned into a slow, romantic ballad, and they made their way back to Abby's table.

"George and Margaret left. I think they had an urgent problem to take care of," Tessa said and giggled. "She asked me and Rodney to take you home."

"She did? We are?" Rodney's glassy eyes focused on something behind Abby and he smiled. "Hey, Joe, have a seat."

Joe sat in the chair next to Abby.

She could smell his cologne. It was nice, masculine. Abby cleared her throat, reminding herself what a crude, rude ass he was. Joe slowly set a fresh bottle of beer on the table, leaning back on the chair.

"Joe, are you heading back to Sentinel tonight?" Rodney asked.

"Yep," he answered.

Abby cringed, realizing where Rodney was going with the conversation. "Rodney, where did Fred go?" She prayed the cowboy who seemed to have a crush on her was still around.

"I don't know. I haven't seen him in awhile." He shrugged. "Listen, Joe. Me and Tessa, we're going to her sister's place when The Sagebrush closes. She thinks I've had too much to drink. Would you mind taking Abby back to Sentinel with you?" Rodney smiled, his eyes pleading.

"Sure," Joe answered.

"I don't want to impose." Abby turned slightly, seeing the handsome cowboy staring hard at her.

"I'm becoming used to it." His eyes fixed on hers.

"I think I'd rather walk." Abby pulled her coat off the back of the chair, putting it on as she walked to the front door.

Hitchhiking looked better than accepting a ride from that egotistical cowboy. Who did he think he was? How dare he say she was imposing on him? She let out a little scream of frustration as she slammed out the door. Obviously the blonde woman had slapped him for good reason. Joe Baer no doubt deserved it.

Only a few pickups were scattered around the nearly empty parking lot. The temperature had plunged from its usual arctic blast to what had to be the beginning of a new ice age, and Sentinel was nearly twenty miles away. Why did she do this to herself? Once again, she'd managed to be stranded in the middle of nowhere in subzero weather. Streetlights didn't seem to exist in this part of the country. She got just a few feet from the bar's door, it was pitch black.

Abby pulled the worn flannel coat tight around her. Damn the Wyoming wind. Damn snow. Damn Billy Butcher and damn Joe Baer. Damn anyone else she couldn't think of at the moment because her brain was freezing, her hands were freezing, and she just wanted to catch the first bus west. Bus? There were no freakin' buses out here. Maybe she could hitch a ride on an antelope. There were sure plenty of them around.

She'd hoped to hitch a ride, but with the parking lot nearly empty, it didn't look good.

Headlights whipped across her from the side of the building. Abby hoped it might be Fred or another cowboy from the restaurant willing to give her a lift. She nearly sprinted to the side of the building before the lights disappeared.

She never saw the blow coming. Stepping around the corner, Abby's world became a kaleidoscope of intense light. Searing pain slammed into her forehead, she crumbled to the ground.

Faint laughter sounded somewhere in the distance. Rough hands rummaged through her pockets. She could not move to stop the assault. Abby felt the envelope with her winnings yanked from her shirt pocket. Then everything went quiet.

Her eyes were so fogged, only the dim image of a dark pickup truck slinging gravel as it raced out of the parking lot filtered through. Abby couldn't determine the color or make, only that it had a single, long mud flap across the back that reflected the Sagebrush's neon sign.

She leaned against the cold, metal building, feeling nauseated and violated. All her winnings were gone. Tears dripped down her face. Everything was gone. Couldn't the world give her a break? Thirty seconds of feeling like Cinderella and then right back into the hell that had become her life.

Abby stumbled around the building. The pounding in her head didn't hurt nearly as bad as the pain in her heart. She had no home, no family, and no money. Snow pelted her face. Hell, she thought, wiping the snow off her face, had just frozen over. She leaned against the building. The snow fell heavy and the wind blew more snow off the roof, covering her body in a cascade of ice crystals.

*****

Joe walked outside, pulling his collar up against the wind. Abby was nowhere in sight. The stupid city girl was going to get herself killed. He grumbled under his breath. If the wildlife didn't get her, the frigid temperatures would. Why should he care? Why should he feel responsible for her?

Abby, with her purple hair, potty mouth, and angelic voice, wasn't his problem. Hell, he didn't even like her.

He zipped his coat. When would he ever learn to keep his smart-ass thoughts to himself? Now, he felt obligated to find her. Abby Clark's death was not going to be on his conscience. Women!

Metal creaked at the end of the pole barn. Joe's senses went on alert. He stood still, listening. A woman's moan echoed across the darkness.

"Oh, damn."

Her body lay in a crumpled heap next to the building. He kneeled beside her, pulling her gently up, and leaning her against his chest. Blood trickled down her forehead.

"I was coming after you. Dumb-ass city girl."

Abby's head fell back over his arm. His eyes scanned against the darkness for any sign of her attacker. Only snow and darkness surrounded them.

"Fluck...uck you," she mumbled.

He scooped her into his arms. Even through the heavy, flannel coat, her ribs poked through. She wasn't any heavier than a fifty-pound bag of horse feed.

"Where are you taking me?"

"To the hospital."

"No. I can't afford go." She wiggled weakly in his arms. "They took my money." Abby grasp at his shirt collar, pleading.

The look of panic on her face caused him to stop in his tracks. Joe couldn't recall ever seeing such a desperate look on a person's face. It was a look that tore at his soul. "Abby, you've been hurt. You need a doctor."

She wiggled harder. He put her down, leaning her against the side of his truck.

"I'll be fine." Her body shuddered. The bleeding had stopped, but a concussion wasn't out of the question.

He slammed a fist into the truck's fender. He'd just wanted to teach the mouthy city girl a lesson, just let her get a little cold from walking, then pick her up and take her home.

"Let me take you to the hospital." He lifted her chin up to see her face. Her eyes seemed to be able to focus now.

"No, please." She touched his hand. "I'm really all right." She reached for the door handle, when her knees buckled.

Chapter Five

Abby woke up in a bed that smelled clean and fresh. An annoying and painful stream of light slammed into her eyes. Her mouth was dry, her body felt heavy, and it was hard to focus.

The bed was soft, so very soft. Abby had spent several weeks on the hard, tiny cot in the back of McIveys' she'd forgotten what a luxury a real bed was.

A flash of panic surged through her stomach. She was in a strange room, in a strange bed. She peeked through one eye. She was in a plain white room, filled with ugly, cheap furniture. No pictures or knick-knacks. In fact, every surface of every piece of furniture was bare.

The room was cold, sterile, devoid of anything other than the basics. Forcing her aching body to sit up, she screamed, as searing pain vibrated inside her skull.

Joe burst into the room. "What? What? Are you all right?" He ran to the bed, sitting beside her, awkwardly patting her hand.

She bolted upright, screaming again at the sight of him. Where had he come from? Her heart sank. She'd been drinking. Not a lot, but enough to -- oh, she didn't. She couldn't have. Abby pulled the covers up. Relief flooded into her veins. She was still wearing her clothes.

"Shh, not so loud," Abby squeezed her eyes shut. "Where am I and what the hell is sitting on my head?" she moaned.

"You're in my bed and it's an ice pack." He inhaled deeply, staring at her. "Don't you remember? You were at The Sagebrush Bar and somebody attacked you and stole your money."

Last night flashed like a bad dream: the bar, the singing, the money, Joe Baer being an ass, and then nothing. How had her life spun so completely out of control? "So why am I at your house?" She whispered. Anything louder hurt like hell.

He kept awkwardly patting her hand. The concern the cowboy was showing for her surprised her. She didn't think he cared about much of anything, especially not her.

"You wouldn't go to the hospital." The muscle in his jaw worked.

"Shh, not so loud." She put a hand to her forehead.

"You weren't in any shape to stay alone, so I iced you down, and you fell asleep," he whispered.

She watched his face. He seemed awfully proud of himself. Smug in fact. She couldn't remember a blessed thing after she'd been hit in the head. Dread seeped in. She stared at him as hard as she was capable of, considering she couldn't focus on anything more than two feet away.

"You iced me down?"

His jaw flinched again. He let her hand drop and crossed his arms over his chest. "Your head, city girl. I put an ice pack on that large lump on your head."

This man had made her pay for a couple of bales of hay. This act of kindness was probably going to leave her owing her soul to the devilish cowboy. "I've got breakfast ready. I'll bring you some." He started to leave then turned toward her, smiling sarcastically. "Breakfast in bed, you're going to owe me big time."

Crap, of all people to be indebted to, Joe Baer was going to be the worst. She closed her eyes. He was good looking. In fact, his blue eyes made Abby's stomach do flips. Yet he was a big, overgrown, muscular, handsome, egotistical jerk, and now she owed him -- probably her life. If the blow to her head hadn't killed her, she'd have probably frozen to death. Joe had taken care of her. He was a damn confusing man.

"Breakfast." Joe set the tray on the nightstand, propping the pillows behind her back, and handing her a coffee cup with a brilliant smile. Heavens, she hoped he didn't whistle. Morning people were the worst.

The man seemed oddly happy to serve her breakfast. The blow had apparently been much harder then she thought. This was obviously a dream. She closed her eyes and inhaled deeply, then opened her eyes and he was still standing there, all dressed in black -- black jeans, black shirt, black vest, black boots, and dazzling blue eyes.

"Do you have any idea who hit you?" he asked

Abby wasn't sure if he was truly concerned or just didn't want her frozen stiff body to be found at The Sagebrush. Dead bodies weren't exactly good for business.

"No. I was walking past the far end of the building and wham. I thought I got hit by lightning." She laid the ice pack on the table next to the bed, running her hand across the bump on her head. "The only thing

I remember was a pickup truck with a long, chrome mud flap. I think that describes every truck in the parking lot," she edged out a smile.

"I called the sheriff. A deputy will be around later today to take a statement and fill out a report."

Abby closed her eyes. Broke, homeless, no money, and now a police report. Being the lead story on the six o'clock news was about the only way her life could get any worse.

*****

She had a nice smile -- one she should use more often. Abby was paler than usual. Her already fair complexion looked nearly transparent. Her purple-streaked hair was a tangled mess, several angry red scrapes marred her otherwise perfect complexion, and her hands trembled as he handed her the coffee mug.

Anyone who could attack someone as defenseless and vulnerable as this lamb deserved to be dragged across the high desert naked.

Last night on stage, she'd looked like a Wyoming girl, born and bred. Although her jeans were a little baggy hell everything was baggy on her. He suspected she wasn't eating much. The woman however, did look damn attractive in her cowboy boots.

He handed her the plate of breakfast.

"What is this?" Her face took on a gray pallor.

"Steak and eggs on toast."

"That is so barbaric. Do you ever eat anything that doesn't have to be whacked in the head first?" She set the plate back on the tray. "Listen, I really do appreciate you fixing me breakfast, but I haven't eaten a piece of animal flesh in ten years."

Joe slammed the plate on the table. Just when he thought Abby Clark might be a decent human, just when he thought she'd look cute in a pair of cowboy boots, just when he was starting to be glad he'd rescued her, that obnoxious, citified mouth of hers struck again. "Barbaric? Did you actually compare me to a barbarian?" He leaned toward her, blue eyes blazing.

"What about those leather boots you're wearing?" He pointed to the foot of the bed. "Do you think that cow just keeled over peacefully and said please make me into a pair of shoes for a stuck up city girl?"

Abby's face went crimson. Her face contorted, and her lips became a thin line as she struggled to sit up. He almost felt sorry for snapping back at her. Almost.

"First, if you were any kind of decent cattle rancher, you would know those boots are made from cheap vinyl, not leather. And a cow keeling over from old age beats the hell out of being axed in the head so you can have a barbeque."

Joe's hands balled into fists. That hadn't happened towards a woman since that ill-fated night with Kelly Childers, the night he'd lost everything that mattered. Pulling to his full height, he leaned into the bed.

Abby stood up on the bed. Her body swayed as she regained her balance. He felt a twinge of pride at her bravado, but this city girl was not going to have the last word. "You're right, a decent cattle rancher would be with the cattle right now, not baby-sitting some stuck-up, potty-mouthed, city girl."

He saw it coming, ducking as Abby's small fist came in a giant arching circle toward his head. With a jerk, he yanked the sheet from under her feet, sending her careening backward onto the bed. Her legs flashed out from under her, her feet snapped upward, and her toes landed a hard blow on his cheek.

A grunt escaped as his head snapped back. The top sheet flew to the floor, winding around his feet. Joe's large body arched back, his hands wildly groping the air, fighting to stay standing, as the sheet wound tighter

His hand gripped the corner of the fitted bed sheet, the weight of his falling body pulling the sheet taut. Two elastic corners on the fitted sheet held firm and the tightly pulled fabric formed a perfect slide. As Joe's body fell back onto the floor, the sheet stretched beyond all logical ability, and Abby sailed down the makeshift slide feet first onto his chest. Her knees crunched against the hardwood floor, her body lurched forward, her legs straddled his body, and her breasts landed squarely in his face.

Her breasts were warm and soft through her flannel shirt. It was a rather pleasant feeling. He let out an oddly satisfied moan.

The bedroom door burst open.

*****

Abby looked into the most disappointed eyes she'd seen since her mother broke Granny Martin's heart. Margaret McIvey stood silently in the doorway.

George peeked over her shoulder, a large grin covering his face. "Would you kids like us to come back later?" he asked, receiving a stinging slap on the arm from Margaret. His grin grew wider.

"No," they shouted, untangling themselves from each other and the twisted pile of bed sheets.

Joe kicked the sheets away, fumbling to tuck his shirt in, backing away from Abby.

Abby would have done anything to erase that look from Margaret's face. Tears were useless. They wouldn't fix her life, and they wouldn't change what Margaret thought of her at this moment. She sat on the edge of the bed, fighting tears, humiliation, and the urge to kick Joe Baer in the same place she'd kicked Billy Butcher. An audible groan escaped before she could stop it. That was how this entire mess had started -- with her temper.

"Dang you, Joe Baer, how could you let this girl get hurt?" Margaret stomped into the room. "You self-centered oaf, I ought to have you horsewhipped. On second thought, that'd be too good for you." Her eyes cut into him as he finished straightening his shirt.

George held his cowboy hat in his hand, shrugging at Joe's bewildered look.

"I didn't do anything wrong. I didn't know she was going to be stupid and storm out of the bar in the middle of the night by herself."

"I am not stupid," Abby shouted, and then grabbed her head with regret. Both her mother and Billy Butcher had called her stupid, and Abby was tired of it. She was never going to let someone call her stupid again.

Margaret rested her hands on her hips, sending horrid looks to Joe. "I trusted you cowboys to get her home safe. It's the first time you've let me down." She sat beside Abby on the bed and tucked Abby's hand into hers. "I'm so sorry honey. I wouldn't have let you get hurt for anything."

"It's not your fault." Abby didn't want to open her eyes.

Joe grunted and stomped down the hall.

Margaret ran a motherly hand across the top of Abby's head, parting her hair, and giving the bump quite an examination. "It's not bad. Just keep putting ice on it," she said, offering her medical opinion.

Abby figured she'd had a lot of practice. "But if you'd like, I can call Doc Barlett and have him take a look."

"No, I'm fine." As close to fine as she'd been able to get lately.

"Did you lose all your money?" Margaret asked, giving her a long, hard look

Abby inhaled long and deep, staring up at the ceiling. "Yeah."

"Here." Margaret handed Abby a large paper sack. "I brought you everything I could find from the storeroom including those go-to-hell orange high heels." She yanked out a pair of jeans and wool socks. "Get these on and we'll get you out of here."

"Margaret, nothing happened." Abby fought to contain the tears that threatened to gush.

"First, it wouldn't be any of my business, and second, I know." A small smile perked up Margaret's face, then an eyebrow arched and her face took on an angry scowl. "It isn't you I'm mad at. It's those cowboys -- particularly Joe. I trusted them to take care of you." Margaret's spine stiffened, her jaw set. "Now, you ain't got time to sit and sulk, get your coat on." She picked up the flannel jacket, helping Abby slide her arms inside. "If you're sure you're well enough?"

Abby smiled at the concern. "I'll be fine, but you can't keep rescuing me like this."

Margaret bent down, staring her square in the eye. "Would you rather stay here with Joe?"

Abby's stomach flipped. "No."

Margaret chuckled, helping her up. "George, get over here."

George appeared quickly, a big smile across his face.

"Help her to the truck," Margaret ordered, picking up the sheets that were still in a bunch on the floor.

George took the paper bag from Margaret and guided Abby down the hall to the front door, his hand at once strong and gentle.

The house was small, cold, and impersonal. A fireplace in the living room looked like it hadn't seen a fire in years. The living room had only an old, worn green couch, one end table with peeling veneer on the top, and a lamp that leaned to one side. There wasn't even a wayward newspaper lying about. The entire house was as barren of personal items as the bedroom. She scanned the house for any sign of Joe. Abby wasn't sure if Joe was that private, didn't care, or he was just that lonely. For a reason she didn't fully understand, his absence left a hollow feeling in the pit of her stomach.

"Where is Joe?" Was she seriously expecting him to be there? Why? The man didn't even like her. She didn't need him or anybody else. Winning last night's talent contest proved it.

"I reckon he's out in the field. I saw him bundle up and head out the back door a few minutes ago." George pulled on the wooden front door. It took a few hard yanks to open. "Better button up, it's cooling off outside." George stopped in midstride. "You got anything else here?"

Abby shook her head no. She didn't have anything except her pride, and that was pretty much gone too.

The front walk had been shoveled, but the long driveway showed only two tire ruts. Any vehicle hung lower than a pickup truck would scrape its underside on the deep snow. George had greatly underestimated the weather. It was way past cool -- it was downright frigid.

Abby's face felt like a thousand bees were stinging it, the air made her nose feel like someone had stuffed aluminum foil up it, and she just knew her teeth were going to shatter at any moment from chattering so hard. How she longed to be in a warm house snuggled next to a raging fire, or even a heater vent blowing hot air.

The chug of a tractor engine coming from the rear of the house caught her ear. George held her hand down the two front steps.

"Where is he going with the tractor in all this snow?" Abby asked.

"More than likely he's taking hay out to the cattle. I'd say its feeding time." George held tight to her arm.

"I'm feeling fine George, you don't have to hold on so tight." She smiled.

He leaned close to her ear. "Honey, if I let you fall, Mrs. McIvey will kill me, so I ain't taking no chances." His eyes twinkled and a dimpled smile reached ear to ear.

"I heard that," Margaret said.

"That lady's got the hearing of a fox. It's scary," he teased.

Abby laughed, stopping as the vibration of her laughter rattled her aching head.

"Uh-oh, don't look now." Margaret tapped George's shoulder, pointing to a pickup coming down the driveway.

A dark red pickup pulled into their path, charged off the drive, and plowed through the snow. *Childers Farm Implements* glistened in silver across the door. The woman driving looked like the one who had slapped Joe at the bar last night.

A tall, well-dressed blonde bounded out of the truck. "Good morning George, Margaret."

The smell of very expensive perfume exploded around Abby. Her eyes filled with water, her nose hairs nearly atrophied. Damn, did the woman bath in the stuff? A perfect salon styled haircut of shimmering blonde fluttered perfectly around her face. A snug fitting alpaca jacket covered an expensive beige cashmere sweater. Abby suddenly felt very drab, frumpy, smelly, and poor.

Margaret stiffened. "So what brings you out here where the little people live, Kelly?"

The woman ignored Margaret, walking toward Abby. She stood just inches from her, a cat-like smile on her gorgeous face, scrutinizing every inch of Abby. This was a woman high on money but low on class. "Aren't you going to introduce me to your friend?"

George walked around her, taking Abby in tow. "She's a family friend here for a visit."

"What's your name, dear?" This Kelly stepped in their path.

"I'm Abby Clark." Abby held her head high, as high as was possible with the searing pain shooting between her temples and the large lump on top of her head.

"I'm Kelly Childers. My daddy owns Childers Farm Implements." Her voice was high pitched and condescending. "My goodness what happened to your head?"

Abby was formulating a sarcastic remark as Margaret grabbed her arm and led her to the truck. "We need to get going."

"Do you two know where I can find Joe?" Kelly asked, the fake smile still plastered to her face.

Abby's stomach churned. Was that jealousy she was feeling? Yes, it sure as hell was. Oh, no. Not over that jerk. She pushed the feeling away.

George smirked. "He just took the tractor out to the west field. You'll have to wait a few hours to see him."

"I just don't think I can wait that long." Kelly hopped in her truck and drove it at a punishing speed across the snow-covered, furrowed field toward the slow moving tractor.

"Idiot. She's going to tear that truck apart." George shook his head, started the engine of his own truck, and pulled out of the drive.

"Her daddy will just buy her a new one. She doesn't care," Margaret chimed in.

They drove slowly down the narrow road -- at least that's what Wyoming people called that narrow strip of asphalt without any lines.

The field ran alongside the road. Abby stared out the window. Kelly Childers pulled her truck in front of Joe's tractor, forcing him to stop. She strutted alongside the tractor as Joe climbed down. Long arms wrapped around Joe's neck, and she gave a grand wave as Abby and the McIveys drove past. The incident at the bar last night must have been a lover's quarrel. She seemed to be forgiving him today.

Margaret let out a humph, and George refused to wave.

"Is she Joe's girlfriend?" Abby quietly asked.

George snorted.

"That little snake is the reason Joe's losing his ranch. He hates her guts." Margaret snorted identically to George.

"He sure didn't look like he hated her."

"You've got to understand the background, honey," George said. "The Childers family is the money in this part of the state. They've got their hands pretty much around everybody's balls, if you know what I mean. Piss off Kelly, her brother Matt, or old man Ben Childers, and you had better hope their bank don't hold your mortgage." George's knuckles turned white against the steering wheel.

"They own the bank too?" Abby asked.

"Honey, they own the bank, the feed mill, the implement store, the repair garage, and the grocery store. *And* Ben Childers is on the county commission," Margaret chimed in.

"But I thought Joe's ranch had been in his family for generations? Wouldn't it have been paid for long ago?" Abby stretched her bruised knees out as far as the hump in the middle of the floorboard would allow.

"You ain't from the country are you?" George laughed. "The ranch was paid for long ago. But when you ranch, you need equipment. You need to replenish your livestock. You need to add barns and make improvements, and all of that takes money. You mortgage the ranch to buy these things, then when the cattle go to market you pay off the loan, hopefully." He scratched his chin, deep into the conversation. "If you have sick livestock, or if the price of beef drops, or you don't get any rain, or you get too much rain, well, honey, you'd better be able to carry that loan to the next year. You get the idea?"

Abby nodded, beginning to understand that ranching wasn't the glamorous picture of the starry-eyed cowboy she'd always envisioned.

"In Joe's case though, he was a good businessman, savvy with the beef market. Until Kelly came along," George said.

Margaret gave Abby a long, hard look, and then glanced around her at George. "I know pretty much everyone in this county, and I don't know anyone who could have done something like this to you."

"Honey, The Sagebrush Bar gets folks from all over. Whoever hurt Abby was probably from somewhere else, saw her win the money, and decided they wanted it." He took in a long, deep breath.

"It just makes me mad." Margaret squeezed Abby's hand. "I hope the sheriff catches the creep."

Snow swirled across the road and crusty patches of ice glazed the asphalt. A long, loud truck horn sent shivers down Abby's spine and abruptly ended their conversation. Abby whirled around in the seat, staring out the back window at bright head lights and a huge chrome grill.

*****

Joe yanked Kelly's arms off his neck. All he wanted to do was slap her, and hard. This woman has ruined his life, his future, and taken away everything important. Her breath reeked of whiskey and her perfume was thick. Joe figured she'd poured on the perfume in an attempt to cover the whiskey smell. Her blonde hair whipped across her face in the wind, giving her the appearance of a pissed-off thoroughbred horse -- all spit, and temper.

"Get your truck out of my way. I've got livestock to feed," he snapped.

Kelly shoved her hands in her pockets, smiling up at him. "I just got a new jacket. Do you like it?" She twirled around. "It's very soft and warm." She rubbed her hands seductively across her ample breasts.

The woman was unbelievable. Did she really think he was that easily seduced? Joe sighed. He damn sure was. She'd suckered him once, and that one time had destroyed him.

"I don't give a damn what you wear." He climbed back onto the tractor. "Move the truck or I'll run over it."

Kelly smiled. "You don't want to do that, Joe. Daddy wouldn't be happy, and I know you want to keep Daddy happy." She flipped the collar of the coat up around her neck, whipping her long, blonde hair back.

Joe slowly climbed off the tractor, pushing his hat back on his head and staring at her. "What do you want?"

She walked back to her truck. Turning to give him a look over her shoulder, she grabbed a cigarette and lighter. After a long inhale, she walked back to him. "I was very disappointed you didn't want to dance with me last night." She blew smoke at him.

Joe squinted, arms folded across his chest.

"I really am a good dancer, and hell, I would have even bought the drinks. I'm an equal opportunity woman."

"We had a business deal. I don't want to dance with somebody who doesn't repay their debts. I don't want to dance with you. I don't want to date you. I don't want anything but Hidden Rock Ranch back."

Her face went crimson and her hands became fists. Kelly Childers had never been denied much of anything. Joe liked being the one thing she couldn't have. The conniving, woman had taken his ranch, but his pride and his dignity were still his. He'd be damned if she were taking them.

"That godforsaken ranch! Is that all you can think about?" She flipped the cigarette away. "Don't I mean anything to you? We meant something to each other once--" she put a hand on his cheek-- "remember?"

He flipped it away. "You just don't get it, do you? You never have and you never will mean anything to me. I helped you because you were desperate and about to be killed. For that, I'm losing the one thing that mattered in my life." He squeezed her hand tighter. "If you want me to feel anything for you, then repay your debt and give me back the deed to Hidden Rock."

He climbed on the tractor. The engine sparked. He backed up, maneuvering around Kelly's truck.

She stomped her foot in the snow, then kicked the side of the truck. "You'll want me, Joe Baer. Very soon, you will be begging for me."

Chapter Six

Margaret hung the upper half of her body outside the truck's window, sitting her butt on the top edge of the door where the window rolled down. George showed no signs of concern about his wife hanging outside a moving truck as a tailgater swerved behind them.

Abby's hand went to the dashboard as the truck slid across the thin ribbon of asphalt, "Margaret?" Abby nearly screamed as George pushed the accelerator and swerved across the road. "Margaret what the hell are you doing? I really think you should get back inside the truck. Road rage never solved anything."

Margaret laughed and banged on the top of the truck. "Mike, you worthless dog. You back that truck off before I tell Stella Parker you've been fooling around."

George chuckled and elbowed Abby. "Mike's got a real soft spot for Stella," he explained. "Mrs. McIvey, get yourself back inside this truck and quit flirting with cowboys. Dang woman, have you no decency? At least do your flirting when I'm not in the truck." He reached across the seat as Margaret slid back inside, patting her thigh.

"Why would I do that? I like the way it aggravates you and makes you jealous," she laughed patting her windblown hair back into place.

Abby ventured a look behind, not taking her hand off the dash. The huge dualie pickup truck had backed off considerably and the driver, Mike Connor, was smiling a toothy grin and waving at her.

Abby's teeth chattered harder as snow blew in through Margaret's open window. George was merrily sliding along the road paying no attention to the deep ditches on either side on the pavement.

"Looks like Mike has come to get you. I guess he thinks you've decided take the job at Hidden Rock." Margaret rolled up her window putting an arm around Abby's shoulder. "Do you want to go there?"

Abby nodded. It wasn't like she had a choice.

"Why don't you spend a few days with me and George?" Margaret offered.

"I'm really fine."

Margaret gave her a sideways glance. "You don't have to play tough, honey." Se gave Abby a tight hug. "You remind me of a lost, little heifer."

Margaret took in a deep breath. Damn, she was about to cry. Margaret was about to cry. Abby couldn't let that happen. Her own emotions were too raw, too close to the surface. She didn't want Margaret to know how fragile she really was.

Instead, she forced out a laugh. "A heifer? A cow? I remind you of a cow?"

Margaret pulled back, staring at Abby. Tears lay in pools in the bottom of her eyes. "A baby, honey. Just a lost little critter that needs some mothering." She brushed a stray hair from Abby's forehead.

"Thank you," was all she could say without unleashing a torrent of ugly emotions. She leaned her head back against the truck seat, pulled her coat tight around her, and prayed her teeth didn't shatter.

George stopped the pickup and Mike's face suddenly appeared at Margaret's window.

She rolled it down. "Mike, I'm sending this stubborn woman with you, but you'd better take care of her or I'll horsewhip you."

Mike adjusted his knit cap to better cover his ears. A mischievous smile played on his face. "A threat like that coming from a woman like you is enough to keep any man in line."

George laughed. "Her threats have kept me in line for years."

"George McIvey." Margaret raised an eyebrow almost to her hairline.

Abby owed the couple more than she would probably ever be able to pay them back. Pulling her sack off the floor of the truck, she folded the top closed, "I'm feeling fine, Mr. Reynolds, and I think you have some hungry cowboys that need to be fed."

"We're here if you need us for anything." Margaret opened the truck door and the two of them got out.

Abby gave her a hug. "I know." "Is there anything you need me to get for you?" Mike asked, staring into the truck, then back at the small, brown paper bag in her arms.

The look in his eyes spoke what he couldn't. She'd seen the look so many times in the last year. Pity. Gut-wrenching pity. "I travel light Mr. Reynolds." She walked with head held high to his truck.

"I meant what I said, Mike." Margaret's eyebrow raised.

He gave her an understanding nod and hopped in the truck with Abby. "Please, call me Mike." He smiled, starting the engine. Making a hard u-turn, the truck slid across the pavement.

Abby fastened her seatbelt and grabbed the handle above the window.

The truck fishtailed across the ice, but Mike didn't slow down. "I hope you don't plan on going shopping very often." He turned the wipers on. They screeched painfully across the glass. "It's a fair piece to the nearest store. We plan far in advance for shopping trips, so you'll want to keep a list for pantry purchases."

They pulled off the main road onto a gravel road. He made several more turns onto smaller and smaller gravel roads, until they reached a rutted, one-lane dirt road. Suddenly the dirt road gave way to a smooth blacktop drive that wound around snow-covered banks, atop which a red snow fence ran as far as the eye could see.

"I think I'm going to have to drop breadcrumbs to find my way in and out of here." Abby couldn't remember ever having been so far from civilization. "Tell me, do you ever get snowed in back here?" As far as she could see in every direction was nothing, absolutely nothing, except hills, snow fence, trees, snow, and huge mountains.

"Occasionally we've been snowed in for a few days. We've got snowmobiles and we can get out for supplies with them."

A lump formed in her throat that refused to be swallowed.

"We've also got the Cat and the Deere with plows and shovels."

Abby had no clue what he was talking about, but as long as those things could get her out of this desolate wilderness, she liked them.

"Nobody's lived at the cottage for awhile. I had the boys go in, knock down the spider webs, and make sure no snakes or anything was living inside, but they don't always get everything. You aren't afraid of spiders and such, are you?"

The lump on her head began to ache. Mike's expression was kind, but odds were she was about to face those things, afraid or not. "I can't say I care too much for them."

"Well, snakes are hibernating this time of year. But they can move about when you start disturbing them. I'll have the boys leave you a hoe just to be safe." The truck slid across the blacktop road. Mike chuckled. "That was fun."

Abby pushed a hand against the dashboard, her mouth becoming suddenly dry. "A hoe? What do I need a hoe for?"

"For hacking the snakes' heads off, honey." Mike was matter-of-fact.

"Hack its head off?" The ache in her head turned to throbbing and was joined by a rumbling nausea deep in her stomach. "Couldn't I just call you or one of the men to come and--" she shuddered-- "hack the thing?"

"Sure, but we're usually out in the field or up at one of the cattle barns. It could be awhile before one of us could get it for you. By then it could disappear under the floor only to pop back out in the middle of the night and snuggle up with you in bed."

"They're cold-blooded, you know, and they like to find a warm spot to sleep. So it would be best if you just hack them when you see them."

Her head swam. Her vision turned gray and began sliding into black. She had gone from a bad dream to a horrific nightmare. Abby pinched her thigh, wincing at the pain. Awake. She was awake. The nightmare was real.

"We're here," Mike announced, parking the truck.

She sat forward in the seat, staring at one of the most beautiful homes she'd ever seen. It could have been on the cover of a national home magazine. A rock and log A-frame snuggled against a high rock cliff. The entire front was nearly three stories of glass and home erupting from of a wall of granite.

"That?" she whispered.

Mike laughed. "No, that's the main ranch house. We have to walk back to the cottage. We don't have a drive back to it yet." He left the keys in the ignition and hopped out of the truck. Without waiting on Abby, he took long-legged strides down a half-shoveled path to the left of the main house.

She grabbed her small sack and trotted behind Mike up the hill. After what felt like a three-mile hike, Abby huffed and puffed to a stop at a small cabin. It wasn't as dire as she'd imagined.

The small, log cottage sat atop a little rise that overlooked an endless vista of snow. A short porch sheltered the front door, and tall drifts surrounded the recently shoveled walk.

Mike opened the door and flipped on a lamp. The living room was small but cozy, with a rock fireplace at one end surrounded by a wide hearth. A large picture window gave an amazing view of a rugged mountain range in the distance. The only furnishings were two well-worn, green wingback chairs, a faded green couch, two corner tables with lamps, and an oak bench that sat in front of the fireplace. A large, black metal bucket for holding firewood, and an ugly, faded floral arrangement graced the wooden mantel. The small cottage looked like the Ritz after the McIveys' storage room.

"Looks like they cleaned pretty good." She was impressed.

Mike laughed. "They're hungry. They want you in the kitchen right away. You want me to start you a fire?" he offered.

"Is there any other heat in here besides the fireplace?" Abby was hopeful. She had no idea how to start a wood fire or how to keep it burning. Western movies had taught her that she needed to live in town with a furnace or she'd freeze to death. In Wyoming, that wouldn't take long.

"Yes, ma'am, we have all the comforts of home," Mike walked to a thermostat on the wall, pushing the switch upward.

Cocking his head to the side, an irritated look crossed his face. "I didn't hear it pop, did you?" He looked at Abby. She shook her head no.

"Well, for now I'll start you a fire that should heat this old place up just fine. It's pretty warm outside."

Abby's head jerked around. "Warm?"

"It's around twenty degrees. That's not bad for January." He pulled on a pair of deerskin gloves. "I'll get some firewood and be right back."

Abby's hands were frozen, her nose was numb, and she could hardly feel her feet -- and he thought it was warm. She set her sack on the old wooden dining table, looking over the rest of the cottage. The kitchen was small and ugly. There wasn't a celebrity decorator alive that could make it beautiful.

She walked down the short hall to the bedroom. An iron frame held a fat mattress and a small dresser was smooshed against the far wall. Across the hall from the bedroom was the bath. Abby inhaled deeply as she opened the door. A claw-foot tub sat ominously against one wall. It looked like a deep, dark pit. A pull chain toilet with no seat lurked in the corner and a sink with yellow water stains standing in it took up an entire corner.

The front door slammed. Abby walked into the living room as Mike began stacking bits of wood in the fireplace.

"Could you show me how to do that?" she asked, walking beside him.

"You mean you've never started a fire?" He turned slowly toward her, a stick falling from his hand onto the hearth.

"No." Abby kneeled on the floor next to him.

For the next ten minutes, Mike showed her the finer arts of fire building, how to pick out kindling wood, which logs to use first, and how to operate the damper. He asked if she had any questions. None entered her mind, as warmth started to come from the fireplace.

"When you get settled, head down the path we came up, go past the main house, and turn south up the hill. That's where the kitchen and dining hall are." He put his gloves back on and walked to the front door.

"Where? What hill?"

Mike patiently explained again. "If you aren't there by four o'clock, I'll know you got lost and come find you. The fire should take off in a bit. Just shut down the damper a little to keep the flames low and the heat inside the house. I also put a hoe on your front porch, just in case you need it." He left her with one of his twinkling smiles.

Abby massaged her temples. How freakin' long it would take her to get out of this place? She never knew her life could slip so completely out of her control so quickly. If only she'd just slipped out of Billy's way like she had done dozens of times before. If only she'd made her mother leave. If only she'd known how heartbroken her grandmother was. She'd made so many bad choices, and all of them lead her to here -- Sentinel, Wyoming, smack in the middle of nowhere. Her world was filled with work, snow, a hoe on standby, and desperate dreams.

She needed to freshen up and head to the ranch kitchen. First, she fished her orange stilettos from the brown bag. She set them beside the dresser in the bedroom. "I'll get there, Grandma. I promise," she whispered.

Abby walked to the bathroom, turning on the hot water spigot in the sink. The water ran ice cold. She'd have to tell Mike. Hot water was a necessity.

She looked at the strange, wooden box above the old toilet. She'd never seen one with a pull chain before. Gently, she gave the old chain a tug. The toilet gurgled, and then it hissed. The water went down, but none filled it back up. Abby stared into the dark hole. A sorrowful groan echoed upward.

Folding her arms across her chest, Abby leaned against the sink, staring into the pitiful toilet. The toilet burped, gurgled, and the last remnants of water disappeared.

"Great, now what?" The words had no more escaped her lips when a pink nose, followed by long whiskers, appeared out of the dark hole in the bottom of the toilet. The huge, brown rat, its fur matted and wet, slipped around in the porcelain bowl.

Like an Olympic sprinter, she tore down the hall screaming.

The living room smelled hot. Flames were bursting from the fireplace. Abby had no memory of what Mike had said to do.

Damn, the place was burning down and she didn't even have a phone to call the fire department. The damper. She remembered something about the damper. Closing the damper makes the flames smaller.

Cautiously, she crept alongside the fireplace, reaching for the metal handle. She pulled hard and quick, and it slammed shut. She leaned against the rock hearth, relieved she had saved the cabin. Abby Clark was becoming a country girl.

Squeals echoed from the bathroom. She squirmed up on the hearth, certain that the ugly, hulking thing was making its way down the hallway toward her.

The fireplace made a weird, belching sound. Abby turned just as a billow of black sooty smoke heaved outward spraying her, the room, everything with black, grimy soot.

She ran shrieking from the cabin. No damn slobbering, rabies-infected rat was going to eat her as a roasted snack. The front door was stuck. Abby yanked, yanked, screamed, and yanked.

The door finally whipped open and she ran face first into the screen door. The toes of her boots caught on the threshold, the screen door ripped from its hinges, and she tripped down the ice-covered concrete steps, falling face first into a three-foot snowdrift.

Her mangled, frozen body lay plastered like a snow angel with rigor mortis in the drift. Her knees screamed with pain, her hands were suddenly numb from the cold, and she gasped for air. Thick, wet snow molded around her face. Dear God, she was going to die in a snowdrift, where no one would find her body until spring.

Strong hands gripped her arms, lifting her out of the white tomb. Blinking the snow from her eyes and spitting ice balls, she looked into the faces of Mike Connor and Joe Baer.

Mike laughed so hard he could barely stand. Joe turned his head to the side, his shoulders trembling with laughter. He swallowed hard, regaining his composure. Abby crossed her arms over her chest. What exactly was so damn funny?

"What in the hell happened? We heard you screaming all the way up at the kitchen." Joe stared at the cabin as billowing, black smoke oozed out what was left of the front door.

Tears begin to roll down her face. They promptly froze on her cheeks.

Fred ran up the hill, followed by Rodney and several cowboys she didn't know. Their eyes went from Abby, to the cabin, and back to Abby. "Whoa."

*****

Joe and Mike coughed through the smoke as they ventured inside. Mike pulled the damper open. "She shut it completely down. I told her how to work this thing. I swear I did."

Joe opened windows, letting the smoke escape. He walked onto the porch, staring at the black-faced lady. The knees of her jeans were torn, her face was black with streaks of frozen tears cutting through the soot, and snow crystals clung to her hair. A smile crossed his face again.

Abby Clark was a living, breathing poster child for calamity. He'd yet to cross her path that some accident or disaster didn't befall him. As if his life needed any more trouble. It had more than enough without this klutz of a city girl adding to it.

Although it had been a long time since anyone had made him laugh the way she did.

Fred took off his coat and wrapped it around a shaking Abby. "Honey, what did you do?"

Abby sniffed. "I didn't do anything. The fireplace blew up, the toilet didn't have any water, and there's a huge rat in it."

Joe and Mike's heads sprung up instantly. Joe sprinted to the bathroom, spying the huge critter sliding around in the slick toilet bowl. With experienced hands, he picked it up -- by its tail so it couldn't bite him -- and carried it to the front door. "Is this the huge rat you were afraid of?"

She screamed. The cowboys laughed and made squeaking noises.

"He won't make much of a meal, but here kitty, kitty, kitty," Joe called.

Abby shrieked, "Don't you dare." She pulled loose from Fred's embrace. "Don't you dare!"

"You want it?" Joe dangled it toward her. The mouse's small legs flailed in the air, its little paws opening and closing, eyes wide with terror.

Abby jumped back. "No, but can't you just turn it loose in the woods with some cheese or something?" Joe handed the wet mouse to Mike, walking down the steps to Abby. Mike looked at Joe, then at the mouse, his eyebrows raised.

"Who is she, Mike?" A cowboy asked.

"She's our new cook." He smiled.

"If she can't cook any better then she can light a fire, we're going to starve to death." He shook his head.

Joe led her to his truck and opened the door for her before he walked to the driver's side. Mike, Fred, and the cowboys stood on the snowy hillside. Black smoke billowed from the cabin windows with Mike holding the struggling mouse.

"Where are we going?" She asked. Her jaw quivered and her teeth were chattering.

Joe turned the heater on high, pulling quickly away. "We're going to get you cleaned up." He slid down the drive, the same way Mike had.

"What is it with you guys and sliding in your trucks?" She reached for the grab handle above the door.

"It helps ease frustration." He gave her a hard glance.

Twenty minutes later, he turned down the two-rut road that led to his house. "You can shower and change here, then I'll take you back to the ranch so you can cook dinner. I'll see about getting the house fumigated."

"And get the furnace to work?" Her eyes pleaded.

"If I have to drive to Cheyenne to get one and install it myself you'll have a furnace. I don't ever want you to start another fire."

Chapter Seven

"You done in there?" Joe's voice blared at the door. "You've got to be at the ranch to cook dinner in less than an hour."

Abby turned the hot water off and then dried off quickly. Her clothes were a black, sooty pile on the floor. Oh, crap. She had nothing to wear. What the hell was she going to do? She wrapped the bath towel tight around her, leaning against the wall.

She was going to have to ask Joe Baer for help again. She reached for the door handle, then stopped. She couldn't do it, not again. Abby stared up at the ceiling, taking in a deep breath. "Humility is becoming my middle name," she sighed. Someone up above truly hated her.

It wasn't as if she had a choice. Abby yanked the door open, facing an empty hall. Her bare feet were cold against the linoleum floor. Why did she have to pick the dead of winter in the freakin' tundra to kick Billy's balls and get her ass thrown off that bus?

Joe was staring out the window over the sink, sipping on a steaming cup of coffee. One foot was propped on a kitchen chair. His jeans pulled tight across his butt and the flannel shirt was taut against muscular arms. A large hand wrapped completely around the coffee cup.

Abby swallowed hard, liking the view way more than she should have. The towel suddenly felt tighter against her breasts. She pulled it hard, tucking it more securely. A sheen of perspiration suddenly enveloped her shivering cold body. Abby cleared her throat.

Joe turned dropping the coffee cup. "Damn." It shattered across the floor.

"I didn't mean to startle you." Abby clung tight to the towel. "Did you get burned?"

"No, I didn't get burned," he snarled. "What the -- what are you doing out here? Don't you know that's not decent?" He picked up the pieces of cup, mumbling under his breath, "City girls."

"It wasn't like I had a choice. If I'd had any clothes, I damn sure wouldn't." She adjusted the towel around her breasts and then adjusted her usual colorful ranting. "Look, the clothes I had on are sooty and everything else is back at the cabin. I don't have anything to wear." Why did he have to make everything so complicated?

"You are...frustrating." He stopped, picked up the pieces of cup, and slammed them on the counter, then stomped out of the room.

*****

The woman was going to be the death of him. What was she thinking, standing in the middle of his living room with nothing on but a towel? She was nearly naked for criss sakes. Nothing but a towel covering firm swells of breasts. And legs -- legs everywhere.

He swallowed, sliding hanger after hanger across the rod in his closet. Abby had great legs. Her eyes were pretty too, framed by ringlets of honey-blonde hair that clung to her face and neck.

Finding a pair of jeans someone had bought him that were too small, he yanked them and a flannel shirt off a hanger and turned to find her standing in the doorway. Joe caught his breath. In the full light streaming through the window, she looked as angelic as she had the night he saw her sing.

"Here's some clothes, hurry up." He ordered. "City girls."

"Hicks." She slammed the bedroom door shut behind him.

Joe went back to the kitchen and wiped the spilled coffee from the floor. What was it about Abby that made him care and made him so angry? He smiled, remembering her sooty face and snow-drenched hair. He wanted to know more about her. Joe slammed a fist against the counter. No, he didn't. He didn't want to know anything about another woman.

Just thinking about her standing in the hallway with nothing on but a towel made his mind wander to places it shouldn't. His stomach became warm, and his groin was taking on a life of its own. What was he thinking? He wasn't. His groin was. Well, that was going to stop right now.

She came into the kitchen, her feet bare, the jeans swallowing her small butt. The flannel shirt was so big it could have been a dress. She looked absolutely stunning. Damn, he was going to have to find something to distract him. Cows, hay, tractors.

"I need a safety pin. I can't keep the jeans on." She interrupted his thoughts, holding the ample material at the waist and staring up at him.

He grunted, rummaging through a kitchen drawer. "I can't find one. Here try this." He held up a wooden, spring-loaded clothespin, handing it to her.

"Thanks." She tried to stuff all the extra material in the clothespin. The pants slipped over her hips, than the spring broke. It careened across the kitchen, stopping with a ping in the kitchen sink.

"I'm sorry," She winced at the noise.

"It's all right, Abby," Joe emptied the drawer onto the kitchen counter. Matches, hardware, twine, and finally a large safety pin appeared. "This should work." He handed it to her.

She folded the denim over and pushed the fabric into the pin. The pants finally stayed put. She rolled up the sleeves of the flannel shirt and then rolled the pant legs up. "This should work, thank you."

"Would you like some coffee before we head over to the ranch?" He held up the steaming pot of coffee.

"Yes, I would." Abby slid into a chair at the small dinette. "I'm sorry about smoking up the cabin. I've never been around a fireplace before that wasn't gas operated. I'll clean up the mess after I finish with dinner."

Joe sat the cup in front of her and sat in the chair across from her, "The boys should already have most of it cleaned." He watched her stare into her coffee. She'd sprung into Sentinnel like a west wind, gusting into the county, getting everyone's attention, and then -- and then what? Would she leave? Would she stay? That was damned unlikely. Abby was a city-girl with talent and good looks -- not the type to stay in the Wyoming outback. "Where are you from?" he asked.

"Indiana." She kept her eyes on the coffee. "What brings you to Wyoming?"

He wrapped his hands wrapped around the coffee mug, wanting to ask her a thousand questions.

"Just passing through, Sheriff." She did a really awful John Wayne impression. "Where are you heading?" Getting her to talk was like extracting teeth from a grizzly. He was stubborn too, and he'd keep asking questions until he knew everything about her. "California."

"What's in California? Family?"

"Yeah." Her eyes went back to her coffee. Damn, she was lying to him.

"How long will you be staying around here?"

Abby gulped the last of the coffee. "I'd better finish dressing. I've got hungry cowboys to feed." She pushed away from the table, walking down the hall to the bedroom, the jeans barely staying put on her hips.

Either she was a very private person or she had something to hide. Hiding something seemed to fit her better. He drained the last of his coffee, slid his jacket on and met her at the door. "I've heard a lot of bull in my time, but that takes the cake." He handed her a jacket.

"I imagine you are pretty familiar with bull." She walked around him, sliding her coat on and heading toward the front door.

"What are you running from, Abby?"

"Perhaps it's something I'm running to." She gave him a hard look. "I'd like for you to take me to the ranch. I have a job to do."

*****

In just a few days, Abby had the meal schedule and kitchen operation down to a science. Breakfast and dinner daily, and occasionally, she packed a lunch for the cowboys. They were well mannered and usually complimentary, but they loved to tease.

They were never going to let her live down the mouse-in-the-toilet fiasco. She'd found fake mice in her apron pockets, mice in a pot in the kitchen, mice hanging by a rope over the kitchen sink, and she'd even found one sunk into the mayonnaise jar. She hoped their supply was running out.

Joe had installed a furnace while she was working. He seemed determined to avoid her as much as possible, that was fine with her. She didn't like the way he made her crazy, mad, and klutzy.

Mike had fixed the toilet and Fred Gillis had brought her a new toilet seat -- a padded one he was very proud of. Her cabin smelled less like smoke each day, but it had yet to stop snowing outside.

The end of the week brought a bright spot: Tessa.

"Hi honey. How are you faring out here?" She wedged herself and those breasts into a seat at the small dinette table in Abby's cabin.

"I'm doing pretty well." Abby filled a kettle with water and sat it on the stove. "Tea?"

"Sure." Tessa was a walking advertisement for spandex. Cobalt blue spandex pants with matching over-shirt, white cowboy boots with rhinestones, and enough gold chains to make the local jeweler jealous. Her red hair was teased high on top of her head, and long dangling earrings whacked the sides of her neck when she talked.

"How's your head? I don't see any bandages."

"It's healing very well." Abby lifted her bangs so Tessa could see.

"Did they find out who did it?" She clicked her long, blue fingernails on the tabletop.

"No." Abby stuffed tea bags into two cups as she talked. "The sheriff has been here, but all I can tell him is that a dark truck peeled out of the parking lot. Maybe that was the person who did it, maybe not." She sighed, turning the heat up under the teakettle.

Tessa strummed her fingers faster, fidgeting. "I need to apologize to you. Rodney and me, we never meant for you to get hurt. I'm so sorry, we just got so horny, you know?" She walked to Abby, patting her arm. "Could you forgive us?"

"Tessa you're priceless. I don't think you could do anything I'd stay too mad at for long." Abby gave her a hug. The teakettle whistled. "Sit and I'll bring us some tea. I guess things between you two are pretty good since you're so horny, huh?" She grinned, handing Tessa a teacup and sitting at the table across from her.

Tessa stirred sugar into the tea. "They're all right, I guess." Then she stared wide-eyed at Abby. "But did you ever think there has got to be more then great sex?" Tessa's Texas accent grew thicker when she got excited.

Abby nearly choked on her tea. She wasn't quite sure how to answer her. "Well, yes," she stammered.

"Haven't you had great sex, Abby?"

She'd had two relationships, neither of which gave her great sex -- or great anything, for that matter. She quickly changed the subject. "Does he still want you to learn how to cook before he asks you to marry him?"

"He just keeps pointing out that I can't cook like his mama." Tessa slammed the spoon down on the table. "He says on a ranch, you gotta to be able to cook. Where I come from, we had a cook. I told him we could just hire one. He laughed at me and said 'I ain't no Texas rancher, honey.'" Resting her elbows on the table, she stared up at Abby like a lost kid.

She had no words of wisdom to give. Based on her life, advice was the last thing she should be giving out. "How about we start your cooking lessons?" Abby nodded toward the kitchen.

Tessa squealed, smacking her hands on the table. "Yee haw," she shouted. "I can pay you." Her eyes were wide with excitement.

"I don't want pay, but I don't have a car. Do you think once in awhile I could borrow yours and go into town?" Abby prayed Tessa would go for the deal. Living on the ranch with no television, no radio, no computer, and barely any company was driving her completely insane.

"Anytime."

"Now? We'll have to go to the grocery before I can start giving you lessons." Abby felt almost as excited as Tessa looked.

"Rosie is ready." Tessa swung on her cobalt blue fake fur coat and stretched the matching gloves over her hands.

"Rosie?" Abby had not heard that name before; then again, she didn't hear much out on this desolated ranch. "Who is Rosie?"

Tessa just laughed and burst out the door.

*****

The Cadillac moved slowly up the lane toward Joe. He was out of options for saving his ranch. Today he would plead and beg. Pride be damned if it meant keeping his ranch. It was probably lost forever, but the blood and sweat that six generations of Baers had put into it wouldn't let him back away without trying everything he could to get it back, including humbling himself before Ben Childers.

Childers was a cold-hearted, unforgiving man whose god was money, and the only thing Joe had to offer was his soul. Ben's car slowed as he approached. Joe stood in the driveway, leaning against his black pickup truck. The garage door opened and Childers drove inside. Joe followed. Being confined in a small place with Ben Childers could be very dangerous. Joe kept a reasonable distance.

Ben pushed the opener, shutting the garage door. He slid on his cowboy hat and stepped out of the Cadillac. The dim opener light gave the large garage an eerie radiance, like a bad horror movie.

"Well, well. Joe Baer, what brings you to my place?" Ben's heavy gold bracelet clanked against the glass as he shut the car door behind him.

"You know why I'm here Ben. I want--"

"Hidden Rock's mortgage," Ben interrupted him and bristled. His neatly coifed gray hair matched his gray eyes.

"This was a deal between me and Tom Talking Horse." Joe worked hard to keep his voice calm. "I made the deal with him, not you. I don't know and I don't care how you came to get the deed, but I want to work out a deal for it."

"The hell you don't care. You'd give your right arm to find out how I got the deed to Hidden Rock." His cold laughter echoed in the garage. "The deed is unpaid at my bank and unless you can pay me one million dollars for it in a little less than two months, it's mine, all legal. We have no further business, Mr. Baer, so see yourself out the side door." He pushed his hat back on his head and walked toward the entrance.

"Ben, that ranch means everything to me. I'll do whatever it takes to get it back."

Childers paused on the top step, turning slowly toward Joe. "That should be plenty of time for a smart man like you to come up with the money."

"I need more time. I can't raise a million dollars in sixty days." Joe felt Hidden Rock slipping through his fingers. If a man ever wanted to commit murder, Joe sure as hell did at this moment.

"I might have a way." Ben's cold eyes fixed on him. "For years I've wanted one of my cowboys to win the Silver Bullet Rodeo Championship for Childers Ranch. I've never had the satisfaction of seeing that." A smile eased across his face. "I'll tell you what, you enter the bull-riding contest under my ranch's name and win, I'll sign the mortgage back over to you, lock, stock, and barrel. Instead of a winning purse, you get the deed to Hidden Rock." He pulled a cigar out of his jacket pocket and slowly lit it, not talking his eyes off Joe. "Now that's one doozy of a deal, boy."

While Joe was one of the rodeo's best bull riders, Ben Childers never left anything to chance. He sure as hell wasn't going to let Joe win if he could prevent it.

"What's the catch?"

"It's just good business." Ben leaned against the Cadillac. "A few investors and I thought a purse of one million dollars would bring the best riders in the world to Sentinel. With the best riders come the best press, the best advertisers; hell we've got ESPN panting at the door and advertisers throwing money at our feet for exclusive rights." He inhaled long and deep on the cigar. "For a purse of one million dollars you're going to have some stiff competition."

Joe watched the coldness in his eyes. "Which bull? And do I get this in writing?"

"Whatever bull you draw. Have your lawyer draw up a paper. I'll sign it." Smoke circled around Ben's sun-worn face. "Hell, I'll even waive the twenty-five thousand dollar entry fee for you, providing you ride under the Childers name. Eight seconds, and Hidden Rock Ranch is back in the Baer family. If you're interested, sign up at the feed store under my ranch name. Now see yourself out," he flipped the garage door light off at the top of the steps and walked inside.

Joe stood in the dark. He'd been in many rodeos, ridden broncos and bulls, and even managed to win a few competitions. The Silver Bullet Rodeo was one of the premier rodeos. Although it was an off-season rodeo, it attracted the best riders from the U.S. and Canada. But a bull ride that carried a purse of a million dollars, even with the biggest advertisers on the planet taking part, felt very suspicious.

Joe stepped out through the small side door, squinting at the sudden brightness. Whatever Ben had planned, he didn't care. The man had just offered him the only chance he had of keeping his ranch, and he was going to take it, even if it killed him.

Chapter Eight

"I have died and gone to Bonanza." Abby slid out the door of the big, black, four-wheel-drive pickup truck Tessa affectionately called Rosie, and into a town that looked like a movie set. The sidewalks were wood, the street was paved but had no lines, and there were hitching posts at the ends of the block.

While there weren't many cars parked along the main street, there was every make and model of pickup truck, in every size, color, and length.

People wore cowboy hats, boots, and dusters. They weren't suburbanites making a statement -- these were ranchers. Abby smiled. It was amazing to see real western cowboys walking down a street then hop into a truck instead of onto a horse.

"Does anybody use those hitching posts?" she asked Tessa.

"In warm weather they do, or when they move the cattle to winter pasture." Tessa seemed to know a lot about ranching. "We have open range in Texas, too. There ain't a whole lot of good pasture in these parts, so you move the cattle to where the feed is."

A pickup truck emblazoned with the sheriff's emblem slowly cruised down the main street. "If Matt Dillon gets out I'm heading to the saloon for a stiff one." Abby laughed.

"The deputy sheriff is Bowdie Tucker, and oh, is he a hottie." Tessa stood like a seductive Greek goddess, leaning against her truck. She gave the passing sheriff a wave.

She was right. Even through the windows of the truck, the man looked like an iconic advertising cowboy. He had a chiseled jaw, dark hair, amazing eyes, and so much testosterone that it leaked out of the truck and left a trail down the street where several women just stopped and enjoyed the view.

The deputy nearly wrecked, checking out Tessa and her *endowments*. The girl knew how to work her assets. He tipped his cowboy hat, giving her a smile as wide as a Texas sunset and continued through town, apparently satisfied that he'd left all the women with racing hearts.

"That was fun." Tessa laughed, then made a hissing sound as she nodded toward a truck with *Childer's Implements* painted on the side. "Too bad our Bonanza has to have those heartless buzzards living in it."

Kelly slid out of the passenger seat and gave a disgusted and bored look down the street.

Tessa grabbed her arm. "Let's do some fun shopping before we head to the grocery store." She opened the door to an inviting shop called Water's Edge Gallery. "Olivia, are you in here, girl?" Tessa's voice was loud and shrill over the soft native flute music that was playing.

The intimate shop was full of silver jewelry, woodcarvings, leather works, and magnificent artwork.

"Tessa? Tessa Marie?" A gorgeous, dark haired woman came from the back room. What the hell kind of DNA was rampant in this county? There wasn't an ugly person to be found, herself excepted. Tessa exchanged hugs with the perfect specimen of womanhood.

"Abby Clark, meet Olivia Talking Horse."

Olivia was tall and slender, with silky black that fell to her waist Her dark native complexion was flawless. Abby felt sorely in need of makeup or a large paper bag.

"Hello." Olivia started to extend a hand, then grabbed a towel wiping her hands off. "I'm sorry, I was painting."

"You're the artist?" Abby wandered around the shop. The paintings were magnificent. Images of the Wyoming plains, the craggy, ancient mountains, the ceaseless snow, and native animals -- those were the ones that immediately captured Abby's heart. A mountain lion hidden in the rocks, a bull elk enjoying a summer stream, and a white buffalo surrounded by a field of Indian paintbrush filled canvases in muted desert colors. The painting of a gray wolf stopped her.

Its eyes were soft yellow, its fur tinged with ice, its face so expressive Abby had to stop herself from reaching out to stroke its fur. "This is absolutely beautiful, and it's so real."

"You like wolves?" Olivia walked beside her, smelling of sweet sage and fresh earth.

"I like this one," Abby said on a laugh.

"I call him *Freedom's Shadow*. He is a great, gray wolf that roams the Wind River Reservation." She leaned back looking at the small canvas on the wall. "He is elusive, stealthy, and brave. Many of us have tried to capture his image. My brother, Tom Talking Horse, actually got close enough to snap a picture. His photo is what I painted this from."

Tessa leaned against the counter. "I put your ranch painting right over my fireplace. It's perfect, and it looks exactly like home." She peeled open a granola bar from the display and took a large bite.

Olivia smiled. "Bring me a picture of those brothers of yours. Your parents' anniversary is only a few weeks away. I am only human."

Tessa nodded as she chewed. The small bell on the door jingled. Olivia's face took on a look of utter dread.

Abby turned as Kelly Childers and a distinguished looking older man entered the store. They had the same eyes, the same facial features, and the same haughty expression.

Tessa cleared her throat and gave Abby a snarling nod toward them.

"Good morning, Olivia." Kelly smiled, sending Abby a sarcastic look.

Abby moved to an out-of-the-way spot near the back of the store. She didn't want any confrontations, particularly not with these people, since everyone she'd encountered seemed to be living in fear of the Childers' heavy hand.

"I'm here for the family portrait I commissioned." The man's voice was commanding. His manner was that of a man used to people jumping to attention when he spoke. He was tall, well over six feet, and his hair was completely silver. Everything he wore, from his jewelry to his boots, was very expensive.

"I'll bring it right out, Mr. Childers." Olivia stepped into the back room.

Kelly made her way to where Abby was trying to remain invisible. "Abby isn't it?" she asked, walking in front of the wolf painting.

While the people in this county might owe their souls to the Childers's, Abby didn't, "Yes, it is. I'm glad I impressed you enough to remember."

Tessa made her way to Abby's side, leaning close.

Kelly's eyes went wide, then narrowed with anger. She grabbed the man's arm and pulled him toward her. "This is my father, Ben Childers."

"Ma'am," he tipped his cowboy hat, giving Abby an even more thorough once over than Kelly. "What brings you to these parts?" He walked into her personal space, obviously used to his presence scaring people into moving away.

Tessa's twangy voice whispered in her ear, as she breezed past. "Don't tell him anything, honey."

"I'm just visiting friends." Abby gave him a pointed stare, standing her ground. She'd been in bars, honky tonks, mosh pits, and some of the seediest dives in the Midwest. He was a long way from being scary.

"You're not from Wyoming?" He smiled, walking back to the counter.

"No," she answered.

"Here's your portrait, Mr. Childers." Olivia came out of the back room with a large canvas covered in brown wrapping paper.

Ben Childers put on a pair of thick glasses and ripped the paper off the canvas. He scrutinized the work with the eye of an art critic.

"Not bad, Olivia, not bad at all." He set it on the floor, taking a few steps back and gave a reluctant sigh. "I reckon I'll have to write you a check for the full price. Re-cover this. I have a long drive back to the Circle C."

Olivia's jaw set tight. She nodded and returned to the back room to re-cover the portrait.

Ben's attention returned to Abby. He walked across the shop, standing inches from her. "Will you be staying in Wyoming long?"

"I don't know."

"I see you're an admirer of Olivia's art." He squinted at the wolf painting. Kelly leaned against his arm, like toddler. He didn't seem to notice.

"I am." Abby turned her attention to a piece of pottery, walking away from the annoying duo.

Olivia returned from the back room and walked behind the counter to ring out his purchase. "Will there be anything else, Mr. Childers?"

Kelly grabbed with wolf painting off the wall. "I want this." She put the painting on the counter.

Ben pulled back, giving the painting a long look. "I thought you hated wolves?"

Kelly pouted. "I think it's pretty and I want it."

Olivia gave Abby a shocked look. "I wasn't planning on selling this."

"Hell, honey everything's for sale." Ben pulled out his calf-skin wallet. "How much?"

"Three hundred dollars." Olivia folded her arms across her chest.

"You want three hundred for that little piece of paint on fabric?"

"It took many hours to paint, Mr. Childers." Olivia smiled.

Ben gave her a look hard look, then a smile washed across his face. "And only a few minutes take advantage of a white man who indulges his daughter."

"The price is three hundred." She stood firm.

Abby gained an instant respect for the shop owner. She'd held both her tongue and her temper, and was going to make a nice, little profit.

"Daddy, I want it." Kelly clung to the painting.

Ben pulled three crisp one hundred dollar bills from his wallet. "Looks like your lucky day, Olivia. I guess it will still be four hundred for the portrait."

"It will." She rang it into the register and handed him a receipt.

"Ladies." Ben tipped his hat, escorting Kelly out the door.

Olivia slammed the register drawer shut, letting out a low, guttural growl. "I'm sorry, Abby. I know you admired that painting."

"I couldn't afford it and you made a profit, what's not to like here?" Abby laughed. "Now I understand why everyone I meet hates that man."

They all stood at the shop's front window watching the two drive down the street.

"Time to perk up and head to that grocery store, Abby." Tessa gave Olivia a hug. "Later, honey." She grabbed Abby's arm and nearly dragged her outside.

"I am not one to let some desert lizard ruin my day. The best grocery store is on the far side of town. This general store doesn't have anything but bullets, salt, and sweet feed." She reached into her coat pocket and tossed the keys to Abby. "You ever drive a truck before?"

Abby looked at the huge black four-by-four with small yellow roses painted behind the side windows, and *Rosie* painted across the nose of the hood.

"No, I haven't." She climbed into the driver's seat. It had been months since she'd driven anything. Exactly eight months ago, when the bank had repossessed her twelve-year-old car. Abby ran her hands over the leather steering wheel, then stared out the windshield and adjusted the power seat to fit her. The seat conformed to her back and rump.

"There's a heater in that seat," Tessa offered. "I saw your teeth chattering."

Abby reached down and pushed the heated seat button. "That is awesome enough to make me say, 'yeehaw'." They laughed as Abby started the engine.

The grocery store wasn't far, but enough of a drive to satisfy Abby's driving lust. The truck was a lot more powerful than her car had been, and as she turned the corner into the parking lot, she plunged the truck through a huge crater of water.

As the sludge settled, she spied one very soaked, very muddy Joe Baer standing on the corner. Filthy water ran in a stream off the brim of his hat. Abby slammed on the brakes, which sent another cascade of water across the man.

Tessa took in a deep breath, then snorted with laughter "Nothing like ticking off an angry bear."

"I didn't mean to." Abby stopped and gave Joe an apologetic wave. He just stared at her through a mud-spattered face. Abby drove into the parking lot clipping a plastic trash can with the fender. She jerked to a stop, taking up two parking places. "Sorry, I guess it's a bit bigger than I'm used to."

Tessa just nodded.

Abby stared at Joe in the rearview mirror. He slung his hat around, trying to rid it of the road sludge, then popped it back on his head and walked down the street. Why did this keep happening? She leaned her head against the steering wheel. The truck horn played Deep in the Heart of Texas. The tune echoed across the parking lot. Every head turned, several dogs howled, and Abby slid low in the seat.

Chapter Nine

The kitchen was warm, despite the snowstorm squalling outside. Alone in the kitchen she worked on her vocals. The low notes were easy -- she was a natural alto -- but those high notes made her throat raw and her voice warble. At least in the middle of nowhere there wasn't anybody to hear how bad they sounded. Abby lingered in the kitchen long after the meal had been served. The kitchen was the only warm place she'd found since landing in Wyoming..

The cowboys loved all the baked goods she was churning out. She'd wasn't about to tell them she was only baking to keep the ovens on, otherwise she'd freeze to death. Plus, she was getting very tired of the smell of searing animal flesh. The baked goods were as much of a diversion for her as they were a treat for the cowboys.

Lately, she'd been adding more and more vegetables to their meals. At breakfast yesterday, they hardly missed the steak with their eggs. Only a few grumbled. Tonight, she was going all the way. She cooked the fresh vegetables that Mike had brought in earlier into a wonderful vegetable soup, minus the beef, and made loaves of sourdough bread to go with it. Beef ranchers or not, these men needed some vegetables. The cowboys came in as she pulled the last loaf of bread from the oven.

"Whew, it is cold out there." Fred stomped his feet at the door, hanging up his brown canvas coat. Abby raised an eyebrow. Hell must be close to freezing over for one of them to say it was cold.

Everyone ate at pine tables in the large dining room, with long, detached seats like a perpetual picnic. Abby put bread, butter, salt, and pepper in the center of each, setting out plates so they could line up cafeteria style and receive their soup.

Other cowboys followed, each cussing and mumbling about the snow, the tractors that wouldn't start, and the cows that were belly-deep in the white stuff.

"What's for supper, Abby?" Hal Tolen asked with a large grin on his face. He was the best-looking cowboy in the bunch, with sandy blonde hair, emerald green eyes, and a smile that could nearly melt the Wyoming snow.

"It's soup." Abby pulled a ladleful out of the big stockpot.

"I love beef stew," Hal held his bowl in front of him like a small boy waiting on a piece of cake. A perplexed look crossed his face, "where's the beef chunks? Did they sink to the bottom?"

"Well, no, not exactly. It's, well, it's vegetable soup."

"Ain't there no beef in it?" The smile dropped from his face like an anchor.

"It won't hurt you to eat a vegetarian meal once in a while." She stirred the soup, looking across the now silent room. Each man stopped where they stood. She thought she could actually hear the snow falling outside, the room had become so quiet. "What?"

Fred Gillis walked slowly to her side, whispering in her ear, "Abby, we're beef ranchers. We eat beef -- the more beef the better." He peered into the stockpot. "Ain't there no beef in it all?"

Abby growled, a habit she'd recently developed living with the constantly growling cowboys.

Fred peered deeper into the pot. "And what's that white stuff a'floatin in there? Don't look like no vegetable I ever saw."

"It's tofu."

A look of utter terror froze across Fred's face. Mike snorted and the others stood completely still.

"Just try it." Abby pointed at Fred with her ladle.

Fred backed up two steps. He looked across the room at the men watching him, and then back at Abby still wielding the ladle.

Mike rolled up his shirtsleeves and grabbed a soup bowl off the stack. "What the hell, I'm hungry. It's been hours since lunch. I could eat damn near anything."

Abby smiled, ladled him a large bowlful, and gave a disgusted look to the rest of the cowboys.

No one moved a muscle as Mike walked to a table and sat down. Taking a slice of bread from the basket, he dipped it in the broth. With a look of mortal fear on his face, he cautiously took a bite.

Three chews into it, a smile erupted across his face. "It's ain't bad and I think it's got beef broth in it." The room buzzed alive as the cowboys lined up for a bowl.

Abby growled again, ladling out the soup.

"Oh, dear heaven." Hal's voice was so slow and low, the room went silent. Everyone followed his gaze out the front window of the dining hall. A large plume of black smoke billowed across the hill.

"The cattle barn's on fire!" Mike grabbed his jacket off the peg by the door. "Abby, call the fire department, then call Joe!" The entire room burst out the door.

Abby frantically ran to the phone and dialed 911. There was no response to the number. The ranch was so far off the beaten path they didn't have 911 services. Scanning through the numbers scrawled on the wall beside the phone, she found the fire department. Thank goodness the dispatcher knew where Hidden Rock Ranch was. Fire would have consumed the place before Abby could have given them directions.

Joe's number was just below the fire department. She dialed, getting his answering machine. "Joe, Mike needs you at the ranch, there's a fire in the cattle barn." She hung up the phone, pulled on her heavy flannel coat, and sprinted outside.

Flames were spewing out the windows of the barn when she arrived. Black smoke grabbed at the sky. The wind had picked up, whipping the snow into huge drifts and flaming the already intense fire.

Fred ran to her. His face was red and small blisters lined his forehead. His coat was black and sooty. "Go up to the equipment barn, grab the blue tractor with the bucket attachment. We got at least twenty heifers inside and, we're gonna have to knock down a wall to get to them." He ran back to the barn.

Every available man was bucketing water. An old pumper truck, its hose ready to dip into the huge pond beside the barn, was stopped short by ice. Two men were slamming picks into the ice, pounding furiously trying to break through. Fred frantically waved her toward the equipment barn, when she just stood there, gaping at the fire.

Abby ran up the hill. With each step, she wondered how to start a tractor. She'd never been on one in her life. The wind was growing more ferocious. Some of the gusts had to be twenty miles an hour. The wind hammered the barn doors. Abby pulled and tugged, fighting against it. She managed to get the small door open, but the large door wouldn't budge.

Inside, she prayed she would find a garage door opener. Even if she managed to get the tractor started, she couldn't get it outside. Groping in the dark barn, she found a light switch. A small, low-watt bulb was the single source of light.

The large, blue tractor sat in the middle of the barn like a man-eating tiger waiting on its prey. With little light, it was all shadows and claws. Cautiously, she climbed atop its cold, metal seat. The wind tunneled through the barn, filling it with drifts of snow and popping the light bulb. Abby was engulfed in darkness.

The barn had no windows, no cracks, no source of light. Abby was completely blind. She had to reach the door. She had to have some light. Climbing off the tractor, her groin impacted with the gearshift. Sparks raged behind her eyes.

She plummeted to the concrete floor, pounding both knees. She growled, crawling in the general direction of where she thought door should be. Her hands landed on small stones that pierced into her palms.

She stood, groping in the darkness for the smooth doorknob. The wind grabbed the door as she pushed it open, whipping her out, sprawling into the snow. Clinging to the doorknob for dear life, she pulled herself to her feet and squinted through the semi-dark barn at the machine. "All right tractor, this is war."

Easing her bruised body back onto the seat, she spotted a key in the ignition. She turned it. Nothing.

The smell of smoke poured inside. Frantically, she pushed all the buttons then tried the key. She located a flat pedal on the left side of the tractor. She eased her foot down, pushing the pedal all the way, hoping it was the accelerator.

Slowly, Abby turned the key again. The engine caught, revving hard. "Yeehaw!" She gave a Tessa yell and let off the pedal.

The tractor heaved, convulsed, coughed, then lurched forward with the gusto of a derby racehorse. The throttle was at full speed, the gearshift was in high, and the shovel was straight out.

In less than a minute, Abby splintered through the barn door and careened down the snow-covered hill, completely out of control.

*****

Ben Childers propped his feet up on the coffee table. Two size-twelve ostrich-skin cowboy boots took up most of the space on the small antique mission table. A cigar in one hand, a snifter of brandy in the other, he sank comfortably into the leather couch.

A crackling fire burned in the huge rock fireplace that covered one wall. His recently acquired family portrait sat above the mantel. The entire Childers clan, minus his beloved late wife, was staring back at him.

"You'd like the painting, Rebecca." He saluted her with his brandy snifter. "I included everyone." His daughter Kelly, son Matthew, and Ben made a proud looking family.

The far wall of the cedar chalet was glass from ceiling to floor, showing the huge expanse of ranch, cattle, mountains, and Wyoming snow.

He sucked in a long draw on the cigar, staring through the windows at his piece of the world. Twenty years in the making, but he'd done it. He'd built an empire in the middle of the high, desert plains. He smiled, sipping the fine amber brandy and letting it rest on his tongue then slide down his throat. Smoke rings curled slowly upward as he rounded his lips, creating two more circles.

The ringing telephone pulled him out of his daydream. Tom Talking Horse's name blinked on the caller ID. "Childers," he answered, sipping the brandy.

Tom Talking Horse's quick, deep voice was on the other end. "Ben, I want you to reconsider."

"Reconsider what? One of the best business deals I ever made?" Ben chuckled.

"Business deal? This is a man's home." Ben listened to the guilt in Tom's voice, amused by it.

"I'd say you've got a big ol' part in this."

Silence filled the other end of the line. "This isn't fair." Tom's voice was heavy with frustration.

"Since when is life fair?" The front door opened with a rush of cold air. "My daughter's here, we'll finish this discussion later." He hung up the phone, not waiting for a reply.

Kelly was a mess. It was a rare sight to see his daughter in a less than perfect state. Her coat was unbuttoned, her hair was windblown, and her boots were muddy.

"Where have you been?" Ben walked across the room as she struggled to pull the muddy boots off. She flung the fur coat carelessly on the floor in frustration. "Sit down," he ordered. She sat on an antique hall chair, cheeks red, lips pouting. Ben put her foot between his legs and pulled off one boot then the other.

"Thanks, Daddy." Moving to the bar, she poured a whiskey with water. After kicking it down quickly, she made a second one.

"Where'd all the mud come from?" He poured himself a fresh brandy.

"Those cows of yours. I was at the horse barn with Jerry, checking that pregnant mare, when one of your cows decided to bolt for the fence where I was standing." She brushed a stray lock of blonde hair off her forehead and sipped her whiskey. "The smelly beast nearly pummeled me into the dirt. I hate cows."

Slamming the brandy snifter down on the bar, he pointed an angry finger at her. "But you sure don't hate this big house, those fine clothes and those new trucks, do you, girl? Those cows are the reason you wear four hundred dollar boots and live in a million dollar house. Don't you ever forget it!"

"I won't, Daddy. You'll make sure of that." She set the glass on the bar and went upstairs. Her door slammed shut.

"I see the diva is home."

Ben turned at the sound of his son's voice. "I didn't know you were here, Matt." He held up his glass. "Drink?"

"No, I better keep my wits if Kelly is on the warpath. I'll need all the agility I can get." He smiled, grabbing a soda from the refrigerator.

"Did you get the bull I wanted for the rodeo?" Ben nervously swirled the ice around in this glass.

Matt walked to the large windows, staring across the fields toward the setting sun.

"Son, did you get the bull I asked for?" His voice was louder.

"Yeah, I got the bull." He sipped on the soda, staring at his father. "Tell me why you wanted Charlie Hoffman's bull so bad."

Ben stared hard into Matt's eyes. "Because I always hedge my bets, son."

*****

"Disaster just follows you like a shadow, doesn't it?" Joe stared at the busted barn door, the trampled fence, and the splintered feed trough. Two gaping holes yawned wide in the cattle barn and the tractor was semi-submerged, its back end sticking out of the frozen pond like a broken skeleton.

"She did save the cows." Fred nodded toward the placid herd of heifers grazing contentedly on a fresh, round bale of hay. "Ramming through the barn with the tractor was the best thing she could have done." Fred put his jacket around her wet, shivering body.

Abby's knees hurt, her butt hurt, her groin was pounding, and what didn't hurt was wet -- a kind of crunchy, frozen wet.

The tractor had raced out of control through the barn doors, skidding down the frozen slope of the hill through the wire farm fence, yanking a sizeable section of it out of the ground.

Continuing its downhill race, the tractor had crushed through a wooden feed trough, showering the cowboys with corn, oats, and assorted grains she couldn't identify. Then it had blasted into the cattle barn right between two cows. The tractor then careened into the frozen pond -- bucket first -- hurtling her across the ice, where she now came to rest flat on her back in the middle of the frozen pond.

The cowboys stood silently as the tractor's front end sank to the bottom of the pond. Abby regained her breath and managed to sit up. The icy pond was littered with cracks. She couldn't get off the pond without risking plunging through the ice.

Mike lassoed her like a prize heifer and the cowboys gently slid her across the pond to safety.

"Putting that old tractor in the drink was the best thing that could have happened. It broke the ice so we could get the hose of the pumper truck down in the water. It saved--" Fred looked at the charred skeleton of barn -- "well, it saved some of the barn."

Abby sneezed.

"It's a disaster. Two barns damaged, fencing yanked up, a submerged tractor, and two calves sprinted from the barn like terrified geese," Joe snarled at her. "Now they're wandering through this snow and are probably going to be dead by morning."

She sneezed again.

"Get her up to the house before she catches pneumonia." Joe ordered, walking past her to the smoldering remains of barn. Fred wrapped an arm around her shoulders, walking with her slowly up the hill.

Abby stopped in mid-stride, turning slowly toward Joe. Did he seriously just order her to the house? Who the hell did he think he was? No one was ever going to order her around again. "What's the matter, Abby?" Fred followed her angry gaze.

"That sarcastic, overbearing ass." The more his words echoed in her ears, the angrier she became.

"Joe?" Fred shrugged. "Heck, don't let him worry you. He just hasn't been himself lately."

"I told you to get to the house and get some dry clothes on," Joe repeated.

Abby's hands went to her hips. "I do not take orders from you," she yelled back. "Frankly, I've had enough of your macho John Wayne attitude."

The men stopped working and stared at them. Joe threw down his shovel, stomping through the knee-deep snow up the hill toward her.

"I want to know where one is supposed to learn to drive a fucking tractor." Abby shouted. "Podunk U, in Tractor Driving 101?"

Fred tensed and squeezed her shoulder tighter.

Joe stood inches from her face. "This may be Podunk, Wyoming, but our women can drive a tractor and they don't have potty mouths."

"Kiss my ass, you Clint Eastwood wannabe."

He bent low, nearly nose to nose with her. "I said get to the house." His voice was low, his blue eyes hard. "You've done enough damage here today."

She stood tall, pressing her nose against his. "You go to hell. I worked like crazy to save that barn and those cows. I'm sorry those two cow-babies bolted, but I don't deserve to be talked to like this."

"They're calves," Fred corrected.

"Calves," she said. "What the hell do the damages mean to you? This isn't your ranch. I don't even know why you're here all the time. Mike Connor signs my paycheck, not you."

The look that swept over his face sent shivers down her spine. Color drained from his face, and his hands clenched into hammer-sized fists at his sides.

Fred took in a large gulp of air. "Come on, Abby. Let it go." Fred shoved her up the hill toward her cabin. She fought against him, but Fred wouldn't let go, practically dragging her along. At the top of the hill, he lightened his grip. "Darling, you really need to learn when to keep your mouth shut."

Abby pulled away, turning to face him. "Not you too? That man had no right to yell at me like that. He deserved to be told off."

Fred stared at the ground. "You're right, he shouldn't have yelled like that. But Hidden Rock Ranch is his ranch, or is until a few weeks from now when Ben Childers forecloses." Fred wiped his nose with the sleeve of jacket. "Now he's just lost his barn. Out here that's a big loss, honey."

Abby's heart nearly broke. "This ranch is the one he's losing?" Fred nodded.

She rubbed her forehead with a wet, frozen hand. Joe was right. She was a walking, talking disaster. In a very short time, she'd managed to wreck not only her life, but the lives of everyone she touched. "How could I have been so stupid?" She had to apologize.

She began trudging back down the hill until Fred grabbed her arm. "Oh, no you don't. The weather is getting real bad. You don't want to be caught outside in this, especially you being wet and all." The snow had begun to pick up in intensity.

"I need to find those calves." She had to make this up to Joe somehow. The only thing she knew to do was find the missing calves.

Fred pushed his cowboy hat down over his face to help protect his eyes from the sudden onslaught of snow.

"Baby cows lost in this snowstorm?" She squinted in all directions. All she could see was white, punctuated by tall pines.

"We'll find them, but right now you've got to get to out of this weather. You need dry clothes. It doesn't take a person long to freeze to death out here." He yanked her along.

The new furnace made the cabin warm and toasty. Abby sneezed and sneezed.

"I'm going to change, Fred," she managed to utter between sneezes. "If you'd like, you can make some coffee." She walked stiff-legged into the bedroom as her jeans were nearly frozen.

The wet clothes felt like they were peeling skin as she stripped them off. She quickly pulled on dry clothes, adding an extra sweater under her jacket. Stuffing her jeans into her boots, she quietly raised the bedroom window and slipped into the snow. Maybe saving the babies would make up for all the screw-ups she'd made.

Chapter Ten

"Get these cattle to the old livestock barn before they freeze." Joe turned the collar up on his canvas jacket, grabbed a lariat of rope, and gave a whistle. The heifers jumped at his approach as he plodded through the heavy, deep snow toward the old, gray barn on the far side of the pasture.

"What do we do about the tractor?" one of the cowboys asked.

Joe stopped and gave him a long hard look. Drawing in a deep breath, he whistled, and then trudged along herding the cows. Nobody else said a word.

As he walked through the snow, he kept seeing her face. All wet hair and mud. Hell, she looked worse than that half-drowned mouse he'd pulled out of her toilet. Her face wouldn't leave his mind, especially those angry, beautiful eyes. Brother, she had a temper.

Her words flooded his mind. This ranch was his, damn it, and he aimed to keep it. Kelly Childers had used him and he'd been naïve enough to believe her lies.

Kelly was a selfish, egotistical brat. Her master was her father -- that, and her father's money. Nothing else mattered. Joe didn't think she had any feelings about anything or anybody, not even her brother, Matt.

Ben had a temper and a taste for making money. According to many in the small county, some of his business dealings weren't always legal or ethical. After his wife Rebecca died, Ben's temper had grown uncontrollable and his appetite for money insatiable. Not long after, he came after Hidden Rock with a vengeance.

When Joe was a kid, their families had gathered for holidays, birthday parties, life celebrations. Then it was as though something snapped in Ben Childers; it was something Joe couldn't quite put his finger on. The man had become more obsessed with getting Hidden Rock. The ranch was Joe's heritage, his life, and his legacy. To Ben it was just another acquisition, land with bragging rights for his big city bankers.

Joe's mother had died when he was young. His father, Joe Sr., had died not long after his brother, Connor, had stormed off the ranch after one of their infamous fights. Damn, he missed his older brother.

That had been five years ago. He'd searched the desert and valleys around the ranch for days after Connor left. He'd called the police who told him that, as an adult, Connor could go anywhere he wanted. He'd tried everything he knew to find his brother. Connor didn't want to be found.

"Joe." Fred's voice snapped him out of his daydream.

Joe stopped and waited on Fred to wade through the snowdrifts.

He was panting hard, his face bright red. He bent at the waist, resting his hands on his knees and catching his breath. "It's Abby."

"What happened?" Snow was falling so hard it was difficult to see the other man's face. Their eyes locked.

Fred looked like his was going to throw up. "She said she was changing. The next thing I know, she's out the bedroom window."

Joe yanked Fred by the coat collar, wrenching it tight against his throat. "What the hell did you do to make her climb out the window?"

Fred grabbed his hand, trying to loosen the grip on his throat. "I didn't do anything to her. She was upset about the calves. I think it's one of those mothering instinct things."

He released Fred, practically throwing him on the ground. "Help move the cattle. I'm going to find her." He slogged through the knee-deep snow, cursing her name with each step.

The storm was raging, the wind chill could freeze the hairs on a polar bear, and the snow was falling in buckets. City girl Abby had no idea how lethal weather like this could be.

*****

A solid wall of white faced Abby. The snow fell harder than she'd ever seen. The wind felt like rock pelting her face. Yet her heart hurt worst of all.

Everything she'd done since landing in Sentinel had ended up hurting Joe Baer. She'd trashed his hay barn, almost burned down his cottage, sunk his tractor, had to borrow his clothes, and now she'd lost two baby cows in a blinding snowstorm.

In spite of all that, Joe had given her a job, and a place to live. Even after she sunk his tractor, he'd sent her to the cabin to stay safe and warm. While his help was usually doled out with a heavy dose of sarcasm and insults, he'd made sure she was safe. Every problem she'd found with the cabin had been fixed. Nearly every disaster she'd created, he'd bailed her out of.

Maybe if she found the calves it would help set things right. She didn't know Hidden Rock was his ranch. Never would she have lashed out that viciously had she known.

The snow curled in hard chunks around her legs, sucking her down to her knees. "Ahhh," she yelled, slamming a fist into the waist-high snow.

She should have been in Los Angeles now. She should never have kicked Billy Butcher's balls. How could she have let herself get stranded here? Tears burst down her cheeks as she laid her face in her wet, gloved hands. She was never going to get back to Indiana, back to fix that tattered part of her life.

Her thoughts went to Granny Martin. She closed her eyes, seeing the kind, wrinkled face of the grandmother who'd raised her. She hadn't seen her mother, Elaine, since she was eleven.

Then Elaine showed up on their doorstep. She gave Granny Martin a long-winded story about how she'd gone through detox, and was clean and sober. Now, all she needed was a chance to redeem herself. She wanted to go back to school, buy a house, and get to know her daughter.

Granny had waited years to hear that. Without telling Abby, she'd mortgaged their home to help her wayward daughter. Within days of getting the money, Elaine was gone again. Granny lost the house. Soon after that, Abby lost Granny to a heart attack

Without any money, she had to give Granny a city pauper's burial, no headstone, no services. Her funeral consisted of an unknown minister who acted imposed upon to be there and a heartbroken Abby.

She cursed herself. Why didn't she just let Billy have his way? Things would have been so much easier. Tears streamed down her face as she thought about Granny.

A small, moaning sound in the distance caught her ear. A speckle of brown was stark against the white snow. Abby trudged toward it.

A small cow, barely the size of a German Shepherd lay almost buried in the snow. Abby dug the snow from around it, freeing its legs. She wrapped her arms around its neck, tugging it out of the snow. It tried desperately to stand, but it was nearly frozen. She picked up the small mass and carried it back in the direction she thought the barn was in. Its weight soon became too much in the deep snow. Abby fell, picked herself and the calf up, and tried again.

A whipping gust of wind fired across the field knocking her face-first into the snow. Curling into a ball, she wrapped herself around the small calf and began to feel strangely warm.

*****

"Why is Hidden Rock so important to you?" Tom Talking Horse asked.

Ben smiled, slowly lighting a cigar. He was an expert at hurt, hell he'd had enough of it to know how to deal it. "Why is that heathen reservation so important to you? I want Hidden Rock." He rolled the expensive cigar around to the corner of his mouth. "I get what I want. I always have."

Tom's hands were hard fists. "This is part of my family."

"The white part." Ben propped his feet up, sipping on a glass of scotch. "I didn't see Big Joe Baer leaving anything to you, my red friend."

"I am not your friend, red or any other color. I never asked Big Joe for anything. All you do is use innocent people to further your ambition."

"Ain't nobody innocent, son. Nobody." Ben blew a large puff of smoke at Tom.

"Turn the water back on to the reservation." Hatred filled Tom's eyes.

It didn't bother Ben at all. He was finally getting Hidden Rock with Tom's help. Hell, this deal just kept getting better for him. "Oh, I will. I wouldn't want those poor little Indian children going thirsty." He propped his feet on his desk. "We made a fair deal." Ben tossed back the scotch, smiling.

"White man's fair is an ever expanding pool to fit what they need at the moment. You have the mortgage. I'll do no more."

"You will get me Chief Harrison's prize bull for the rodeo." He blew another long stream of blue smoke from his cigar.

"I thought your son was getting Charlie Hoffman's bull for this rodeo?

"He did." Ben smiled.

"Chief Harrison's bull is a killer." He folded his arms across his chest.

Ben blew a smoke ring, still smiling."You just make sure I get that bull."

"And if I refuse?"

"Then there's going to be a lot of thirsty Indians at the Standforth Reservation."

*****

Ice had frozen on his mustache, his hands were nearly numb, and his boots crunched in the snow when he walked. A song whispered on the wind. Was that a lullaby? Abby? The fierce wind made it hard to find the source.

A dark clump in the snow caught his eye. Joe put his face against hers, relieved she still had some warmth. The small calf let out a gut-wrenching bawl as the cold air rushed across it. Abby had laid her body over the small creature. Joe shook his head. The city girl had found her wayward calf and saved it.

He was proud of her. She had wandered several miles across the frozen landscape. Her lips were blue, and the tips of her ears were bright red. He yanked off her gloves. Her fingers were as blue as her lips. Her body shivered hard, but she didn't open her eyes, and she didn't stop humming the lullaby. Hypothermia was setting in, and it wouldn't take long for her to succumb to its effects.

Carrying her to the main house would take too long. He had to get her warmed up fast. He headed for an old feed barn. The spindly-legged calf followed and bawled with every step.

The barn was dark but filled with hay that provided some insulation against the savage cold. Joe scrounged a few old saddle blankets from the tack box and made a nest in the middle of hay bales.

"Abby," he called softly, lying down next to her and brushing the snow from her hair. Her lips were blue, the cheeks of her face white, and her eyelashes crusted with crystals of ice. "Abby," he whispered, pulling off his coat, hat and gloves. "Come on city girl, don't you die on me."

He pulled off her coat, unbuttoned her shirt, and unzipped her jeans. With little effort, she was completely naked on the hay bed. Quickly, he removed all his own clothing. Laying her on top of one of the saddle blankets, he scooped the hay close around them and layered the two other blankets over the top of them. Her body was freezing. No warmth came from her at all. He nuzzled her frozen face into his bare chest, wrapped his muscular arms around, and pulled every inch of her as close against him as possible.

"Come on, Abby, hang in there." The calf bawled, chewed on a shaft of hay, and lay down beside them. Joe threw an old blanket across its back.

For hours, the white flakes piled higher outside the barn. Abby slept deeply. Joe smiled at the little snore she had. It wasn't an actual snore, just a little snort. The calf's head nuzzled close to hers and it, too, slept peacefully. He propped up on an elbow, watching her in the hazy morning light. When he moved away, she nuzzled tighter against his chest. On her right shoulder was a tiny red rose tattoo. A spray of blonde hair zigzagged across his arm, and a strangely contented smile danced on her lips.

He brushed the hair from her face. He let out a breath. She was warm and her cheeks were pink again. Last night, his only thought had been to save her life. This morning, however, the swell of her chest when she breathed and the fullness of her lips stirred a very different emotion.

He told himself it was lust and nothing more, but every inch of him knew better.

Abby's eyes fluttered. The small calf greeted her with a long, rough, wet tongue across her face. "Yeck." She wiped her face, and the calf licked again. "Stop it." She turned away, shoving her face into his chest. Joe took in a deep breath. This wasn't going to be easy.

Abby looked up, her gray eyes wide, meeting his gaze head on.

"Good morning." Joe liked the look of her tousled hair. Waking up beside Abby wasn't a bad thing at all. "It seems you made a mess in another one of my barns."

He was starting to get used to that crimson wave of anger covering her face. She bolted upright. The horse blanket fell from her shoulders. Her small hands thrust out to catch it. Those eyes bore down on him like mortars.

"You bastard," she yelled, landing a well-placed fist in his lower ribs. His hands came up defensively, grabbing her wrist. He pulled her toward him, her naked butt sliding easily across the slick hay.

"How dare you take my clothes? You no good, lousy jerk." Her fists thrust upward, not making contact. He put an arm in front of his face, blocking her weak blows.

"If it's any comfort to you, I'm naked too." He smiled.

Abby growled. When had she started growling? Then she landed a punch on his cheek.

"Ow, stop that." Again, he grabbed her small fist. Her knee slammed into his stomach, causing him to expel a large burst of air. Joe'd had enough.

He pulled her legs straight underneath him, pinned both arms to the floor and straddled her body with his. "Now stop and let me explain." She was stronger than she looked. He had to add some force to hold her in place. "I had to take your clothes. Dang, you fight harder than a Brahma Bull." Joe caught his breath. "Since you decided to wander off in the middle of a snowstorm and I had to come to your rescue, taking your clothes off was the only option I had to save your life."

She looked away from him. He gently pulled her face around making her look at him.

"You don't have any recollection of last night, do you?"

Her eyes spit fire at him.

"I do," he said. "You were close to freezing to death when I found you. There is no electricity in this barn. The only warmth I had was body heat. I didn't take your clothes off from pleasure. I took them off because I had to."

A flash of hurt crossed her face. "It's not like I wouldn't want to for pleasure." His eyes did a quick survey of her naked body beneath him. Instantly parts of him came to attention. He cursed himself and his aggravating appendage.

Her eyes widened.

"What I mean is I took your clothes off for medicinal purposes only."

Abby drew in a deep breath. Damn he liked being on top of her. Their eyes locked and he lowered his lips toward hers. The calf bawled and planted a large, wet tongue down the length of her face. Joe laughed as she grimaced.

"You want to get off me now, Doctor Baer?" Abby growled at him.

Joe rolled off, lying on his back in the mound of hay. She wiped the calf slobber off her face, tugging at the blanket. The calf tucked itself in next to her, demanding attention.

"Did you find the other one?" She asked, stroking the soft fur on the calf's head.

"No."

Abby turned toward Joe, averting her eyes from his naked body. "You want to put some clothes on, or at least cover up?"

"Why? Does my being naked bother you?" Joe smiled, rolling onto an elbow and watching her. The calf rooted around and found a morsel of hay. Abby scooted away from him, struggling to keep the blanket around her and rummaging through the hay, looking for her clothing.

Joe moved closer, leaning his bare chest against her bare back. Her breath quickened. "I believe my nakedness does bother you."

He didn't think it could be bothering her nearly as much as her warm, naked body was bothering him. The moment she found her jeans, his hand reached around her, grabbing them. She turned, her eyes meeting his.

"I'm glad you're all right."

"Thanks for rescuing me."

He pressed closer, his lips fluttering across hers. Despite the cold, the heat of her lips was searing. He stroked her face, her lips parted just for him. Joe traced the outline of her face, pulling her close to his chest.

The barn door burst open. Joe sat straight up and his body tensed. He squinted at the bright light streaming through the door. It was impossible to see anything.

Abby pulled away, wrapping the blanket tighter. She groped through the hay for her clothes.

The calf's loud bawl echoed across the barn, followed by a high-pitched whistle and dirty laughter.

"Sorry, Joe." Mike cleared his throat. "We got worried, thought maybe you were in trouble when you didn't come in last night."

Abby groaned, pulling on her boots and trying to yank on her clothes.

"Guess we shouldn't have worried." They laughed.

"It's not what you think. I found her half frozen and had to warm her up." Joe stood, pulling his jeans on.

"Looks like you did a real good job too, boss." Hal snickered.

"All of you, out of the barn," Mike ordered. "Joe, there's a spare snowmobile waiting outside whenever you're ready." He snorted and left.

Abby rested her head in her hands.

"I'm sorry. I never meant for the crew to walk in."

Abby said nothing.

The roof of the old barn sent out a loud, angry groan. There was a shudder and a puff of snow through the ceiling. With another groan, the barn trusses splintered and the old roof collapsed onto them.

Joe leapt on top of Abby, his body protecting her from the full impact of the avalanche. She choked through the heavy, wet snow that covered her face.

Mike held her hand tight, pulling her through the wet mounds of snow. He smiled, as she gained her footing.

"You all right, Abby?" He looked her over.

"Where's the baby?" Abby asked, her voice hoarse.

"Standing pretty over there in the corner." Mike pointed to the calf that was safe and dry near the door.

Joe dusted the snow off. "I'm fine too, Mike."

Mike smiled. "That's good."

Abby moaned, shaking snow from inside her frozen jacket, yanking clumps of hay from her hair. She stomped outside. "I hate snow, and I really hate Wyoming."

Joe and Mike shrugged at each other and grinned as the calf followed her outside.

Chapter Eleven

"Hi, honey. I heard you had a rough time a couple of days ago?" Margaret wiped her feet as she stepped into Abby's cabin.

Abby smiled. "One among so many," she groaned, taking Margaret's coat.

"I brought you something." Margaret handed her a still warm bowl. The smell coming from it was nothing short of nauseating -- beef, and plenty of it. "I figured you were probably getting sick of your own cooking by now. I know I get that way. After a few weeks, I just gotta eat something fixed by somebody else."

"Thank you, Margaret." Abby forced herself to be polite. She wasn't a vigilante vegetarian, just an objector to eating a flesh and blood creature. But since getting stranded in Wyoming, she'd come to despise meat-eaters. The cowboys wanted it for every meal, steak and eggs for breakfast, steak sandwiches for lunch, T-bones for dinner. She couldn't stand the sight or smell of it.

"I had a hard time getting up here. The boys have been plowing, but the snow is deep out there. They'll be out all night just keeping a pathway clear."

A loud bawl sounded from down the hall.

"Is that what I think it is?" A quizzical expression covered Margaret's face and she marched off. Abby followed Margaret down the hall into the bathroom. A scrawny calf, swaddled in blankets lay in the deep, claw-foot bathtub, sleeping peacefully on a nest of straw. "What is that thing doing in here?"

"It's a baby." Abby smiled, stroking his head. "I saved him, sort of."

"All right, but what is it doing in the bathtub?"

"I'm going to take care of it until it gets big enough to go out with the other cows." Abby answered.

Margaret laughed, snorted, and laughed some more.

"What? What's so funny?"

A loud knock at the door ended the laughter.

"Knock, knock. It's just me," Tessa yelled. Abby and Margaret left the calf to sleep, and joined Tessa.

"Hey. After I heard what happened, I thought I'd better pop in and see if you were all right." Today Tessa sported a fur coat, pants, boots, and hat, all in a very bright purple. With the snow covering her shoulders, she could easily have been mistaken for a grape popsicle.

She slammed a fist down on the counter. "Does everyone know I was almost frozen to death?"

"You were?" Tessa's eyes grew wide. "I just heard you were bumping with Joe in the feed barn and the whole ranch sneaked up and caught you."

"What?" Abby nearly screamed. "I was not bumping with Joe! Who told you that?"

"Honey, calm down. It's cowboys talking," Margaret walked past her into the kitchen and poured some coffee.

Tessa perched at the kitchen table, pulling the foil up on the casserole and grabbing a hunk of beef between long, purple nails. She ate the seared flesh and then licked her fingers clean.

Abby grimaced, rubbing the throbbing pain that had begun behind her eyes. "I went looking for some calves and I got lost," she said through gritted her teeth. "Joe rescued me, sort of. But I was not bumping with him, do you understand me?"

"Sure honey." Tessa swallowed another hunk of beef.

Abby pulled several plates from the kitchen cabinet, gathered some forks, and set them on the table.

Margaret poured coffee all around and sat at the table. "She's got one of them in the bathtub."

"A calf? You're kidding me? A calf in the bathtub?" Tessa jumped off the chair, nearly running to the bathroom. "Hot dog, what a cutie," she shouted down the hall, then headed back to them. "What are you gonna name him?" She returned to her perch beside the beef stew.

"Him? It's a him?" Abby asked.

Margaret and Tessa exchanged shrugs. "It's got all the right parts, honey." Tessa laughed.

"Frosty. That fits him."

"Getting back to the barn," Margaret said on a sigh, "I was referring to the incident at the cattle barn. Haven't you ever driven a tractor before?"

"Is there anything the two of you and the rest of this godforsaken county haven't heard about?" Abby swallowed a gulp of black coffee, wishing it were something much, much stronger.

Margaret laughed, "This is a small town in the middle of winter. We're bored as can be, so when somebody does anything a little off-the-wall, everyone -- and I do mean everyone -- knows about it."

"Even before phones and e-mail this county could spread a story faster than a hooker could spread K-Y Jelly," Tessa added with a perfectly straight face.

Abby choked on her coffee. Margaret nodded in agreement and patted her back.

Tessa popped another taste of beef, then a smile spread across her face. "But I tell you what, I cannot wait until Kelly Childers hears you were naked in the hay with Joe. Dang, that heifer is going to go stark raving mad with jealousy."

"I was not naked in the hay." Abby rubbed the raging pain between her eyes. "Well, technically I was, but it wasn't why you think I was. I mean, I was cold," she sputtered, making the situation worse. She poured some more coffee. "Besides I don't think Kelly would ever be jealous of someone like me. Since you two seem to know so much, can you tell me why Joe is losing this ranch?"

"Nobody's real sure. We all speculate about it, but it centered on Kelly." Margaret forked spoonfuls of the casserole onto a plate. "I've heard she had gambling debts from Vegas. She came to Joe all beaten up, and he mortgaged Hidden Rock to save her life because she was afraid to tell her daddy. Personally, I don't buy that one." She forked several large hunks of beef into her mouth.

"I'll bet she's pregnant." Tessa shook her head, chewing on a hunk of beef.

Abby's heart sank.

Margaret frowned. "Nah, Joe went on a few dates with her, but nothing ever sparked. According to some of the cowboys, Kelly worked him into bed. Then she mentioned marriage and moving to Hidden Rock. Joe backed away real fast." Margaret raised her eyebrows over the rim of her coffee cup, taking a sip.

Tessa laughed. "Reckon he didn't want no mobile mattress for a wife."

Abby nearly snorted the hot coffee up her nose.

"Honey, are you all right?" Margaret gave her a quizzical look. Abby nodded.

"Fact is, Kelly had never been denied anything in her life." Margaret pulled the foil completely off the casserole, forking several hunks of beef onto her plate. "You can pretty well figure if Joe turned down her marriage proposal, she is out for blood. Joe is a strong man without many sins in his closet. She went for his weakness, Hidden Rock. How she did it, nobody but her and Joe know."

"If Kelly gets word of you and him in that barn, you'd better watch your back," Tessa warned. "It's cold in here. Why don't you start a fire?" "No!" Abby and Margaret yelled in unison.

Another knock at the door ended their conversation. Abby answered as a flush-faced Fred stomped his feet on the porch.

"Come in, Fred." Abby opened the door wide. "You look frozen. You want some coffee?"

"No thanks." He pulled off his cowboy hat, holding it limply in his hands. "I just wanted to tell you we found the other calf this morning."

Abby smiled. "You did? I'm so glad." She shut the door behind him.

"Well, you won't be. It was dead, froze to death." He licked his lips, swallowing hard.

Abby sat in a kitchen chair. Margaret patted her shoulder. Would the bad stuff ever stop happening to her?

Fred pulled a huge, plastic baby bottle from his coat pocket. A bright red nipple stood at attention on the top. "I brought you something for the little bull you got. He'll like this." He handed the bottle to Abby. "I'll bring you up the feeding mix. You'll have to give him a bottleful every four hours or so."

"I'm sorry the other one didn't make it," she whispered, twirling the bottle around in her hands.

"All part of being a rancher." Fred fidgeted at the door.

"If I had only known how to drive a tractor, this wouldn't have happened."

"Honey, if I had a dime for every critter I've lost, I'd be richer than Ben Childers," Margaret said. "They were born mid-winter, their odds weren't real good from the start. Besides, you managed to save one of them. You start feeding him and in no time, he'll be chasing the heifers."

"I've got to be going. I'll bring the mix by later." Fred pushed his hat down on his head and left.

Margaret pulled back the blinds on the kitchen window. "Look, the sun is out, it's stopped snowing, and me and Tessa love you. What more do you want?"

"I'll let you wear my new coat if it'll make you feel any better. I know it makes me feel much better." Tessa rubbed an affectionate hand on the purple fur coat.

Abby laughed, walking to the bathroom with the calf's food. The little calf drank hungrily from the bottle. Abby rubbed a gentle hand across its soft ear.

Tessa and Margaret followed. Tessa sucked her belly in hard and pulled her truck keys out of the pants pocket. "I got my four-wheel drive pickup, honey, and it's full of gas."

Margaret fluffed Abby's hair. "Tuck that baby in and let's shop, girls."

*****

Joe couldn't keep his mind on his work. Soft, hazily lit images of Abby's body kept flooding his mind. He skewered a pitchfork of hay into the feed trough. His horse snorted a thank you as it reached over the stall door with its nose.

He remembered the tiny red rosebud tattoo on her right shoulder. He'd never known a woman with a tattoo before. It was kind of sexy. Joe stroked the stallion's velvety muzzle. It reminded him of Abby's warm breaths against his chest. Brother, he had to stop this.

How had that inept city girl gotten under his skin? What would it be like to have her sing just for him? He pitched hay into the stalls of two more horses. Why would she want him? He had no money, he was probably going to lose his ranch -- he didn't have a thing to offer. He was just a haymaker with nowhere to set his boots. Just as well. He didn't need her or anyone else in his life.

George McIvey crushed out his cigarette before entering the barn stomping it out in the snow. "How are you, Joe?"

"I've had better weeks, George. What brings you out here?" Joe raked the last of the hay into a stall. Hefting a small mallet, he busted the inch or so of ice that had formed on the top of the horses' water buckets. The last one took several good hits before cracking. "What was that I saw you smoking?" Joe grinned over his shoulder at him. "I bet Margaret wouldn't be too happy if she saw you puffing away."

George popped a piece of mint gum into his mouth, stuffing the papers into his pants pocket. "She'd skin me alive, so if you value our friendship you'll keep your mouth shut." He winked. "I guess it's a bit of curiosity that brings me out. That, and the fact that this is the first day in almost a week the roads have been clear enough to go much of anywhere. Cabin fever, I reckon." He leaned against the stall door, reaching through to give the brown horse inside a good scratch behind the ears.

Joe busted another bucket of ice water.

"I've heard some rumors about you and Abby."

Joe inhaled deeply. The cowboys had been all over him about what happened. It was only a matter of time before the rest of the county did the same.

"George, there is nothing between me and Abby. She got this bright idea to go find two calves in a snowstorm and nearly wound up froze to death. When I found her, she had wandered too far to get her to help in time, so I went to the old range barn and got her warmed up. That's all." He hung the mallet up on the pegboard inside the tack room. "Abby's a city girl, I'm a rancher. There is nothing there."

George smiled, chewing the gum. He made his way to each stall, giving every horse a scratch. "Margaret told me one of those tour buses pulled into the café early this morning and the man inside it was asking about Abby. She wasn't sure if it was that Billy Butcher fellow who dumped her on the road. She warned me not to tell you. She thought you might be interested in Abby and his arrival might make you jealous." He leaned his back against the wall and crossed his arms over his chest.

"Dumped her?" Joe felt a protective rage build.

"Didn't Abby tell you how she came to Sentinel?"

Joe shook his head. For the next half-hour, George related the incident that had brought Abby to their small community. Joe stacked hay as he listened. It was none of his concern, Joe kept repeating to himself with each bale of hay he threw into the loft. He put up an amazing amount of hay bales in the short time it took George to finish the story.

"From the way she talked, he should have been kicked in the family jewels a long time before Abby did it. Well, I don't know if this fellow's him or not. But Margaret couldn't imagine who else would know Abby was around here." George slowly opened the barn door, spitting his gum out into the snow. "I'm making a beef stew special tonight if you need some dinner." He pulled on his cowboy hat and let the door softly shut behind him.

Joe stood on the hay wagon, sweating and breathing hard.

*****

The price was right -- three dollars for the softest, warmest cable knit sweater Abby had ever laid eyes on.

"You know, I've never shopped in the second hand store before." Tessa said carrying an armload of clothes. "These prices are amazing. I can buy three times the stuff I normally do."

"Does she work?" Abby asked Margaret.

"Doesn't have to, her daddy's rich. He just sends her a check every month. Wouldn't that be a kicker?" She held a dress up to Abby. "This is pretty."

Abby looked at the price tag and shook her head no. She was hanging on to every dime she could. The sweater and a pair of jeans that actually fit were going to cost her fifteen dollars, and that was too much in her opinion. She had no use for a dress.

After a whirl through a card shop, the ladies returned to the McIveys' café for lunch. "Do you have anything besides beef stew, Margaret?" Abby swallowed hard at the heaping bowl sitting on the counter in front of her.

"Well, I got a couple of really good mincemeat pies. Does that sound better?" She smiled, tying an apron around her waist.

Abby eyed her suspiciously. "Isn't that made with beef?"

"Yes, ma'am. USDA prime Wyoming beef." She made a yum sound and smacked her lips.

"How about a cup of coffee?" Abby slid the bowl away.

"Ain't you gonna eat that?" Abby motioned for her to help herself. She dug in with the zeal of a wolf cub.

Several posters had been plastered around the café, tacked to the walls and sitting on the tables and the counter. Abby reached around Tessa picking up the plastic framed poster. *Silver Bullet Rodeo, sponsored by Childers Ranch*. It listed times, events and in large, red letters -- "A One Million Dollar Bull Riding Event."

"Oh, I meant to tell you." Margaret stopped wiping the counter, interrupting her reading. "There was a fellow in here looking for you a couple of day ago just before that snowstorm hit. I thought it might have been that idiot who dumped you, so I said I didn't know you."

Could it possibly have been Billy? How the hell did he find her? "What did he look like?" She set the poster on the counter. Margaret rested her hands on the counter. "Let's see, he was taller than George, nicely built and dressed, with dark hair and dark eyes. He was good looking, not the sort one would take for dumping a lady along the road."

Abby's began to breathe again, "That's not Billy. Billy's not even six-foot tall, with hair that could be white, orange, or purple. He's got a dozen pierced places on his face and he's skinny as a skeleton."

"Then who was this guy?" Tessa grunted over a mouthful of food.

"I don't know." Her only thought was that someone from Indiana had found her and was trying to collect on her mother's debts.

The doors of the café burst open as the evening dinner crowd began to appear.

"Rodney," Tessa squealed, jumping off the barstool and rushing into his arms.

Rodney blushed as she wrapped her arms tight around him, much to the amusement of the three other cowboys that had entered with him. "Hey, Tessa, guess who I ran into on my way over." He smiled, nodding at the three men. Tessa had a blank look on her face.

One sauntered over to Abby. She had a moment of recognition, but couldn't place his face.

He reached out a hand to shake. "I'm not sure if you remember me. My name is Tripp Tanner." Abby shook his hand. "We met at The Sagebrush Bar and Music House. You won the talent night."

"Oh, yes. I'm sorry I didn't recognize you at first."

Tripp sat on the stool beside her.

"It's the Swinging Huskers, Tessa." Rodney grinned.

Tessa giggled. "Well, ain't that something? She shoved herself into a booth with Rodney and the two other Husker band members.

Margaret sighed, taking four cups and a pot of coffee to the booth.

"I dropped by to see if Jack Spencer had been over to talk with you?" He set a coffee cup upright, looking hopefully toward Margaret.

"Who's Jack Spencer?" Abby had not really taken much notice of him the night of the talent show, fear blinding her.

"Jack Spencer is the assistant of Winslow Dodge." He raised an eyebrow, staring expectantly out the window.

"The country singing star?" She didn't understand.

His eyes shot toward the parking lot. She followed his gaze out the moisture-fogged windows as a gray two-seater Mercedes pulled up outside. Two men came in the door. The first man had taken no more than two steps inside the door and the café became dead silent.

Winslow Dodge took off his hat and smiled at Abby. The café fell silent, except for Tessa's muffled whimpers.

Tripp whispered to Abby. "The guy with Winslow is Jack Spencer." He nodded at Jack and went to the booth joining his band members.

Jack whispered to Winslow and gestured toward Abby.

She felt a sudden rush of heat that started at her toes and ended at her forehead. Winslow Dodge was a damn good-looking man, even without the help of makeup artists, airbrush photography, or computer enhancements. He didn't seem to need any enhancement anywhere.

He was tall with coal black hair, a trimmed-to-perfection beard, and a matching mustache. Her heart palpitated. Abby followed the splendid lines of his body up to his killer face that flashed her a million-dollar smile.

"Howdy, I'm Winslow Dodge. You must be the lady I've heard so much about."

With the grace of a ballet dancer, his huge frame floated onto the barstool. Her heart skipped several more beats. Her mouth opened but nothing came out.

"What would you be wanting with Abby, Mr. Dodge?" Margaret put herself between him and Abby, holding a pot of steaming coffee in her hands.

"Nothing harmful, ma'am, honest. My assistant, Jack Spencer, got a call from Tripp about Abby. According to Mike, she can sing one of my songs better than I can. From his raving reviews, I thought I should come and hear her for myself." He peeked around Margaret's shoulder, smiling at Abby.

"Oh, my god, I just can't stand it any longer," Tessa squealed, breaking into a run across the room, her cowboy boots clicking on the linoleum. Her purple fur jacket fell to the floor, exposing her ample chest through the flimsy spaghetti-strap top.

Winslow jumped at the sudden rush as Jack bolted toward his side too late.

Tessa wrapped her arms around his neck. "Winslow, I love you. I've waited years to squeeze myself around you."

They both tumbled into a heap on the floor, Tessa's chest surrounding Winslow's face. Jack pulled the purple mass off the smiling singer. Tessa pushed Jack Spencer halfway across the café. Then Rodney made his way over to her and loudly cleared his throat.

"Oh, shut up, Rodney." Tessa swooshed her hair back out of her face, glaring. "I'll bet his woman doesn't have to cook to get a marriage proposal."

The room erupted into a chorus of laughter.

Winslow raised an eyebrow, giving Rodney a quizzical look as he stood up, dusting the seat of his pants off. "My advice, mister, would be to take a lady who looks like this one home for keeps."

Tessa stuck her tongue out at Rodney. A wave of red crept up his face.

"I'm glad you like my music, honey. I'm playing in Omaha in two weeks. Jack will be happy to give you a couple of front row tickets."

Tessa jumped up and down. "And an autograph, please, an autograph." She smacked Rodney's shoulder, snapping her fingers. "Give me that notebook you always keep in your shirt pocket." Rodney obliged and Winslow signed it for her. She stood on tiptoe and placed a kiss on his cheek. Then, reluctantly, she let Rodney lead her back to the booth.

"Well." Winslow took a sip of coffee, cleared his throat, and gave a quick glance in Tessa's direction. Margaret stood behind the counter. Winslow smiled at her, but she didn't leave. The entire room was tuned into their conversation, and no one was budging.

"Abby, I'd like to offer you an audition. If you're as good as Mike says you are, there might be a future for you in the music business. I'd like to help make that happen. Are you interested?"

Abby could not utter a single word.

The door to the café opened with a loud rush of wind. It slammed shut even louder. Joe stomped the snow from his boots. His eyes met Winslow's then locked with Abby's. In an instant, every person was focused on Joe.

"What do you say, darling?" Winslow smiled.

Abby returned her attention to Winslow as Joe sat on a stool at the far end of the bar. "I've got a few weeks before my Cheyenne concert with nothing to do but listen to you." Heavens, his smile could melt butter in Anchorage. She smiled back.

Margaret nudged her arm. "What have you got to lose?" She shot an almost imperceptible glance toward Joe, who sipped his coffee and ignored her.

"Um, yeah, well, yes, Mr. Dodge. She leaned an elbow on the bar, grabbing the edge to keep from trembling.

"Great. We'll hold the audition at my private recording studio in Cheyenne. How about this Friday?"

Abby nodded. Her voice refused to work, her brain was complete mush, and Winslow was spewing enough testosterone to make the entire female population of Wyoming and Montana very happy.

"I'll have a plane at the airport in Lander, and my limo will take you into Cheyenne." Winslow nodded toward Jack who typed notes into his cell phone.

Tessa waved widely from the booth, pointing to herself. "Take me with you," she mouthed, as Rodney grabbed her flailing arms out of the air.

"I need my...makeup person with me. Would that be all right?" Abby cocked her head to the side, trying to look as pouty as Tessa could.

"You can bring whoever you need." He put his Stetson back on and extended his hand. "It's good to meet you. I look forward to hearing you sing."

With that, Winslow Dodge and Jack Spencer were out the door. Tessa sprinted across the room, hugging Abby until she could barely breathe.

"Down girl," Margaret ordered.

Rodney stomped across the room. "I don't like this one bit, Tessa Marie Springer. You running off to Cheyenne with Winslow Dodge."

Abby eased herself between the feuding couple. "I really do need her, Rodney, if it would be all right with you. I'm scared. I could use Tessa there for moral support." She put a hand on his shoulder.

He fidgeted for a few minutes, staring at his boots. "I never thought about it like that. I guess you are pretty scared. Well, it's all right with me if Tessa goes."

"Well, if Tessa doesn't want to go, I'll take her place," Margaret shouted from behind the counter.

"Oh, no you don't," George yelled from the kitchen. "You see them young cowboys out there in those tight jeans and suddenly I got a wife who's a roadie. You need to stay here and take care of your man."

"Are you scared or jealous, old man?" she laughed and yelled back.

"Both."

The café erupted in laughter.

"Guess it'll be you who takes care of her." Margaret glanced at Joe who was staring into his coffee mug. "Sometimes we ladies just need to hear that we're wanted." The volume of her voice increased.

Abby inhaled deeply, wondering just what she had taken on. She knew one lousy country song and she was supposed to audition for a living legend of country music in two days. Her heart palpitated. "Tessa, could you give me a ride back to the ranch?"

Joe stood up, laying a dollar on the counter. "I'm heading out there now. I can give you a lift." He lazily popped his hat on, giving her a long stare through those blue eyes.

"Thanks." Abby pulled on her coat and retrieved her bag of shopping goodies from Margaret's back room.

"We'll all be rooting for you, Abby." Margaret hugged her.

Joe held the pickup truck door open for her. Did she owe this to the appearance of Winslow Dodge?

She glanced back at the café to see every head in the entire place staring out the window.

Snowflakes fell as he pulled out of the parking lot. The ride was quiet for a long time. He fidgeted with the heater, he flexed his hand around the steering wheel, and he kept annoyingly clearing this throat. Obviously, Joe had something to say but wasn't quite sure how to say it.

Abby looked out the window across the vast expanse of land. Snow and more snow. Still, Joe remained quiet. She nodded toward the clock on the dash. "I guess I stayed in town too long. I don't have much time before I need to fix dinner."

"Not much," he answered.

"Is this snow ever going to quit?" She squinted out the window.

"Not soon."

This was becoming a hellish trip very quickly.

"Thanks again for rescuing me." She smiled.

"Yep, couldn't afford to lose the best cook the ranch has ever had. The boys would skin me." A dimpled grin spread across his face.

"The best cook you've ever had, huh?" She relaxed a little. "So it wasn't my brains or body you were interested in, just my wealth of culinary knowledge?"

"Well, it wasn't for your tractor driving skills."

"I'm sorry I caused that baby cow to die and for what I said about your ranch. I didn't know." She folded her hands in her lap staring at her laced fingers.

"It wasn't your fault. That's just ranching, it happens." A gust of wind blew a curtain of white across the truck. The wipers squealed and nearly melded to the windshield. He turned the defroster on high. "As for your comments about my ranch, well, it's probably not going to be mine much longer, so don't worry about that either."

He turned off the main road onto the small lane that went back to Hidden Rock. Rounded snowdrifts had wandered across the plowed path. He burst through them without any hesitation.

"I wouldn't have said anything like that if I'd known what happened." She put a hand on the dashboard.

"What do you know about what happened?" Anger rose in his voice.

"Nothing. Don't be so damn defensive. I just didn't mean to hurt your feelings." Her eyes shut tight as the truck went blindly into the white wall of snow, sliding haphazardly on the other side.

"Do you know why they call it Hidden Rock Ranch?" He continued up the lane toward the big ranch house instead of pulling off toward Abby's cabin.

"No." Abby suddenly felt nervous.

"Let me show you." He swerved hard, causing the truck to skid into a parking place at the side of the house.

She'd spent the night naked with the man, so why was this making her nervous?

"Come inside," he nodded toward the house, stretching after climbing out of the truck.

"Said the spider to the fly." Abby mumbled, getting out to join him.

Chapter Twelve

"That tramp." Kelly stomped across the tack room. "Who does that dime-store whore think she is?" She pulled a saddle off its wooden holder and slung it to the floor.

The barn was a palace of wood, cedar, and the latest technology in horse management. The tack room was huge, with twenty-five saddle holders displaying some of the most intricately carved leather to be found anywhere. Childers Ranch also possessed several inlaid silver beauties that gleamed under the row of overhead lights.

"I didn't think it'd make you mad. I just thought it was a funny story." Fred Gillis picked up the saddle and placed it back on its holder, then filled his toolbox with the necessary equipment to fit her horse for shoes.

Even though he worked for Hidden Rock, he supplemented his income doing horseshoeing for most of the local ranchers. He was the best farrier for several counties, if not in the state.

"Funny?" she screeched. "I don't see any humor in the fact that Joe Baer has become so low class. I mean, doing it in a barn with that dime-store tramp." She pulled cigarette from a silver case in her jacket pocket and lit it.

Fred snatched it from her lips and walked to the barn door, flipping it outside. "Not in here, Kelly. Do you want to burn the barn down? There are almost four hundred bales of hay in here."

"Well excuse me, Smokey Freakin' Bear." She put her hands on her hips. "Since when did you become so conscientious?"

"Since Hidden Rock's barn caught fire. There was a cigarette butt found in the ashes, you know."

Kelly folded her arms across her chest, dropping the subject.

He pulled horseshoes off the shelf, finding the right size, and checked the length of his nails. "I really don't like you talking bad about Abby either. She's a nice girl."

"You've got a crush on her." She circled around him, watching a crimson blush wash over his face. "You've got the hots for Dime-Store Abby."

"Stop it, Kelly." His voice grew angry. He picked up the toolbox and stomped toward the barn door, running into Kelly's brother, Matt. Fred pushed past.

Matt backed up a step, letting him through as Kelly leaned against the doorframe and watched Fred's truck disappear down the drive. "What did you say that ticked him off so bad?"

"Why do you always blame me?" She rolled her eyes.

He gave her a baffled stare. "Because it's usually your fault."

"How you got to be a part of this family, I'll never understand."

"Genetic mutation." He smirked. "I understand Hidden Rock's livestock barn burned." A cold look glared from his eyes. "I wonder how that happened in the middle of a snowstorm?"

"What do you want?" She buttoned her jacket, heading toward the door.

"I want to know why Joe put the mortgage to Hidden Rock on the line. I'd like to know just what could have made him do such a thing. I find it utterly amazing that dear old Dad now holds the mortgage to a ranch that he's been wanting in the worst way." He plucked a piece of hay from a bale, chewing on it.

"I'm also pretty amazed by Joe's cousin, Tom Talking Horse, selling the mortgage to Dad. That must have been one heck of a conversation. Joe and Tom were always pretty tight. Tom wouldn't hand something that valuable over to our dad." He spit out another piece. "Not without a damn good reason. You wouldn't know anything about that, would you, sis?"

"How should I know?" She glared at her brother. Kelly adjusted the collar on her coat, pulled the gloves out of the pockets, and stretched the fine cowhide over her hands, not bothering to look up at him.

"Wouldn't have anything to do with that thing you've got for Joe, would it?"

Kelly glared at him. "I don't have anything for Joe Baer." She stomped toward the barn door.

"That's good, because he's going to die at the Silver Bullet Rodeo. I'd hate to see you brokenhearted over it."

Kelly stopped dead in her tracks, turning slowly. "Joe's been doing rodeo for years. There isn't anything he can't ride." She smirked, pushing the door open.

"Except you." Matt shot her a sarcastic look. She slammed out of the barn.

She stomped through the snow, shoving the truck into gear. The tires clawed into the snow, spinning harshly as she raced down the lane.

Everything was going wrong. She slammed a fist against the steering wheel. All she wanted to do was make her father proud -- to show him she could be as cunning as he could. She wasn't quite as shrewd as he was, and she'd made some dangerous mistakes and some seriously lethal enemies. Matt knew too much already, and if he started asking questions, daddy would know just how much trouble she was in.

*****

Joe's huge ranch house was warm, despite the arctic weather outside. The interior was straight out of the old west. A twenty-foot high post and beam ceiling spanned a huge great room, and a wall of river rock included a massive fireplace. The wide set of arching stairs made of logs cut in half was flanked by a handrail of burled wood with knots, shined from years of use and layers of shellac.

Clay pottery filled corners, antique Winchester rifles hung above the mantle, and half a dozen tomahawks crisscrossed the far wall. A full Indian headdress of feathers sat like a prized museum piece in a recessed nook.

"Come out here and let me show you the Rock." Joe took Abby's hand, sending a warm tingle up her arm. He led her up two steps into the kitchen. His voice became nearly a whisper. "Look out the window."

Abby's breath caught.

A huge outcropping of granite cliff circled around the back, forming a natural grotto. The south corner of the house had been built right into the cliff. The grotto was a rock palace covered with frost and long tendrils of spun ice spiraling down to the ground. Wispy loops of snow circled around the jagged rocks. A dozen full glasses doors separated the house from the grotto.

Just then, the sun burst from behind a cloud and illuminated the entire grotto in a halo of silver mist. Spider webs of fine ice glistened in remote recesses like fairies peeking from their igloos.

Abby remembered to breathe. "It's absolutely beautiful."

Joe walked up behind her, his lips close to her ear. "You should see it in the summer. Long ferns grow from the rocks and it takes on a deep emerald color. Sitting in there with a tall glass of cold water on a hot August day is just about perfect." He put a hand on her shoulder.

"This was the hill my mother picked out for the house. The original homestead was built much closer to the main road. When mom and dad got married, she told him she wanted a hideaway among the rocks, so he built her Hidden Rock."

Abby turned toward him. "Are both your parents dead?"

"Yes." He took in a deep breath.

"Any brothers or sisters?" She returned her attention to the grotto.

"An older brother, Connor. I haven't heard from him in five years. Dad and he didn't get along. He wanted a different life, a life that didn't include living on Hidden Rock Ranch. He wanted to see the world, and my father was determined both his sons would stay on the ranch. Connor just wanted to know if there was more out there, so he left one day and never came back.

"How awful." She turned around, staring into his face. "Don't you know where he's at?"

He shook his head no.

"I'm sorry. That must be hard."

"I'm used to being alone. I don't need anybody." He went to the sink, filled a pot with water, and scooped some coffee grounds into the pot.

She pulled her flannel coat tight around her and sat on a barstool at the end of the kitchen counter.

Abby stared at the chiseled man. Thick, muscled arms led to large hands covered with many scars. He had a broad chest, thin waist and very long legs. Joe wasn't pretty and drop-dead gorgeous like Winslow Dodge, but he had a rugged sex appeal that Winslow could never hope for.

He straddled a barstool next to her, folding his arms over the back of it and staring at her with those damned eyes.

Her gaze shifted to the grotto out back. "How big is Hidden Rock Ranch?"

"There's eighteen thousand, five hundred and forty two acres of prime Wyoming ranch land." He stared out the doors into the distance. "There's generally about five thousand head of cattle running, seven barns, and three houses."

He left the room without saying a word and returned carrying a large picture frame. Laying it very carefully on the counter, he stood beside Abby. His eyes sparkled, his cheeks were slightly flushed, and he began to talk in a low, almost church-like voice.

"This is the Sweet Water River. About four miles of it meander through the ranch." Inside the frame was an original survey map of Hidden Rock Ranch, circa 1860. His large hand traced the river across the map. "Through here are some of the grandest bluffs you'll see this side of the Badlands, and down over here toward the western edge, there are still ruts from the Oregon Trail. Right here along the river the Pony Express riders used to make a quick stop to water their horses before riding on to the next station."

A gentle hand glided along the map, pointing out the history of the land he loved so much. "The first homestead deed dates back to 1842, when my great-great grandfather, Larsen Baer, came here. Of course the other half of my family wasn't so glad to see him." Joe laughed.

Abby was confused. "Huh?"

"The Shoshone. My great grandmother was a Shoshone."

Now Abby understood the home's mix of western frontier and Native American pieces.

"In fact, they hated each other. From stories my father told me, they had shot at each other for years until the day my great-grandfather, Max Baer, got deathly ill. He was a small boy, only around six years old, and everyone had given him up for dead. After much fighting with his father, my great-great grandmother took the buckboard and rode right into the Sioux encampment. She knew they had healers in the tribe that could save her son.

"The story goes that as the Chief was about to kill both of them, the Chief's wife stepped up, took one look at the boy, and carried him into her tepee. Well, he of course lived, and members of the Shonshone and Baer families have been marrying each other since." A sweet laugh erupted from him.

"You really love this ranch, don't you?" she chimed in.

He stared at the map, his eyes tracing every inch of the yellowed paper. "More than anything. Hidden Rock isn't just a place, it's who I am, what I am, where I have been, where I'm going. It's part of my soul."

She felt the same way about Granny Martin's house. It was supposed to have been hers, but in an instant, it was gone.

She understood how a place invaded your soul, invaded your spirit so totally that your identity was as intrinsic to the place as it was to you.

Clearing her throat, to end the painful memory, she smiled. "So, tell me, do you always bring girls you rescue up here and tell them the history of Hidden Rock?"

A smile crossed his lips. "Only the ones who break my tractor, destroy my barns, blow up my cabins, and have mice in their toilets."

They stared silently for a few seconds then burst into laughter. The laughter turned to uncontrollable hysterics. Abby grabbed her sides, wiping her cheeks as tears rolled down them. Joe snorted and they laughed harder.

The coffee was done by the time they regained control. Joe wiped a speck of tear off her cheek as he poured some coffee. "Thanks."

Her face felt warm where his hand had been. "For what?"

"I haven't laughed like that in a very long time." He swallowed hard, pulling two cups from the cabinet. A small dimple played on his right cheek from the grin he still had. "Are you going to Cheyenne to audition for Winslow Dodge?" His eyes locked on her again as he set the coffee down, sliding the cherished map out of harm's way.

"Yes, I am." She looked up. "I can't pass up a chance like this."

"The way you sing, I can't blame you." He took a long sip.

She pulled the flannel coat tight around her. The fact that he liked the way she sang made her oddly happy. She didn't understand the feelings she was having for him. Joe Baer was nothing she'd ever wanted. He was brash, egotistical -- a cattle rancher for heaven's sake. The man raised cows for slaughter, and she refused to eat any creature.

She wanted to sing, see the world, and be a star. He wanted his ranch, cattle, and tractors. They just weren't meant for each other.

Yet here she was, completely enamored of him, his ranch, and his damn fine body.

"Are you cold?" Strong hands held her shoulders, rubbing them to warm them up. He turned her chair around so she faced him. "I'm very glad you got dumped in Sentinel, Wyoming, Abby."

Slowly, he bent his head down. His lips touched hers, warm and soft, lightly caressing hers as a hand went to either side of her face, pulling her closer. Her lips opened, inviting him. A hand went behind her head as his lips slipped down to her neck.

Joe made tiny nibbles on her earlobes, her neck, her eyelids, tasting her, feeling her, caressing her with his lips. A small moan escaped from her throat as her arms wrapped around his neck. His hands went inside her coat, massaging the small of her back, making tiny circles up her ribs. Her hands thrust up into that thick mane of wavy hair. She pulled back. Their eyes locked. Then his lips slid down the bridge of her nose, to her chin, to her throat.

"It's not yours yet, and I'll be damned if you'll come up here without me."

Voices in the living room jarred them both back to reality. Abby squeezed her jacket closed as Joe bolted into the living room.

"What the hell are you two doing in my house and on my property?"

"Very soon, it's going to be my house." Ben's voice boomed in the living room, as Abby quietly walked to the door watching.

"Don't bet on it, Childers. You've got two months until that mortgage is due, at which time it will be paid in full. Now, get off my property." Joe's voice grew dark and deep, like a primal growl.

"No harm done. I was just coming up to get some measurements for the addition I'll be putting on."

The two men stood inches from each other. Abby walked around the corner, praying her presence would calm them both.

"Well, now I know why you're so anxious to get rid of us." Ben smiled at her. "Nice to see you again, Abby." he tipped his hat. Abby nodded.

"I asked you to leave." Joe never took his eyes off Ben.

Ben took a long look around the room and walked outside. "I can get what I need when you've vacated the premises."

Tom Talking Horse stood silent at the far end of the room.

"You're not welcome here either." Joe's voice deepened even more.

"You don't understand. I had no choice." He took a step.

Joe's angry gaze fell on him, daring him to take another step. "I asked you to leave."

Abby squeezed his arm.

"If you'd only give me two minutes." Tom pleaded.

Ben popped his head back in the door, a large grin spread across his face. "Coming Tom?"

"Your boss is waiting."

Tom slapped his hat against his thigh and walked out the door.

"Are you really going to lose the ranch?" Abby stared up at him.

His eyes squinted, staring across the room into the dark fireplace. "I will unless I'm very damned lucky."

"Who was the other man?" She let her hand slide down his shoulder, clasping her hand in his. His grip tightened around it.

"My cousin, Tom Talking Horse. The man who sold the mortgage note on Hidden Rock to Childers." A cold look glazed over him as he stared down at her.

"Why would he do--"

"Millions of reasons," he interrupted.

Chapter Thirteen

"Tessa I know one, just one, country song." Abby paced the room, sipping really awful, cheap red wine from an ugly mug with a damn tractor on it.

Tessa smiled. "There ain't no problem that can't be solved if you use a little ingenuity." She sat an iPod and a set of speakers on Abby's small kitchen table. "I am full of ingenuity. In this little gizmo are probably three hundred of the world's best country songs." She pulled off her coat, hanging it on the hook. "You listen to them while we cook. You get a record contract, I get a husband."

Abby breathed a sigh of relief. "God bless you, Tessa." She pulled out a baking dish to prepare their latest creation. "If I have anything to do with it, that boy will be married to you before Christmas."

Tessa turned the volume up high, and began Abby's indoctrination into the world of country music. Sift flour, add one cup of olive oil. One, two, three, sing the refrain, bury the dog, and watch the wife drive away. By the end of the day the kitchen looked like an ad for Third World disaster relief and Abby knew about four lines from every country song Tessa owned, but not one entire song.

They sprawled onto the living room floor, finishing off one bottle of wine, opening a second one. "I did good, Abby. That was the best dang casserole I ever ate." Tessa held her tractor mug up in salute.

Abby saluted back. "And you made it yourself." She chugged. "Now you can fix breakfast and dinner."

Tessa sat forward, eyes glassy. "Oh hell, what do I do about lunch?"

Abby laughed. "Send him to Margaret's place."

"I think I'll like lunch better than any meal." She filled both their mugs again. "Yes, lunch will be my best meal. To lunch." She made a toast.

"To lunch." Abby toasted back.

Tessa laughed, than eyed Abby with the scrutiny of a judge. "You need some clothes. You can't go to an audition with Winslow Dodge looking like a farmhand." She sipped more wine, looking at

Abby over the rim of the wineglass. "We need to shop, and I don't mean at the half-price stores. I'll loan you some money."

"I can't."

"Listen, put me on salary as your makeup artist when you get that recording contract." She giggled. "Then I can be close to Winslow."

"But I thought you wanted to marry Rodney?"

"I do, I just want to have sex with Winslow." They laughed. "Speaking of sex, how was it with Joe?"

Abby choked, coughed and her eyes began to tear. "How should I know?"

"You were naked in the hay loft with the man."

"So?"

Tessa snorted, pouring another mugful for each of them. "The way that man looks at you, I'd say he's having a real hard time keeping his hands off you."

Abby's face flushed. She remembered his kisses, his caresses. How far would things have gone if Ben hadn't interrupted? She felt an attraction to Joe like no other man she'd ever met. His touch was so comfortable and easy.

His life was Hidden Rock Ranch and nothing would ever be as important to Joe Baer as his ranch. Besides she was getting the audition of a lifetime, a chance to make more money than she could imagine, a chance to be a star, and the chance to fix some screwed up things in her own life.

*****

Cheyenne loomed in front of the limousine's windshield. Tessa hadn't stopped giggling the entire flight. Tessa packed Abby a complete wardrobe with underwear, bras, makeup, fancy cowboy boots, and some pants so skin-tight that eating one large meal would send the buttons popping across the room.

The limo was long, black, and carried a fully stocked bar, which Tessa was emptying very quickly.

"Tessa, I think you'd better lighten up on the booze."

"Ah, honey I'm fine. There hasn't been a man since my seventeenth birthday that could drink me under the table." She put the decanter back into its slot in the wet bar. "But if you feel better with me quitting, that's what I'll do. This is your day and I want you to go in there and sing like a Texas Mockingbird," she yelled.

The driver flinched, glancing into the rearview mirror. Tessa waved and winked. The driver blushed.

He was a young man of maybe twenty-one. The poor thing had tried to be a perfect gentleman and keep his eyes at face level. But Tessa's low-cut, body-hugging blouse was proving a most difficult challenge. Tessa knew it. She scooted forward, leaning across the back of the driver's seat.

"How much longer till we get there, honey?" Tessa slid closer to him, one of those massive breasts just grazing the top of his shoulder.

"We...we, we're here," his voice squeaked like it was changing.

Tessa kissed his cheek.

He missed the entrance and circled once around the block. Tessa had a way with men.

The building was unimpressive from the outside -- a huge, steel building that could have passed for any industrial pole barn in Wyoming. The limo stopped in front of a gray, metal door.

Winslow Dodge and Jack Spencer exited almost immediately.

"Hello, ladies." Jack said as he opened the door, his blazing smile greeting them. "I hope your drive out here was a good one." The smile increased when Tessa got out. Abby hoped her voice had the talent to compete with Tessa's breasts.

The outside proved to be a well-designed façade for the state-of-the-art recording studio inside. "This is where all my recordings are made." Winslow explained, taking Abby by the elbow and leading her inside.

"Not in Nashville?" Tessa sounded disappointed.

"I haven't recorded there in years. I'm from Cheyenne. I find this is more convenient and less restrictive than Nashville. Also, nobody knows I'm here." His million-watt smile flashed at them. "That helps when you've got a few neurotic fans out there."

"I sure hope you don't ever consider me neurotic, honey." Tessa planted a kiss on his cheek.

Winslow shook his head, Jack smiled really wide. Abby sighed.

"Well, I imagine you're a little nervous." Winslow's hand rested on the small of Abby's back. "I have a fully equipped kitchen in here, so if you'd like to eat or have something to drink before we get started, just let Jack know and he'll make sure you get whatever you want."

"Oh, honey, I could get used to this." Tessa mumbled to Abby, as they meandered through the small group of musicians, engineers, and other personnel.

The males smiled, following her finely sculpted butt that was cinched into bright, neon green spandex pants. The ladies of the studio weren't so impressed. Several walked to the coffee pot, two or three took off glasses to get a better look, and one just returned her attention to the engineering board she'd been working on.

Jack left Winslow and followed Tessa like a contented puppy. "Come on, Abby, let's get you comfortable." His office was modern in design, not the country decor she would have expected for the reigning earl of country music.

"Whiskey?" he asked. She declined. He poured himself a snifter, threw his jacket across the back of a black leather easy chair, and loosened his bolero tie. "Have a seat."

Abby walked cautiously across the thick silver carpet, hoping she hadn't stepped in any cow dung before they'd left Sentinel. He pressed the answering machine button and listened through the first four messages, a banker, a promoter, an irate record distributor, and one call from a little girl.

"That's the one I was looking for." He smiled, "My daughter."

"Hi, Daddy," the little voice continued, "I miss you. When are you coming to get me? Mommy says this weekend is yours. Bye, Daddy, love you." The machine beeped.

"Her mom's got custody and I get to see her when I can. As my schedule allows and her mother allows." The resentment and frustration in his voice was hard to hide.

"You're one of the most famous men in country music. Why don't you take the money you've got, run away, and spend some time with her?"

Winslow smirked. "I've got money and a whole lot of it, but not enough to run away. I'm not just a singer anymore. I'm also a celebrity spokesperson, a partner in one of entertainment's top ten talent management agencies, and I have over twenty endorsement contracts. Hell honey, I'm a conglomerate. If I quit, almost two hundred people would be out of a job just here in Cheyenne, and they've got kids too."

Abby never realized so many people could depend on one celebrity.

"Do you have any songs you'd like to sing for me?" He sat on the edge of his desk, looking down at her.

Abby understood why women clamored for the man. Just his smile was intoxicating.

"I really only know one country song all the way through -- your song, *Tears*." She looked at her hands, waiting for him to tell her to get out.

Instead he laughed. "It's all right. I only knew one song when I started too." He stood up, offering her a hand. "Let me show you this new computer we've just installed. It's like karaoke on steroids. Sure you don't want a drink?"

She shook her head no again.

Double doors led into a glass-enclosed room where one wall was computers and a row of perfectly aligned chairs circled around the back. Microphones hung from the ceiling and instruments sat on their stands. Directly in front of the one stool at the center of the room was a large television screen.

Outside the front window, three men and two women sitting at the control panel, bored looks on their faces. From those expressions, she'd bet Winslow had brought more than one person to audition through this studio. Obviously, most of them had not been impressive.

Tessa sat perched on top of an office desk, surrounded by six men who were eager to serve her every need.

"This screen will show you all the words to any song you choose to sing. I have one of the largest databases of music lyrics in the world. Do you want recorded music or our house band?" Winslow rested his hand on the small of her back again. She liked it.

"Can I use the house band?"

"Your wish is my command. Have a seat on this stool and the boys will be right in."

Abby's heart raced, her vision blurred, and her palms were nearly dripping with sweat. Stage fright was taking over again. Her shaky hand missed the seat of the stool. She plopped into a perfect heap in the middle of the floor, turning over the stool and sending it crashing into the band's chairs. The bouncing stool caught the first guitar and its stand and sent the rest of the guitars falling, one after another, like dominos into a wreckage of glitter and steel strings.

Abby wished she could disappear. Winslow stood at the door, his mouth hanging open. She pulled herself off the floor.

"I'm sorry." She whispered and attempted to set up the guitars. They ended up in such a tangle that each time she moved a guitar its strings pinged and broke.

The traumatized musicians burst in the room in an effort to save their beloved instruments. After restringing several guitars and setting everything upright, Winslow's voice echoed into the studio. "What song do you want on the screen?"

Abby hesitated.

"She does a real fine job on Kentucky Boots," Tessa chimed in., "You should do that one first, Abby."

"What key do you want it in?" A band member asked.

"That's Jason, my band coordinator." Winslow offered an introduction.

"Whatever key it's written in." Abby whispered.

Jason rolled his eyes and nodded to the band members. They began the intro. The words appeared on the screen. Abby's eyes wouldn't focus. Three more times the band began, three times she couldn't sing a word.

"Abby." Tessa called gently to her. "Just like in the kitchen, honey."

Abby nodded and closed her eyes.

The music began, and in a few beats, she was flowing like an artisan well. She opened her eyes to Winslow Dodge smiling through the glass.

Twelve songs and three recordings later, the band and engineers applauded.

Winslow burst into the booth, picked her up off her feet, and twirled her around. "I think Mike underestimated your talent. If you liked our applause, just wait until a full stadium cheers like that." His embrace was tight and more then friendly. "You did beautiful, Abby." He kissed her forehead.

"We'll make some demos, and then I'll play them for my partners at King Management. More than a few agents will be knocking each other out of the way to represent you. Once those demos make the rounds in Nashville, I'd say you'll have more than one label offering you a contract. He laughed, his hand never losing touch with hers. "You'll need to stay here a few days so we can cut a couple of first class recordings. While you're here, I'll arrange for a couple of agents to fly in."

"You don't have your own record label?" She really didn't understand how the entire business worked.

"I only record here. My label is RBA Records in Nashville. They basically distribute my records and inundate the world with

Winslow publicity." He laughed and led her out of the studio. "I am a silent partner in King Management. King Management is always looking out for new talent. In fact, we manage the Swinging Huskers. That's why they called me about you."

"So you really think I've got potential?" She'd been almost afraid to ask.

Winslow glanced around the room at his entourage, all of whom laughed at the question.

"The potential of selling multi-millions of dollars worth of music." He leaned close and whispered, "Abby, honey, welcome to the big time."

*****

"I thought Jack and Tessa were supposed to join us?" Abby asked nervously as she slipped into the chair Winslow held out for her.

The restaurant was grand. A small, three-piece string ensemble played soft jazz in the background and waiters in tuxedos served the patrons. An onyx fountain tinkled in the center courtyard just a few feet from their table and a menagerie of birds sang in an enclosed solarium behind her. The table was very private, surrounded by tropical foliage, and tucked away in a small alcove.

"There were some last minute details that needed to be worked out for next week's concert." Winslow smiled, sitting across from her. "Jack went to take care it and Tessa asked to join him."

The waiter arrived, showing Winslow a bottle of wine. After a nod, he poured their glasses full and left.

"I think the two of them have formed a friendship." Winslow gave a sly look.

Abby was uncomfortable, and Winslow was making her feel that way He pulled his chair close to her, was overly attentive, brought her flowers, picked her up in a limo and damned if she didn't like it. What girl didn't want that kind of attention?

Yet there was a thread of guilt in the pit of her stomach. Her thoughts kept turning to Joe. She didn't understand why. It wasn't as if they were dating. Remembering the feel of his hands gently pulling her face to his and his lips, she took a sip of water, feeling suddenly warm.

Winslow was her ticket out of the hell her life had become. His way out was paved with money. Abby never wanted to be without money again, never wanted to endure the kind of humiliation she'd endured over the last year and she certainly did not want to live on a ranch in Wyoming.

Did Winslow look at all women the way he looked at her? It was a look of pure, unadulterated desire. If it was a practiced look to seduce women, the man had perfected it. She felt hot all over, deciding against the wine. A little too much alcohol, a little too much Winslow, and she didn't even want to think about the consequences.

What would Joe think? Abby nearly groaned aloud. She shouldn't care what Joe thought. Correction: she didn't care what he thought.

Winslow slid a little closer, motioning for the waiter. "How about if I order for us?"

That instantly broke his seduction spell. Take-charge men were one thing, but domineering ones were quite another. "I'll order for myself." She glanced at the menu, sliding her chair a few inches away from Winslow. The waiter left with a curt nod, and Winslow's gaze grazed every inch of her face.

"I meant what I said about your singing talent" He leaned back, one arm casually draped across the back of her chair. "If you decided to let King Management represent you, we'd arrange some additional recording studio time and hire a composer to work up some material specifically for you."

Abby twirled the wine glass around, straining not to dance with joy in the middle of the restaurant. "That would be great." She tried to act nonchalant, taking a sip of the wine. One sip wouldn't hurt anything. She was celebrating. The sip turned into a long drink. The wine was full, sweet, and addicting.

"I've got two shows next week, but Jack can make arrangements for you to be in the studio and you can work with the composer to get the sound you feel comfortable with." He refilled their glasses.

She tried to stop him. "I really don't want any more."

Winslow smiled and kept pouring. "It's all right. We have a designated driver in the limo."

Too bad we don't have a designated chaperone.

The appetizers appeared, as did another bottle of wine. The string ensemble circled their table. Winslow gave them an almost imperceptible nod, and Abby's personal serenade of seductive love songs began.

An attractive woman walked past the table and Winslow's eyes went straight to her butt. Decked out in an orange silk dress, the woman did have a very good ass, but Abby's eyes went to her shoes -- orange stilettos, nearly identical to the ones that were sitting in a cherished spot in her little cottage.

A pair of shoes and a push of fate had led her to this place, this moment. Nothing, not the overwhelming charm of Winslow Dodge, not the amazing kisses of Joe Baer, and not the ceaseless snow of Wyoming would change her course.

"I have something for you." He reached into his jacket pocket and pulled out a long white box.

The size and the shape of the box meant it was jewelry and, coming from Winslow Dodge, it was probably very expensive jewelry.

He squeezed the box into her hands. "I just wanted to welcome you to King Management."

Abby's alarm bells sounded. "Are you trying to bribe me, Mr. Dodge?"

"It's Winslow, and you would be correct. It is a bribe. I do not want you signing with anyone else." A gorgeous smile covered his face, "I am a partner in one helluva good management company, and I know a good investment when I see it."

What the hell? She opened the box. The glitter from inside nearly blinded her. A necklace of large emeralds surrounded by diamonds filled the box. It literally took her breath away.

"You certainly know how to bribe a woman." Abby sounded more excited then she meant to.

Winslow reached over to take it from the box. "Let me put it on you."

Abby snapped the box shut. "Winslow, I can't accept this."

"Whether its diamonds or a meal, I've always earned it." She slid the box back across the table. "I don't intend to change now." Sipping on the wine, she laughed. "Besides it's not diamonds I need, it's a car. Do you know what it's like to be stranded on a ranch in the boonies of Wyoming with no wheels?"

Winslow laughed. "Actually, darling, I do. I come from these parts."

Several long fronds of the potted palm next to her moved. Giggling feminine voices echoed around their table. Winslow cursed under his breath. The faces of several women pushed through the foliage as a flashbulb exploded.

Winslow slammed his wineglass on the table. Grabbing Abby's arm, he yanked her from her chair. They raced out the front door of the restaurant, jumping into the waiting limousine as flashes of camera bulbs erupted in a frenzy around them.

"I'm sorry." He knocked on the window, getting the limo driver's attention. "Get us the hell out of here." He shoved her into the backseat. "I thought we could have a nice dinner out, but I should have known it would be impossible."

"Does that happen everywhere you go?" She glanced out the back window as the flashes still went off. A dozen people ran down the middle of the street, chasing after them.

"Actually, that was a small crowd." He laid his cowboy hat on his lap, leaning his head back against the seat. "The worst thing about it is that tomorrow, you will make headlines around the world."

"Me? Why would I make headlines?"

"Take us to Abby's hotel and we'll order dinner in her suite," he instructed the driver, then turned back to Abby. "Because darling, you were seen at dinner with me. Therefore, you must be my newest flame, we've been sleeping together, and you're pregnant with my child."

"What?" She sat forward.

"Don't worry about it." He held her hand in his. "This might work to your advantage, give you some instant publicity."

"You know what they'll think?" Abby's mind reeled, knowing what the press would do to her.

"They'll think you slept your way to a recording contact." He answered flatly, then a worried look crossed his face. "You are over twenty-one aren't you?"

Abby leaned back against the seat. "I'm twenty-eight," she robotically answered. This was not how things were supposed to happen.

"I'm sorry, but no matter what I say or how hard I deny the accusations, they won't go away." He slid closer to her. "In a few weeks, it will be forgotten and they'll have moved on to someone else. My advice, and believe me, I've learned it the hard way, is just to smile and not say anything back. Everything you say can and will be misquoted." His arm slipped across her shoulders, then brushed a stray hair from her face.

Drop-dead gorgeous Winslow Dodge leaned toward her and kissed her. Her. He was kissing little Abby Clark from Indianapolis. Her arms wrapped around his neck as if they had a mind of their own. What was she doing? She had no idea. Yes she did. She was kissing a totally gorgeous man. A superstar who thought she was talented.

Then Joe's face invaded her thoughts.

"Mr. Dodge, we're at the hotel," the driver's voice crackled through the intercom.

Abby pulled away, staring into his face. "I, um, need to be alone for awhile." She fumbled for the door handle. "I'll see you tomorrow." She bolted from the limo through the hotel's front doors.

Chapter Fourteen

The small town of Sentinel was buzzing with news of Abby's recording triumph, told with flair, drama, and ever-changing details by Tessa.

Abby hadn't seen a trace of Joe since returning to town. Her mind wandered to his face, to the small dimple in his cheek when he smiled, to the warmth of his hand on her face. Then she remembered the moist lips of Winslow Dodge. Her head swam.

Tessa drove into the McIveys' parking lot. Her huge truck was nearly impossible to get out of without falling flat on one's face. The body of the truck was a good four feet off the pavement. Abby assumed it was built for straddling Wyoming snowdrifts. The parking lot was surprisingly full. Hardly a spot was vacant.

"Well, look at you." George shouted, grinning across the counter at her. "I have to say, Tessa has done a fine job on your makeup. You look prettier every time I see you."

Abby bounced around the counter and gave him a hug.

"Stop flirting, old man, and come pick up this order," Margaret shouted from the kitchen.

"See how she treats me?" He shook his head, kicking open the kitchen door.

Margaret squealed and dishes hit the floor with a clatter. "Stop that, you dirty old man." She giggled.

Abby and Tessa exchanged grins. Tessa perched on a stool at the counter while Abby poured them coffee.

George stumbled out of the kitchen, sporting a huge grin that was covered with a blushing shade of pink lipstick. Margaret followed, squinting at Abby. "I'll be darned if George isn't right. You do look pretty. You did a real fine job, Tessa."

"I told you I was a professional." Tessa held up three fingers. "Three years as a makeup girl, remember? I have made some of the ugliest women you ever laid eyes on look good."

"So when do we start hearing your records?" George leaned on the counter next to Margaret.

"I'm not sure. Winslow left for Nashville with some demo tracks that we made. He wants me to be part of the opening act at his Cheyenne concert."

Heart-stopping terror engulfed her when she thought about it. She was terrified to sing onstage and to face Winslow again. He had been right. Her face was on the cover of every tabloid paper in the country. That had to be the reason Joe had been avoiding her. Those damn pictures made it look like she was wrapped around Winslow. The press had followed them to her hotel. There were pictures of the hotel and Winslow's limo at the curb. Not one tabloid mentioned that she'd gone in to that hotel alone. He'd probably never speak to her again.

"Really? His opening act? Any way we might be able to finagle tickets to this concert?" George smiled, raising an eyebrow.

"I will see what I can do," Abby promised.

The café door opened, and Mike and Hal stomped inside.

"You know, Abby, I really hate it when you take time off." Mike pulled his hat off, hanging it on a hook by the door. "When you're gone, I have to subject myself to having a meal here. This is not good for a man who has had the pleasure of your fine culinary talents."

"If you're trying to get me to stay, it's not going to work." Abby laughed.

Tessa twirled around on the barstool, smiling at the cowboys. "Let's see, millions of dollars and someone to cater to your every whim, or cooking three meals a day for a bunch of boys that smell like cows." She held up her hands, weighing them in the air. "I don't know, Abby."

The boys laughed, gathering in a booth.

"You got to come to the barn tonight. That little bull is bawling like crazy. If he don't see you he gets off his feed." Mike shook his head.

"I'll be up tonight, to feed him and tuck him in."

Tessa rolled her eyes. "I'm just glad he's out of the bathtub and in the barn."

"Bathtub?" George didn't understand. "Looks like we've got us one of those tourist buses pulling in." George straightened up, wiping the counter where his elbows had been.

"Mrs. McIvey, we'd better get braced for some assembly line cooking because that's one big bus out there."

"If you need help, Margaret, I'm not too big a star yet. I can still put on an apron." Abby teased, sipping her coffee.

Margaret pulled the apron over her head, tying it around her waist. Everyone shuddered when the door opened, letting in the frigid air.

"What in the world is that?" George mumbled, looking at the door. Abby turned around. Her throat went dry as her past came stomping in the door.

*****

Abby's coffee cup shattered against the floor.

"Hello, beautiful. I'll bet you never thought you'd see me again, did you?"

"You may be getting very popular," Tessa whispered beside her, "but I think you should pass on this one, honey." Tessa folded her arms across her chest.

The café was silent as every eye was on Billy Butcher and his muscle men.

Billy was a younger, thinner, uglier, wanna-be version of Mick Jagger. He had the body, the clothes, and the lips thanks to Botox, but he had very little talent.

Darrel and Mark, his bodyguards followed closely. The only time Abby remembered Billy being without them was when he had a girl in his bedroom. After her well-placed kick, she figured they now probably followed him in there too. They were the ones who'd thrown her off the bus.

"Who's your new friend with the excellent hooters?" Billy leered at Tessa.

Tessa cleared her throat, looking at him like a bug under a microscope.

"What do you want?" Abby folded her arms across her chest.

Billy smirked, straddling a bar stool next to her. "I was feeling very guilty, baby. What I did to you was wrong." He touched her arm and she pulled away.

Mike slid out of the booth, walking toward Billy.

Two bodyguards shadowed him.

Mike turned slowly, giving them a long, hard stare. "Abby, would you like for me and Hal to make this, whatever it's supposed to be, leave?" Hal stood up.

"No Mike." She held her hand up. "Darrel, Mark these folks don't want any trouble," she told the two bodyguards. They nodded, but didn't move. "Billy, tell me what you want and back your boys off."

"Well, I've got fresh coffee. Who's in need of a caffeine fix?" Margaret burst out of the kitchen, setting a cup in front of Billy and smiling as she poured a steaming cup. She offered Darrel and Mark a cup. They declined.

"Looks like your tour bus didn't have any trouble making it through the snow. Does it handle well in the snow?" George chimed in right on cue.

"I wouldn't know. You'd have to ask my driver." Billy's voice became agitated.

"Is he still on the bus? Bring him in." Margaret turned to the cowboys who were poised for a fight. "Hal, go get this man's driver. It's not polite to leave him on that bus in this cold weather." When he hesitated, she waved him on with a hand. "Go now, get him."

"Lady, my driver doesn't need any damn coffee. Come on, Abby, we need to talk." He grabbed her wrist, yanking her off the stool.

"You take your hands off her," Tessa yelled in her thick Texas drawl.

"Shut up, ho." He yanked harder. Abby swung a foot around, missing his groin.

"Not this time, bitch."

Mike, and Hal stood shoulder to shoulder in front of the café door.

Billy smirked. "All I need is a couple of Podunk hicks in their little cowboy boots trying to act like John Wayne. Look boys, my men will tear your redneck heads off, so save yourself some trouble and move."

"Abby doesn't want to go. So I suggest you let go of her unless you want to see what I can do with my size twelve, pointy-toed cowboy boots." Mike tapped his toe against the linoleum.

"Billy, stop this," Abby pleaded. "I've moved on with my life and so have you. These people don't want any trouble--"

"Shut up." He squeezed harder on her wrist. The smell of whiskey on his breath was strong. "I just found out who you moved on with." He pulled a rumpled newspaper out of his jacket. A picture of her and Winslow were on the cover. "You, baby, are going to pull some strings with old Winslow for me."

"Not a chance in hell." She tried to pull away. He backhanded her across the cheek. Stars obliterated her view. She felt her knees bang into the floor. A bell tinkled. The café door? Was that Joe?

Her eyes watered from the stinging slap. She rubbed them, forgetting about the mascara Tessa had put on her until it stung her eyes. Then they watered harder. Squinting through the tears and mascara, Mike and Hal were in a tangled gnarl of bodies with Darrel and Mark. A gunshot rang out. Abby's heart sank. Dear God what had she brought to these people?

Looking through the blackened tears, there stood George McIvey holding a pistol in the air, white drywall dust covering his head, shoulders, and the counter. All the bodies wallowing on the floor went still.

"Now that I have your attention, I want you bus riding morons out of my establishment or I might have to shoot again, and I don't plan on wasting any more bullets on the ceiling. Do I make myself clear?" He cocked the gun again.

She picked herself up off the floor, wiping the side of her face. Joe was poised to deliver a brutal fist to Billy's face.

He held Billy by the collar of his coat. Blood trickled down Billy's face. One eye was puffy, and his lower lip was bleeding profusely. She wondered how Joe had managed to inflict so many bruises in such a short time.

Too bad George hadn't waited about two seconds longer so Joe could have slammed Billy with another punch. Mike and the boys had fairly well demolished Billy's highly trained bodyguards.

Darrel was lying in a heap with one leg grossly twisted between two table legs, a hand ratcheted at an odd angle behind his back and nearly unconscious. Mark had been thrown face first over the back of one of the green booths, his face red, nose bloody, with Mike's hands clasp around his neck.

"Joe, let go of him." George stood beside him, trying to pry Joe's hands off Billy's collar. "Come on, it's over."

Joe dropped Billy in a heap on the floor. He went to Abby, rubbing a hand on her reddened cheek. "Who is he?"

"Billy Butcher, the guy who dumped me here," Abby confessed.

Margaret spit at Billy.

Tessa handed Abby a napkin. "You've got a tiny bit of blood on your cheek there, honey. And heavens, have you got raccoon eyes." She dunked the napkin in a glass of water and began cleaning up Abby's face.

Mike picked up his hat and adjusted it to fit his head comfortably. "You know, I think it's only fair that we escort Mr. Butcher out of town the same way he escorted Abby into town." He glanced over his shoulder out the window. "Yes sir, looks like some nice snow is going to be falling for the next few hours."

"Let me get my coat." George grinned. "I'll help you."

"Wait." Abby followed them out the door. "I want my things off that bus."

After a few minutes, she stepped out with a small suitcase and her purse. Joe stood on the restaurant's porch, arms folded across his chest, his jaw set tight. "Come on. I'm taking you home." He held out a hand.

She smiled, reaching for him. Home?

Billy's voice screeched from behind her. "I'll get you for this, you bitch."

Mike kicked him in the butt. "You better watch you language or next time I'll shove this boot up your fanny." He pushed Billy in front of his pickup truck, yanking off his warm jacket and throwing it in the bed of his truck. "What do you think, boys? Should I let him keep his shoes?"

Billy's eyes grew wide. He screamed for his bodyguards. They had been hog-tied and thrown none too gently in the bed of Hal's truck.

"Let him keep his shoes. This county smells bad enough," Hal shouted.

"You stay here until I come back for you," Mike ordered the bus driver. "You try to leave any sooner, and Hal over there will blow your tires out." He tipped his hat and climbed behind the wheel of his pickup.

Hal sat on a wooden porch bench and patted the small handgun in his belt. "All right, Billy boy, it's time to pay for your sins."

Mike honked his horn, just touching the back of Billy's legs with his bumper.

"You can't do this. I'm not moving!" he screamed.

Mike pulled his leg up, letting his cowboy boot dangle out the window. Billy screamed. "This is illegal. I'm calling the cops."

"The nearest phone is eight miles up the road, just over the county line." Mike laid on the horn. It blared across the frozen ground.

Billy sprinted a dozen steps then stopped to catch his breath. Mike drove down the narrow road, horn honking, laughing while Billy screamed and trotted.

Chapter Fifteen

Joe placed the icepack on her reddened cheek, brushing a stray hair from her face. "I wanted to kill that man." He repositioned the ice pack so that it fit against the side of her face better.

Abby touched his hand. "That wouldn't have been good. You'd be in jail. I'd have to slip a file to you in a cake Tessa made -- that would be the safest way because no one would taste it -- and then you'd have to go on the lam."

Joe laughed. "You always know how to make me laugh."

"You always seem to know when I need rescuing." She leaned her head back against the soft leather couch. "It's starting to become a habit."

"You're becoming a hard habit to break." He leaned close to her face.

Abby turned away. "So, why did you bring me to Hidden Rock instead of the house you live in over by the McIveys?"

He handed the icepack to her, then with experienced skill and a few long matches, he stoked a fire to life in the massive fireplace. Sharing his feelings wasn't easy for him, particularly with a woman. Abby had just dropped into his world and suddenly he found he wanted to be wherever she was. Yet he hardly knew her. He longed to know her every thought, every feeling, and every inch of her sexy body. He shoved the wood around with the poker, increasing the flames. "This place is special. I thought you needed someplace special at the moment."

She went to the fireplace sitting next to him.

"I've been staying at the other house because it's easier than staying here. Too much to lose here. Too many memories."

Her hand rested on his arm. He bent down and planted a kiss on her cheek. Her eyes closed as his lips found hers. He was lost in the warmth of her, lost in their hunger for each other.

"Abby, how do you do this to me?" Her lips trembled against his. He stepped away. Too many feelings were rushing inside him.

"Get your coat. I'll walk you over to your cabin." The hurt look in her eyes shattered his heart. "Damn it, Abby, I find myself caring a whole lot for you. But, in a few weeks I'm going to be a drifter cowboy without, a ranch, a job, hell I won't have two cents to rub together. You've got Winslow Dodge. I saw the paper."

The picture of her in the limo wrapped around Winslow Dodge haunted him.

"It's not what you think. We went to dinner after we finished the recording session. That's all." She pleaded, squeezing his arm. "Then photographers surrounded us. It was a mob scene."

He rested both hands on the fireplace mantle. "Abby, I don't blame you. He's a good looking guy worth millions. He can give you everything you've ever wanted, everything I can't."

She pulled his hands off the mantle, staring up at him. Before she could speak, he blurted out how he felt. "Abby I think I'm falling in love with you." He put his hands around her waist possessively. "When Billy slapped you, I never wanted to kill somebody so badly in my life." Her body pushed into his, the warmth of her surrounding him. She lightly ran her hands through his hair. "I knew then, right then, how much I care. You make me laugh, you make me crazy, you make me mad, and I want to be with you -- but you deserve better."

She stood on tiptoe, nudging his chin. "Kiss me." She pulled his face to hers.

Their lips touched, playing a dance with each other. At first soft and lilting, then the kisses became forceful and passionate. She pulled back, staring at him with a look that he prayed no man but him was ever privileged to see. "I don't care about having a ranch."

For the first time in his life, he needed to confess his feelings to someone, to her. "It's not just the ranch, Abby. I have nothing else. Ranching is all I know. I don't know how to do anything else. I couldn't even support you."

They sat on the leather couch in front of the fireplace. "I'm not looking for a paycheck. I need someone who wants to share dreams, support each other's dreams and make new ones together.""

"I am my job, Abby. I've been on this ranch my entire life, twenty-nine years. I am my ranch. Without it, I don't know what I am."

She laid her head on his shoulder. It belonged there. The fire smelled of pine and sage, its crackle comforting. "You're a good man, an honorable man, world's greatest defender of inept city girls."

Their lips met. The kiss was gentle, tender, and genuine. He pushed her down on the couch, pulling her tight against him. "I love the way you can always make me laugh."

"You aren't your job and you aren't this ranch. You're so much more than that." Her head fit perfectly into the curve of his elbow.

Joe wished she were right, but he was Hidden Rock and Hidden Rock was him.

They adjusted on the couch, his back pressing against the back of the couch, her back tight against his chest.

"You know, you could always become an organic ginseng farmer." She turned, smiling up at him. "You could buy a few acres and grow organic herbs."

He laughed nuzzling her hair. Then he realized she wasn't joking. "You're really serious aren't you? Herbs, organic herbs?"

"I don't know what cattle bring at market, but American-grown, organically-raised ginseng can bring two to three hundred dollars a pound."

"A pound?"

"People are clamoring for organic." She turned back toward the fire. "If you do that, then you won't have to eat Frosty. He can be part of a petting zoo or something."

Joe laughed. "Me, an organic farmer? Whew, my father would turn over in his grave." He could picture Big Joe throwing his cowboy hat on the ground, shaking his fist and raising hell about how badly his sons turned out.

"Would he feel better about growing lavender?"

He turned her around to face him, kissing her lips, his tongue teasing hers.

He wanted her, needed her now. Her body went rigid, not soft and inviting like he'd expected.

"Joe," she mumbled under his onslaught of kisses.

He didn't want to let her go. The taste of her lips was intoxicating and he wanted to taste more, sample every inch of her.

Her leg jerked from underneath him. He expected those warm thighs to wrap delightfully around his back. He felt her yanking her right leg.

Joe gave her a sinfully dirty look. "That anxious are you?"

A look of utter horror covered her beautiful face. Her eyes were wide and her hands went to his shoulders pushing hard against him. Didn't she want him? Why was she pushing him away? A loud thud, then a sickening snap sounded over his shoulder.

He turned toward the sound. Her boot flew toward the ceiling and slammed like a sledgehammer against the large buffalo head that hung above the fireplace mantle. Then it banked left and clanked against the thick wood mantle.

"Up, get up!" she screamed at him.

Joe threw Abby to the floor as the huge buffalo head unhinged from the wall and charged at him. One horn gouged into the couch right between his legs, just missing his most cherished muscle. "Ahhh," he cried out.

"Joe?" Abby jumped up.

The couch was a mass of dried fur, mounds of dusty buffalo hide, and pieces of artificial, glass buffalo eye. The stuffed head was huge and heavy. Abby strained, pulling hard, struggling to get it off him.

"No, Abby, stop."

"Did I hurt you?"

"No." He sneezed. "But if you keep pushing, things are going to get hurt." He spit pieces of buffalo hair out of his mouth. "Try pulling from the side."

She tugged at the massive head but it didn't budge. "It's too heavy, I can't lift it."

"I think the horns are embedded in the couch." Joe tried to slide from underneath it. Every move he made caused the horns to shove tight against his groin. The left horn of the nasty beast felt like it was slicing through the crotch seam of his jeans.

The right horn was buried in the back of the couch, trapping his right arm between his hip and the horn. It was impossible to escape.

"I'll get Mike. Wait here, don't move." She pulled on her wayward boot.

"Not a problem. Do you think you could get this hair out of my eyes first?" The old hair was thick, and coarse and scratching badly.

Abby pushed the mangy hair from his face, planting a kiss on his forehead.

"I'll hurry." She sprinted down the stairs.

Joe cursed the buffalo and the grandfather who'd shot the damn thing. Now he was going to be caught with his pants down, again, with Abby, again, and this time the circumstances wouldn't be so easy to explain.

*****

Trucks outfitted with halogen work lights on tripods sliced across the desolate piece of land that comprised Standforth Reservation. It was an eerie site, with derricks of lattice steel, lights breaking in the vast darkness of the desert and modern noise on ancient ground.

Tom Talking Horse paced across his porch.

"Have some coffee before you wear the boards out." His wife, Naomi, handed him a steaming mug.

He leaned against the porch railing, staring at the derricks in the distance. They were the last hope his tribe had of finding water and being free of Ben Childers. If hatred could send a man to hell, Tom would have long ago carved out a place for Childers. "I hope Matt didn't get close enough to see them when he was out here this morning. If Ben gets winds of this....."

"From a distance, they look like oil derricks. Let him think that's what they are. Then Ben will be tripping over himself to buy the mineral rights from us dumb Indians." Naomi always knew what to say to ease his mind.

Tom sipped the coffee, loving his wife's calmness in the face of devastation.

Naomi leaned against him, resting her head on his shoulder. "Do you think we'll find water?"

"I hope so. I pray so. I don't think I can take any more of Childers's maniacal demands. The man is enough to make me want scalping to become legal." They sat on the front steps, watching the drilling rig in the distant light. "He wants me to get Chief Harrison's bull for his rodeo."

Naomi shuddered. "That bull is evil -- a killer. Why would he even consider that bull?" She looked at Tom. "Dear heaven, he's not going to put that beast in the rodeo?"

The chief's bull had mangled more than a few riders -- not only mangled, but he liked to charge them and gore them. The bull had only been on the circuit one season and the chief had yanked him. A rowdy bull was good rodeo, but this bull was pure meanness.

"With Childers, you never know."

"You told him you wouldn't do it didn't you?"

Tom swallowed. He couldn't bring himself to look at her.

"Tom?"

"Don't judge, Naomi. There's a lot more to this than you think."

"Like the Hidden Rock mortgage?" She stepped off the porch, her finger pointing at him like a loaded gun. "You should have said no to him. We would have survived. We always do. Look where our people have been stuck for a hundred years, and we're still here."

Tom walked toward her. He didn't often see her this angry. "Naomi, it wasn't that simple."

A pickup truck came down their lane, hitting the horn a few dozen times.

"Who's that? I don't recognize the truck." Her anger turned toward the newcomer.

"That is my ace in the hole." Tom walked beside her, sneaking a kiss on her cheek.

"What did you do? Tom?"

"I needed some insurance and we desperately need some help. So for a change I called in the cavalry." The truck door opened. Naomi drew in a hard breath.

"Connor Baer," she whispered.

*****

All talking stopped as Abby came into the kitchen to fix breakfast. Huge grins covered the cowboys' faces. Her face flushed so badly that even her ears felt hot.

Fred let out a snort like a bull and Hal pawed at the floor with his boot. Mike had to ask for their help in removing the buffalo, and nearly all of the cowboys had made an appearance to see Joe trapped on his own couch.

The buffalo horns had driven deep into the couch. A large hunting knife had to be used to pry the marauding beast loose. Joe had held up remarkably well, considering Mike had to cut away couch and buffalo just inches from his manhood.

As if the entire incident weren't bad enough, Mike and Hal had dropped the heavy head as they were pulling it off. Its sharp horns had skewered Abby's purse. Hal, always being the most helpful cowboy, yanked the purse off the horn, only to find her brand new, bright red bra swinging wildly from one of the buffalo horns. It was a bra that Tessa had bought her, and the thing pinched horribly. She hated wearing it, so she'd whipped it off and tucked into her purse, thinking it was safe. Hal had snatched it and run. Now he bowed his head, mooed, and used her bra like a red cape, taunting the bull. The cowboys erupted in gales of laughter.

Abby wanted to die. She turned around, facing Joe. There was no escape. He smiled at her. It was an apologetic smile, but it didn't help.

Mike cleared his throat. "Boys, are you as hungry as I am?"

"Maybe Abby could whip up some buffalo steaks with those eggs this morning," Fred said and they all laughed.

Abby pulled an iron skillet from the stove, pointing it menacingly toward the cowboys. "If you want to eat, then I'd better not hear another damn word."

Rodney walked into the dining hall carrying a huge vase of red roses. "Hey, Abby, Margaret asked me to bring these up to you." He stomped the snow off his boots and took the vase into the kitchen. "There's another ten of these at the McIveys'. Looks like somebody is trying real hard to impress you."

She pulled the card from the nearest vase, forgetting their teasing. "Where did they come from?"

"We've got several recording labels interested in you darling. Congrats, Winslow."

"Damn," she mumbled through a smile.

What is it?" Mike asked.

"I think it's a bribe."

Joe pushed his hat back, his eyebrow raised, and he looked mildly pissed. "Winslow Dodge?"

Abby nodded. She had a lot to figure out.

Chapter Sixteen

Mike pointed into the stall. Joe peered inside. Abby and the little bull were sound asleep. The calf snuggled against her leg, the empty feeding bottle lying next to him. As they curled together on a pillow of straw, a dim light in the stall made the scene warm and homey. It was one of the most beautiful things Joe had seen in a long time. His city-girl was doing pretty damn good on the ranch. His girl? Where had that come from?

"I got worried when I didn't see any lights in her cabin. I figured she might be with the calf," Mike whispered. "Took me some serious negotiations to get her to put the critter in the barn and get it out of her house. After a week, when the fertilizer got a bit more potent, she saw the logic."

Mike pushed his hat back. "She reminds me of Margaret's daughter, Joyce, always in the barn with a critter. You know she named the thing Frosty?" He chuckled. "Frosty. What a name for a bull."

"She said it was because the calf was very frosty when she found it out in the snow," Joe explained. "Why don't you head up to the house and start a fire? I'll see if I can get the calf to let her go."

Mike pulled his gloves on. "I'll make sure and check for low flying buffalo while I'm at it."

Joe shot him an angry look. Mike chuckled all the way out the barn.

He watched her sleep. Abby groaned, holding tight to the calf. It didn't seem to mind, pulling closer to her, not bothering to open its eyes. He wondered what she was dreaming.

There were so many questions he had. Just weeks ago, she'd trashed his hay barn and didn't know a heifer from a bull. Now she was holding a calf she'd help save in her lap. He leaned against the stall railing.

Strands of blonde hair peeked from under a dark blue stocking cap. Her mouth was slightly open. She wore only one glove, the bare hand resting on the calf's neck. Weeks ago, he couldn't stand her potty mouth or brash attitude or the fact he was attracted to her.

Since Kelly, he'd fought being attracted to any woman. Abby was a walking disaster area on the ranch. But she had persevered through it all and thrived. The cowboys adored her, the McIveys would adopt her, and heaven help him, he was falling hopelessly in love with her.

He opened the stall door. Its rusted hinges squealed, startling her awake. "Hey," she whispered, looking up at him.

"The baby seems to be sleeping. Would you like to come inside where it's warm?" He lifted the calf's head off her lap, laying it gently on a mound of straw. It continued to sleep peacefully.

He pulled Abby to her feet and they slipped from the stall. A whinny from the dark end of the barn drew her like a magnet. She dusted the straw off her jeans and peered inside a darkly lit stall.

"Wow, who are you?" she whispered. A beautiful buckskin horse with silken black mane and tail and a few black spots sprinkled perfectly across his romp snorted at her.

"He's a stallion with attitude. Leave him alone. He's Tom's horse. I'll feed him, nothing more."

"How could you do that? It's not the horse's fault your cousin is an ass." Abby sighed, then corrected herself. "A jerk, I mean."

She slid open the stall door before he could stop her. Joe was blindsided by the running weight of a hundred-fifty pound calf bolting past him into the stall.

He panicked, grabbing a rope. The stallion was a wild one and didn't take well to strangers being inside his stall. Bursting inside, he found Frosty and the stallion nose to nose and Abby stroking the horse's ears, cooing to him.

"He is so beautiful." Her smile lit up the entire barn. Joe reached around the corner and flipped on the stall light. "What's his name?"

"He's got some long, meaningful Indian name. I just call him Mugs."

"This is just the sort of horse you could ride off into the sunset on."

Joe walked up behind her, wrapping an arm around her waist. "Would you like to ride off into the sunset with me?" He kissed her neck.

"Only if you bring Mugs." She laughed, turning around and planting a kiss on his cheek. Did he just ask her that? Yes, he did. Did she understand what he'd meant?

"So, if I rode up on Mugs, you'd go off into the sunset with me?" There was a shocked look in her eyes, and he saw her indecision.

A smile played across her face. "Well, you'd have to have a white hat."

"A white hat?" He had just asked the women to spend forever with him and she was talking about a hat? She confused the hell out of him.

"You always wear a black hat." She flipped his brim. "Don't you know the good guys always wear white?" She seemed very determined not to let him get serious. Was she scared or did she just not want to be with him forever?

Joe sighed, adding a little growl. He looped the rope around Frosty's neck.

"Come on." He tugged on the rope. Frosty would have none of it, planting its small hooves, and refusing to budge. "This is ridiculous." Joe grunted.

Abby walked past him, gave Joe a wink, and called. "Frosty."

The calf shifted gears and bounded out of the stall, yanking the rope out of his hands and following her across the barn back into its own stall. Joe growled, hung up the lead rope, and closed Mugs stall door.

*****

The ranch house was toasty warm when she stepped inside. The huge fireplace was blazing with sparkling flames. Only the kitchen light was glowing and the smell of coffee filled the air.

They kicked off their boots and coats at the door. "Coffee?" Joe asked.

"Yes." Abby found a warm spot on the intricately woven Indian rug in front of the fireplace and propped her feet on the hearth. "I love sitting in front of this fireplace."

Joe joined her, handing her a steaming cup of coffee. They both stared silently into the flames. Abby sipped on the coffee, giving him a sideways glance. She remembered the look on his face in the barn. He had asked her to ride off into the sunset with him. She'd made her usual jokes, and he had looked so wounded it broke her heart. Abby didn't know if he was the one.

Yes, she did. Damn, she didn't want this, a ranch, a life in the country. A record deal loomed in her future. Could she have Joe and fame?

She'd wanted a recording contract her entire life. It's all she ever wanted, until now. Her brain spun in so many directions, she was dizzy. Maybe she didn't know what she wanted -- stardom, adoring fans, a chance to redeem her past. Winslow was waiting in Cheyenne. Joe's smile invaded her every waking thought. His touch made her feel loved and safe. Those were feelings she'd never known.

"The calf seems to be coming along real nice," Joe said, breaking the silence.

"Yes, he is." She sat up, clearing her throat. "I'm sorry about the buffalo thing."

"It's probably a good thing it happened. You would have had some serious regrets the next morning."

She sat the cup on the hearth, sliding next to him,."Only if you lied."

"Lied?"

"When you said you thought you were falling in love with me," she whispered.

Joe shot her a hard, serious look. "I'd never lie about something like that, and I'd never lie to you." He pulled her close, wrapping his arms around her shoulders. His lips found hers. "Abby, I do love you." The kiss was long, tender, and gentle. His lips lingered. She touched his cheek, staring into his eyes.

Their hands intertwined. His kisses covered her face and her neck. His caressing fingers eased open her blouse, kissing her chest lightly after each opened button. He tucked an arm under her neck, easing her back onto the soft Indian rug. He kissed her, soft and slow, every inch of her face from her eyelids to her earlobes.

With a flick of his fingers, the front snap on her bra opened. Very slowly, he pushed one strap, then the other down her arms. The zipper of her jeans opened, then warm hands slip them over her hips, down her legs, and onto the floor.

Soft, wet lips found her breasts. She let a soft moan escape. His rough tongue made lazy circles around her nipples, caressing, stroking, tasting. He wrapped a large hand around one breast, cupping it, suckling her. Then his hand caressed the other breast as a low growl escaped from his throat.

The smell of him was intoxicating, sweet hay, leather, and a hint of cologne. Her fingers played across his wide back, up into his thick, curly hair.

His lips moved ever so slowly down her chest, over her stomach, lingering at the top of her pelvis. Wonderful tingles crawled down her legs. Buttons popped across the hardwood floor as he yanked his shirt off. With quick movements, off came his jeans and he was back beside her, naked and warm.

He stared appreciatively down her slender body. "You are one beautiful lady."

She looked into his face. The dimpled smile filled her heart with joy. Again, his lips traveled down the course of her stomach to stop between her legs. She arched her back, the wanting becoming unbearable.

His hot breath played across her pelvis, as gentle hands spread her thighs and a probing tongue plied into her. She gasped as a wave of pleasure ignited a fire in her belly and a searing wetness flashed from within her.

Joe moaned, hungrily eating the essence of her. She pulled him tight against her. She wanted him, needed him inside her. His tongue invaded her groin, his fingers slid inside, and his hands were everywhere at once.

Jolting spasms of undulating pleasure she'd never known possible seized her body. She succumbed and came over his expert hands, arching her back, pushing against his hand, extending the pleasure as long as possible. Just as she caught her breath, he rolled on top of her. Their eyes locked as they became one.

Joe was gentle, slow, and pleasing her in ways she never knew existed. Their rhythm synchronized and her body moved to accommodate his. Her legs wrapped around his waist. Her hands squeezed his back, lingering across his sinewy buttocks, feeling every inch of him.

The pulsating rhythm increased and the room became a blur. She knew she screamed, but she couldn't hear it.

They lay spent in a tangled mass of sweet sweat and satisfaction. Curled around one another, they were two lost souls who'd finally found shelter, sharing each other's body, touching each other's hearts. Their spent bodies sent them into a satisfied sleep.

A cold breeze traveled up her naked back. She rolled over, missing the warmth of Joe's body. She caught a glimpse of his silhouette in front of the fireplace as he added logs to the flames.

His naked body was a joy to watch. Thighs taut, arms well-defined as he stoked the fire to life. The room became warm and light.

Abby pulled a coverlet off the couch, wrapped it around her, and walked up behind him.

He turned, planting a kiss on her nose. "Drop the cover," he ordered with a smile.

She obeyed. He pulled her to the floor, laying her in front of the fire. He snuggled against her back and pulled the coverlet over them both. He nuzzled her hair. "Any regrets?"

"No. Do you?" She pulled away from the embrace, resting her head on his shoulder, watching the flames.

"None." He toyed with her hair.

"Why are you losing Hidden Rock?" He inhaled sharply. "You don't have to tell me if you don't want to."

He stretched out on the woven rug, locking his hands under his head and staring at the ceiling. "A stupid mistake, I'd like to say Kelly Childers is the reason, but it was my own stupidity."

Abby stretched out beside him, resting on her elbow, and watching his face. "Did you love her?"

A shocked look crossed his face. "No. I only went out with her a few times." His jaw flinched. "In those few dates, she cried a lot. She told me her dad, good old Ben, beat her. She talked about love and said she thought that she and I getting married would be a good idea."

"Did you sleep with her?" Abby held her breath, unsure if she wanted to hear the answer.

"Things never got that far." His eyes reflected the firelight. "There just wasn't anything there."

"I didn't see her for a few months, and then one night a couple of months ago, she's pounding on my door in tears, nearly beaten to death." Joe shook his head. "Her face was bruised, her mouth was split, and God, she looked like hell. She said she'd been gambling and owed some brutally vicious guys nearly a million dollars in gambling debts and interest."

She whistled. "A million dollars? That's a lot of debt."

"She said if she told Ben, he'd kill her. She had me convinced. Everybody in Sentinel knows Ben's temper. A little later, these guys showed up right behind her. I couldn't let them break her legs in my living room, so I arranged to mortgage Hidden Rock to pay her debt." He stared at the ceiling. She could see the regret in his face.

"That's a lot of debt to take on for somebody."

"Our families go back generations. Ben had been best friends with my father. Hell, he'd bailed my dad and Hidden Rock out more than once or twice for more than a million. I figured after I talked to him, softened the blow a bit, he'd understand and pay me back. I wasn't stupid enough to trust him. I sold the mortgage to Tom Talking Horse, my cousin. Tom's a wealthy man. It wasn't much of a strain." Joe tucked a pillow under his neck. "Then I got word that Tom sold the mortgage to Ben."

Abby rested her head on his chest, hearing the strong heartbeat beneath her ear.

"Now, by the terms of the mortgage note, I've got less than two months left to repay the lien or Hidden Rock becomes the property of Ben Childers." He gently stroked the back of her head. "For the last few years, Ben has tried everything to get Hidden Rock. It's like something inside him snapped. He's a different man from when I was a kid. Tom, well, so much for family loyalty." His voice was angry.

Abby rolled onto her back. "I know all about family loyalty. My mother stole the mortgage from underneath my grandmother."

She turned to stare into the flames. "I don't know who my father is, and my mother, well, her best friend is anybody who'll buy her a drink." Abby had never told anyone about her life. Yet, here she was, lying naked beside a man she'd just made love with, spilling her guts. No matter how hard she tried, the words wouldn't stop flowing.

"Granny Martin raised me." Abby smiled remembering the small, happy home they had shared. "She had an old Victorian house. It had been in the family for years. Granny would tell me stories about family gatherings at Christmas and I wanted them so bad, but it was just me and her."

Joe held her tighter.

"I hadn't seen my mother since I was eleven, then one day she shows up on the doorstep, gives Granny a long-winded story about how she'd gone through detox, and was clean and sober." Damn, the words poured out like a dam had broken inside her.

"Granny mortgaged the house to help her out. Once my mom got the money, she was gone. Then came the bills. I couldn't keep up and Granny lost the house. Then I lost her. I didn't have enough money to bury her." She turned, staring at him. "I had to let my grandmother be buried in a city pauper's cemetery, no headstone, no services. Her funeral consisted of an unknown minister, who acted imposed upon to be there, and me. I'm saving money." She choked back the tears, not about to cry on top of long-winded confession. "I'll fix it."

He pulled her tight arms in his arms.

Abby took in a deep breath, pushing back the grief and pain. "I guess we're two of a kind. It seems family ties are not in the cards for us."

"Too bad. I'd like a family."

The fire crackled warmly, the snow fell softly outside, and for a few brief moments, Abby was the most contented woman on the planet.

Chapter Seventeen

Abby had spent the day at Winslow's recording studio, practicing for next week's concert. How to enter the stage, remember the intro music, remember the words, nausea rose in her throat as she prayed she would remember the words.

Now, she stared into the mirror in her hotel room mortified by her own reflection. She looked like the love child of Liberace and Dolly Parton. White denim jeans she couldn't breathe in with the sides slit out, laced with red leather to her upper thigh. This was paired with a white, western-cut silk blouse covered by a dark red leather vest, and topped off with a red cowboy hat and matching boots. "Oh, Tessa, what have you done to me." She talked to her reflection.

Tessa had done a great job on her hair and makeup, but the outfit felt wrong. Then again, the punk rock look didn't feel right either. Hell, she didn't know what felt right. Nothing seemed to suit her. Not punk, country, city life, and definitely not ranch life. Yet it felt so right in Joe's arms.

There was a knock on her door. She glanced at the clock. Winslow was early. Now, she was stuck answering the door in this ridiculous outfit. His face lit up when she opened the door.

"You look amazing." Winslow took off his hat and bowed, his smile generating its own wattage.

Abby tugged at the skin-hugging vest. "This is way too much."

"Not on stage. Folks want you to be a little eccentric. It's what they pay for." He walked behind her, wrapping his arms around her waist. "Besides, once you start singing, they won't even notice what you're wearing." His hug grew tighter.

Abby took a step forward, pulling out of his arms. Why did she feel so awkward? She wasn't some sixteen-year-old who didn't know how to handle men. Although her track record with them hadn't been exactly stellar.

Winslow threw his hat on a chair. "Shall we discuss the contract King Management wants to offer you over dinner?"

Abby's breath caught. Did she hear him correctly?

"When I sent the flowers, I told you several records labels were interested." He sat on the arm of a chair, smiling at her. "A damned good agent at King Management wants to rep you to those labels. Interested?"

It took every ounce of control she had to not dance, jump, and scream, "Yes!" Instead, she toyed with the cowboy hat and said quietly, "I'm interested."

Winslow nodded, giving her a look that sent shivers and sparks down her spine. Abby wasn't sure if he was flirting or annoyed that she was so calm. Either way, she liked keeping him guessing about her decision.

"Would you like to try dinner with me again? Since my last attempt didn't turn out so well, I'd like the opportunity to make it up to you."

"Let's just have a simple dinner here in the hotel room." After the night she and Joe had shared, she wanted to make very sure Joe didn't see any more incriminating photographs.

"Great. Do you want me to order?" He flashed her a sideways glance. "Or do you want to order yourself?"

She smiled. "I'll let you order this time."

He picked up the phone as she slipped into the bathroom to change back into her comfortable blue jeans and flannel shirt.

She twirled in front of the mirror. "Ahh," she grumbled, yanking off the vest. Next went the boots, the hat, the ridiculous blouse, and the skintight jeans.

Never again was she going to wear someone else's idea of stage clothes. She slid into her jeans and flannel, wrapped the clothes in a bundle and dropped them on the couch. "Winslow, I'm not wearing these," she announced. "I will wear what I want to wear, or I'm not going onstage."

Winslow gave her a mega-watt smile. "Darling, you can wear whatever you want. Those weren't my idea. They were Tessa's, although I admit I did like those jeans."

Room service arrived with dinner.

He answered the door and pulled the cart inside. "I just ordered some soup and sandwiches."

The suite had a beautiful table for two in front of a huge window that overlooked Cheyenne. The soup warmed her up and tasted wonderful. They made short work of the sandwiches, and Winslow had thought to include a bottle of wine.

"King Management wants to represent me. I'd like to discuss the details." She went straight to the point.

"King would front the money for your band and your initial concert expenses. Your agent will book all your shows, put together promo packages with radio stations and concert halls, arrange media interviews. In fact, the only thing you would have to do is show up and sing." He reached across the table, dabbing a bit of soup off her chin.

It sounded too good to be true, which in her experience usually meant that it was. "What does all this cost me?"

"King Management would get twenty percent of everything you make." Winslow leaned back, staring at her over the rim of his wine glass.

She whistled. "Twenty percent, isn't that a little steep?"

"It's standard throughout the industry."

"I will want prior approval on every expense, hotel, band, and show." She'd watched her mother walk away with everything. She wasn't about to let the same fate befall her again.

"I'm not a shady businessman, Abby. I can't afford to be. I've been in this business for over twenty years. King Management represents seven major performers. One of their agents represents me."

"But you're an owner." She was skeptical.

"In paper only. I helped financially launch the company, for which I get a percentage of the profits. I don't deal with the performers or the agents." He leaned forward, pushing the wine glass away. "Abby, you can talk to any performer under contract to King Managment before you sign on the dotted line and you are welcome to have an attorney look over the contract."

"I've had some bad experiences in the past. I don't want to repeat them." Visions of the sheriff's sale of Granny's house played over again.

"So have I, darling." He snagged the last sandwich on the tray. "I make money. I won't lie. You won't find a more honest management company, I guarantee you."

A knock on the door caused Abby to flinch.

Winslow nearly danced toward the door. "I've got a surprise for you."

He opened the door and the waiter arrived with a food tray. "Oh, darling, you are gonna like this." He lifted the lid, revealing a huge platter of strawberry shortcake slathered with whipped cream.

"Oh, my." She ran a finger through the strawberry glaze. She was just about to the lick the delectable nectar off her finger when

Winslow caught her hand in mid-air. He put her finger in his mouth, slowly licking it clean.

She yanked her hand away, going across the room. "Winslow, don't do this."

"I'm sorry. Did I make you angry?" He wiped his mouth with a napkin.

"I want to keep our relationship strictly professional."

Winslow nodded and sat down at the table again. "If that's what you want."

She cleared her throat, still standing behind the couch. It had happened. Her heart was back on that damn ranch. Winslow Dodge, the most eligible bachelor in country music had just hit on her, and all she could think about was Joe, the little bull, and that ranch.

"I wouldn't do anything to upset you or put you in a situation where you feel uncomfortable." He finished the wine in his glass. "Although you are a woman I could get used to having by my side."

Abby went back to the table and sat down. "Winslow, you are a remarkable man, but this is way too fast." She couldn't just blurt out that her heart belonged to someone else, to Joe. Winslow could have any woman he wanted. She would just be a girl-of-the-moment for him, and she wanted more than that, much more.

She sat up straight and met his gaze head on. "Getting back to the contract. How long do you think it would take me to earn, say, one million dollars?"

Winslow forked strawberries onto a plate, plopping whipped cream on top, and pushed the plate toward her. "With recordings, royalties, product tie-ins, I'd say a year, less, probably six months. It's hard to say. Why?"

"Is there any way I can get an advance?"

"You want a one million dollar advance?" He filled another plate and forked mouthful of strawberries. "What do you want the money for?"

"Stage clothes," she lied.

Winslow nearly choked on the strawberries, he laughed so hard. "You're a hell of singer, Abby, but an awful liar."

"Let's just say I want a place to call home."

"Well, the best I can do is offer you a personal loan from me to you."

Abby wasn't sure if being in debt to Winslow was the smartest thing. "I'll take it if there is a legal contract with loan terms."

"Honey, I never buy toilet paper without a legal contract. I'll have Jack draw up a loan agreement. It'll take a week or so." He suddenly stopped talking, giving her a quizzical look. "This is for a cowboy, isn't it?"

She didn't answer.

"It's that cowboy at the cafe who could've killed me with a look." He stared at her long and hard. "You're in love with him."

Winslow leaned back in the chair. "I didn't even stand a chance, did I?"

She ate a mouthful of strawberries, staring at her plate.

"Well, I'm glad I know before my heart got ripped all the way out of my chest." He picked up a fork. "You know, cowboys are notorious heartbreakers. I sure hope he's worth it."

*****

A few days later, she was back in her cottage on the ranch when Tessa came squealing inside without so much as a knock. "Grab your boots. You gotta come into town with me."

"What? Why?" Abby pulled on a pair of socks and tried to remember where she'd taken her boots off.

"There is a big ol' surprise for you at the McIveys', but I'm not supposed to tell you," she squealed again.

Abby found her boots under the kitchen table, but wasn't about to put them on. "Tessa, if all of you planned some sort of party for me, I'm not going."

"It ain't no party, now get your boots on," she ordered. "Time's wasting and I got a date with Jack later." Tessa had been spending an awful lot of time with Jack.

"What did you do with Rodney?" Abby pulled the boots on, tucked in her thermal underwear top, and reached for her jacket on the back of the chair.

"I'm still sort of hanging on to him." She toyed with her truck keys. "I know I'm bad, but Jack just makes me so happy and, well, I'm just not sure if he's the real thing yet."

Abby knew how that felt. "You're not lying to me? This isn't a surprise party?"

Tessa made an exaggerated cross over her heart. "I swear, there is no party, but you are gonna be surprised." She nearly crashed her truck into the McIveys' front door as she braked to a stop in the parking lot.

It was surprisingly full. "It looks like business is good." Abby nodded toward all the cars

"It the rodeo, honey. There are cowboys, vendors, judges -- you name it coming to town. The town's busy as a hooker on a Navy ship. At least Ben has done something good, even if he don't know it." She laughed and pointed to the far side of the lot. "There, that's for you."

Sitting by the bait cooler, nearly blocked from view by the stacks of cordwood, was a shiny black Porsche with a huge red ribbon across its hood.

Tessa jumped out of the truck, yanking open Abby's door, and sprinted in her bright red boots across the lot. "Get your butt over here and let's go for a drive."

"How do you know this is for me?" Abby walked to the car.

"Jack told me and he gave me these." She dangled the car keys. "Isn't it gorgeous?"

Tucked just behind the ribbon was a large, white envelope with her name on the outside. Abby opened it.

You didn't want the necklace, you didn't want me. Maybe this will fulfill your wishes. Winslow.

"I can't keep this."

Tessa stomped a foot. "What? Oh, yes you can. You have to. You just have to keep it." Her voice was a desperate whine. She grabbed the keys from Abby's hand, clicked the doors unlocked, and climbed into the passenger seat. Through the glass, she crooked a finger, smiling and coaxing Abby into the driver's seat.

What could it hurt to sit in it? She'd never sat in a car that cost this much. The door shut solidly and the new car smell enveloped them.

"Oh, oh." Tessa moaned, groaned, and moaned again.

"Are you all right?" Abby wasn't sure if she was excited or having a heart attack.

Tessa's face was flushed and her breath was short. "I think I just had an orgasm sitting in the seat."

Abby laughed until tears swam in her eyes. "Stop. I'll have to steam clean the thing before I send it back."

Tessa caressed the dash, touched the knobs on the stereo. "At least drive it once."

Abby shook her head no.

"Just once." Tessa shoved the keys into the ignition.

"You are a bad influence." Abby started the engine. Tessa screamed and they left rubber burning out of the parking lot.

*****

Kelly knew Rodney was getting drunker by the glassful. It wouldn't be long before he was drunk enough to do everything she needed him to do.

"I really like her." Rodney took a sip of beer, elbowing Fred. "I mean, I really like her." His speech was slurred. "Hell, I think I might even love her, but I don't know if I want to marry her."

"Haven't saddled all the fillies in the county yet, huh?" Fred snickered, chugging a drink from the beer bottle.

"Maybe that's it. Shit I don't know. Then again, she's been going over to Cheyenne with Abby and I don't see her for days. Do you know what that does to a man's libido?" He belched.

Kelly winced. This wasn't going to be easy.

"When she is back, its Jack Spencer this and Jack Spencer that." He downed his beer, his voice growing angry. "Oh, let's not forget that Jack Spencer sends her flowers. Like I've never sent flowers."

"Have you?" Fred asked, leaning across the bar and pulling a bowl of peanuts from underneath.

"Whose side are you on anyway?" Rodney sat upright.

"Don't get your chaps in a wad. Maybe all she wants is a little extra attention from you. Women like that stuff you know."

""Hi, Rodney." Kelly cooed in her sexiest voice over his shoulder. She let her hands wrap over his shoulders then move with familiarity down his chest.

Rodney swallowed hard then smiled. "Hey, Kelly."

"Will you buy a lady a beer?" she purred.

Fred snorted, chugging his beer.

Kelly gave him a spiteful glare, and then returned her attention to Rodney.

"Sure. A beer for the lady," he ordered, blinking hard.

Kelly pushed against his shoulder, keeping him upright on the barstool.

"You've put away a few too many beers, Rodney. Come on, I'll take you home." Fred stood, putting his hat on.

Kelly eased comfortably onto his vacated bar stool, her arms still wrapped around Rodney's neck.

"Buddy let's go home," Fred pleaded.

"I think I'll stick around awhile." Rodney grabbed her hand and planted a kiss on it. She playfully touched the end of his nose.

"You go on, Fred," Kelly said. "I'll make sure Rodney gets home safe and sound, don't you worry." She nuzzled her forehead against Rodney's.

"Rodney, buddy, she wants something. Run while you have a chance. There's no way this heifer actually wants a cowboy like you, but she wants something, that's for sure."

Kelly turned slowly on him. "You'd better watch your mouth, Fred Gillis. It's not safe to talk like that to me."

"Rodney?" Fred reached around her, tapping his friend's shoulder. Rodney brushed him away. "Your choice." He plunked a couple of dollars on the bar. "Good luck, you're gonna need it."

"Well, he was in a shitty mood wasn't he?" She nudged Rodney off the barstool. "How about we have a couple more beers and move to a booth so we can talk a little?"

Rodney staggered into a booth with her. His eyes were glazed, and he smelled sweaty.

"The word around town is that you and Tessa are having some problems." She patted his thigh. The beer bottle teetered in his hands.

"I guess we do." A bit of drool slid from the corner of his mouth. Kelly swallowed hard to keep from gagging.

"That's a shame." Rodney chugged the last of his beer. She motioned for another one to be sent to the table. She slid tight against him.

She swirled the beer bottle slowly around in her hand. "From what I hear, it's Jack Spencer that is piquing Tessa's interest." She inched even closer, resting her head on his shoulder. "I'd hate to see a nice guy like you with a broken heart."

"Probably, just as well." He stared at the beer bottle. "Jack's got money and all."

"Yes, he does, and he's not some dirty old cowboy. I mean you're a good old boy. You'd just step aside for him the way a cowboy should." Kelly leaned forward, her elbows on the table, her voice quiet and low. "I think that's a fine and honorable thing to do."

He wiped the slobber from his mouth with the back of his hand. "Heck I ain't just gonna stand to the side. What's so wrong with a cowboy anyhow?"

"I didn't say anything was wrong." She played with the beer bottle. "Are you sure she's worth fighting for? I mean, Jack would probably win."

"He would not." Rodney slammed the beer bottle on the table. "I could kick his ass."

"Rodney, if you're serious about winning Tessa back, I can help." She flashed her most beautiful smile. "Tonight Abby and Tessa are fixing dinner for Joe and Jack."

"So?" He shot little droplets of spittle on her forehead.

Kelly winced, taking the napkin from under her beer bottle and wiping it off. She forced a smile. "If we leave now, we might just be able to make Hidden Rock Ranch about the time they sit down for dinner." She twisted her watch in the dim light of the bar. Just an hour was all she needed. "You do want to keep Tessa don't you, Rodney?"

"Of course I do. But I still don't understand how--"

"Shh." She stroked his lips with a finger. "You just let Kelly do her magic and I guarantee a certain lady will be running into your arms. Are you ready to fight for your woman, tiger?"

A determined look spread across his flushed face. "Ain't no city boy walking off with my girl without a fight."

"You are my kind of man, Rodney." Kelly slid out of the booth, leading a staggering Rodney out of the bar.

"I have some dry cleaning in my truck, so you'll have to ride in the bed." The snow was falling as they left the warmth of The Sagebrush. "It shouldn't be too cold if you stay close to the back window." He obligingly climbed into the bed, slumping over, barely able to sit up.

Kelly slammed the tailgate shut. Inside, the cab was empty. She wasn't about to let that drunken, smelly cowboy ride inside with her.

Rodney slid the back cab window open. "Where are we going again?"

"We're just going to dinner." She spun gravel, tearing out of the parking lot.

Rodney slid flat on his back in the truck bed.

She glanced in the rearview mirror, laughing. "And I'm real hungry."

She laughed harder at the prospect of ripping Joe's heart apart, just like he'd done to hers. With what she had planned, she'd get two broken hearts for the price of one.

Chapter Eighteen

Abby had dropped Tessa off and taken the Porsche for a long drive. She was giving the car back, but a few miles on it wouldn't hurt.

She'd driven to Riverton and shopped alone. No satins, no rhinestones, and no spandex were on her shopping list. Tonight was special, and she wanted to feel special.

She slipped on a soft ivory sweater over a pair of new, well-fitting jeans. There would be no cowboy boots for this city girl. Tonight, she slipped on her orange stilettos. They'd been packed away too long.

Staring at her reflection, a giggle bubbled up. She couldn't wait to see how surprised Joe would be when she handed him the check -- a check that would keep Hidden Rock Ranch right where it belonged.

Earlier she had left a roasting pan of seasoned winter vegetables in the oven of the ranch house. She hoped he wasn't too disappointed that there would be no beef on tonight's menu. She did a final check and walked the shoveled path toward Joe.

*****

The aroma coming from the kitchen was intoxicating. Joe smiled looking over the perfectly set table. Abby had found his mother's stoneware dishes. The two place settings, complete with familiar, old napkins, looked very inviting.

He thought about what it might be like to share his ranch, a family, a life with Abby. He liked the idea of having children with Abby. A fleeting thought of Christmas lingered about him. A tree, decorations, children, and maybe Connor would come home.

Then reality rushed into his mind like a hell storm. How was he going to keep Hidden Rock? He tried to understand why Tom had surrendered the mortgage. The man had just hung his head and walked away. Joe had pleaded with Childers for more time, only to be offered a rodeo spot. He didn't know if he had what it took to ride the bull, particularly any bull that Ben Childers had selected.

The National Rodeo Association had rules and even Ben had to abide by them. Yet Joe couldn't stop the nagging feeling in his gut that something was wrong. Ben had been too easy, and the man never let anyone off easily.

Joe had signed up under Childers colors at the feed store. He read the form, he read the small print, and he asked the store manager for details. Nothing was unusual. All he had to do was ride a bull. All he had to do was last eight-seconds.

He'd done it before for prize money. Doing it for Hidden Rock would glue his butt onto that bull. Joe skipped up the stairs, grabbing a hot shower before Abby arrived.

*****

Undetected, Kelly sat in her warm truck patiently waiting, watching Abby walk down the path. She'd let Rodney sit in the cab when his shivering turned to loud complaining. Now, his head drooped to one side and he was lightly snoring.

Abby moved gingerly down the path. Kelly snickered, at the sight of her bright, orange heels.

The ranch house was brimming with light, and wood smoke curled from the huge chimney. It looked like Joe and Abby were starting to play house together. Kelly's hand shook as she pulled out a cigarette and lit it with the trucks lighter.

Most ranchers never locked a door, and she knew the house very well. She'd carefully plotted every detail of tonight. She'd brought more beer for Rodney, keeping him happy without letting him pass out. All she needed was for him to be just sharp enough to follow directions, but drunk enough to not ask questions.

Kelly smacked Rodney's arm, pulling him awake. She opened the truck door, gathering a small ball of snow and rubbed it against his face. "Rodney, we're here. I want you to sit here. Understand? Just wait right here."

"Why can't I come inside? I thought Tessa was here." He squinted out the truck window. You said we were gonna get Winslow and Jack." His voice grew loud.

Kelly clamped a hand over his mouth. "If you want to keep Tessa, you need to stay right here, do you understand me?"

She rubbed more snow on his face. "Climb over here. When you see Abby come running outside, you just start the engine and call her over. That's all you have to do. Do you think you can handle that?"

"I thought Tessa was here." His speech was slurred, his eyelids half-closed. "I came for Tessa."

"When Abby comes out she'll take you right to Tessa. She's here to take you to your girl."

An idiotic grin spread across his face and he nodded.

Kelly slid quietly out of the truck and disappeared into the darkness toward the ranch house. Being sneaky was one of her better talents. She crept with familiar ease inside the front door.

A clatter of pans sounded in the kitchen. Kelly took her shoes off, tiptoeing across the great room and up the stairs. Joe's bedroom was at the end of the long hallway. Light glowed under the door, she quietly turned the knob. The shower was running in the adjacent bath.

Kelly yawned and turned off the bedroom light.

*****

Abby cracked open the oven door, satisfied her creation was nearly perfect. She tossed the ingredients together for a salad and sliced a loaf of fresh baked bread.

Pulling the card that told him she was giving him a million dollars out of her pocket, she laid it on his plate, studied it, and then picked it up. She folded it inside his napkin, then took it out again. She placed it in the center of the table, stared at it, and then put it back in her pocket.

There wasn't a right place to put it. Maybe she should just hand it to him. When should she give it to him? Over the salad, dinner, dessert? She sat at the table, staring into the grotto. It was dark, with only small reflections of light from the kitchen. Large, glass doors were pulled across its opening, blocking the cold of the rocks from the interior of the house.

Abby imagined it with tiny, white Christmas lights strung through it and homemade decorations tucked into its recesses. Could she have it all -- Joe and stardom? Could she survive living on a ranch? Could the ranch survive her? Would their relationship survive her stardom, the media, and her being on the road?

She thought of making love with Joe, of his touch, of his kisses, of his gentleness. Whatever it took, she was determined to make it work.

Checking the table one last time, she ran up the stairs, opening the bedroom door as the water in the shower shut off. She flipped on the bedroom light as Joe exited the bathroom. He stood naked except for the thick, white towel hanging around his waist.

"We may not make it down to dinner, Mr. Baer," Abby teased.

"Huh? Who turned on the light?" Kelly Childers sat up in the bed. The comforter fell from her shoulders, baring her naked breasts. "What are you doing here?" She yelled.

Abby's heart shattered into a million pieces. Pain raced through her veins as she looked at Joe.

He stood speechless, fumbling to wrap the towel around his waist. Turning on her heel, she ran from the room and down the stairs, nearly falling in the stilettos.

Joe screamed her name, but she didn't stop. She burst out the front door into the snow.

"Here. Over here, Abby. I'm waiting."

Abby bolted for the familiar voice, jumping in the truck and slamming the door, shutting out Joe's voice behind her.

"Go, go, get out of here," she yelled.

"I think I'm too drunk to drive." Rodney's head wobbled like a noodle.

Abby ran around the truck, jumping under the steering wheel. She floored it, spewing snow, gravel, and ice everywhere as she slid down the drive.

*****

Standing barefoot in the snow, a towel wrapped loosely around his waist, Joe watched the flickering red tail lights disappear into the darkness.

He turned toward the front door of his house, murder in his heart. The bedroom was deserted as he kicked open the door.

The rumble of another truck engine thundered outside. He ran to the window, watching the Childers Company pickup groan through a snowdrift and speed down the drive.

Joe leaned his forehead against the windowpane. Kelly Childers had taken everything -- his ranch, his heart, his soul.

*****

McIvey's Café was nearly deserted. Closing time was in a half-hour and only two cowboys sat quietly in a booth sipping their final mugs of coffee.

Abby pushed the numbers on the pay phone, trying to keep her hand from shaking. She wiped her eyes, dialing the number for the third time.

A familiar voice finally answered on the other end. "Winslow, its Abby. Can you have someone come and pick me up tonight?" He cleared his throat.

"Sure, honey. Are you all right?"

"Yeah, I just need to get out of here and get on with my life, the sooner the better."

"I'll be there as soon as I can."

She slowly hung up the phone, staring at the wallpaper. A small corner had started to peel away from the wall. She pushed against it, trying to put it back in place, pushing it harder and harder while fighting the tears. No, she would not cry.

The sight of Kelly naked in Joe's bed wouldn't leave her mind. What a damn fool she'd been, actually believing everything he'd said. He was a jerk when she first encountered him. Did she really think he would change?

He had touched her heart in ways she'd never imagined. Why? Why would he do this to her? Was she just another notch in his belt? Kelly held the deed to his ranch, which meant she held the key to his heart. Joe had told her he'd do anything to keep Hidden Rock. Clearly, he meant *anything*.

Abby wiped her face. Margaret was at the kitchen door. Rodney was half-collapsed in a booth, looking ready to hurl, and the two cowboys made a hasty exit.

"Abby?" Margaret stood beside her. "What happened, honey?" Her arm went around Abby's shoulders.

She pulled away, leaning into the wall. "Nobody's ever really gave a crap about me except my grandmother and she's dead."

"Where's Tessa? She said Tessa would be here." Rodney stood up, staggered, and fell in an unconscious heap on the floor.

"George?" Margaret yelled. "Get that drunken cowboy out of here."

George wiped his hands on a bar towel and half-dragged, half-walked Rodney into the back room.

"Tell me what happened."

Abby yanked her shoulder away from Margaret's hand. She was in no mood for mothering. "I don't want to talk about it."

Margaret slid a chair from a table and nodded for Abby to sit. Abby leaned tight against the wall.

"Not talking about it won't make it go away or make it get better."

"I'm done talking. I'm done believing in anyone except myself." Abby stood at the front door, staring into the darkness. "Trust doesn't exist, you know. There is no such thing."

"I trusted you."

"Yes, you did."

Margaret always knew the perfect thing to say. "Was it Joe?"

A shudder crackled down her body at the mention of his name.

George grunted, coming back into the diner. "I got him on the cot. Whew, Abby, you been feeding them boys too good. He weighs a ton." He rubbed the small of his back. "Abby?"

"George." Margaret's voice was soft.

George began filling the coffee pot with water and wiping down the entire counter.

Headlight beams swept through the window.

"Thank you for everything, Margaret. I don't know what I would have done if you..." The tears began to spill.

Margaret pulled a napkin out of the stainless steel dispenser and wiped the tears from her face.

"I will call you and explain. I promise. I just can't tonight."

"I'll be here." Margaret gave her a long, strong hug.

George sprinted from behind the counter, his arms open wide. Abby fell into them, squeezing him tight.

Winslow stomped the snow from his boots as he entered the cafe. "Good evening, Margaret, George."

Abby shoved past him, running from the diner. From the limo's backseat, she gave a last look back at McIvey's Café. They were both standing in the window, George's arm draped across Margaret's shoulder. The snow was falling in huge flakes, and the café window that disappeared into the distance felt like the last shelter she might ever know.

"My helicopter is just up the road at the county airport, in case you were wondering how I made here so fast." Winslow explained. "I was on my way to Cheyenne when you called."

Abby stared out the window, watching the snowdrifts pass, watching her past fade away with them.

Winslow reached across the seat and held her hand. "Darling, are you all right?"

She nodded, the lump in her throat preventing speech.

*****

"I assume she did it for you." Matt handed the cigarette butt to Ben. The older man looked at the white piece of filter, pink lipstick etching the outer edge.

His son mixed a tall bourbon and water, swirled it around, and downed it in one shot. That was a rare thing for the boy to do. Ben knew finding the cigarette was the reason.

"My sister is pretty damn desperate for Daddy's approval." Matt poured another shot. "I think you enjoy keeping the people around you desperate."

"Watch your mouth, boy. You're treading a very fine line." Ben turned slowly toward him. What the hell had gotten into him? His son had never talked to him like this.

Matt chuckled, sipping on his drink. "Kelly, me, Tom, Joe Baer, who else do you have on that list of minions who have their souls leased out to you, desperate for you to turn loose of their throats?"

Ben slammed his hat on the bar. "What the hell has gotten into you, boy?" No one talked to him like that. "You're crossing the line."

"I've already crossed that line, Dad." Matt leaned against the bar. "I just want to know why? What has caused you to be such a bastard?"

Ben lunged at him.

Matt jumped back, barely escaping his fists. ""Instead of answering me, you're just going to beat the crap out of me." Matt snickered and poured another drink.

"I don't owe you or anyone else an explanation for anything I do. You just keep drowning yourself in liquor." Ben's eyes bored into him. "See how many problems that liquid courage solves for you."

The front door slammed and Kelly waltzed in, throwing her coat across the back of the leather couch. A broad smile covered her face as she danced lightly around the couch.

"Well, good evening, Daddy, Matt, well it looks like it's family night at the Childers Ranch. How sweet."

Ben realized for the first time how very much like him she'd become. He slammed his glass down on the bar.

Kelly reached across the bar, grabbed a bottle of brandy, and a glass.

Ben yanked her around, slamming her back against the bar, his temper barely controlled. "As much as I want Hidden Rock, even I wouldn't burn a man's barn to get it." The bottle of brandy, glasses, and ice shattered on the floor.

"What are you talking about?" Kelly's eyes were wide. She trembled beneath his hands.

Ben laid a cigarette butt on the bar. She glanced at it and shrugged. "So?"

"It's a French cigarette. I doubt anyone else in this county has ever heard of them, much less smokes them. Matt found this near Joe's barn."

Kelly's eyes landed on Matt. A wicked smile made her beautiful face seem ugly. "Well Matt, the Baer in you is beginning to show."

Ben backhanded her across the face. Kelly staggered on her feet from the impact, knocking over a barstool.

"Baer?" Matt walked to her putting a hand on his sister's shoulders. She was having a difficult time staying on her feet. Ben's handprint was already imprinted on her cheek.

Kelly snickered. "Come on, Dad. Explain to your son. Oops! I forgot, he's not your son, is he?" Kelly covered her mouth with her hand, looking from one man to the other.

Ben pulled his arm back to deliver another blow. Kelly closed her eyes waiting.

Matt grabbed his father's arm in mid-air. "No more, Dad. No more. You're not going to hit her again."

Ben pulled against Matt's younger, stronger grip.

"Instead of slapping your family around, why don't you just explain what's going on."

Ben backed away, picked up his cowboy hat, and slammed out the front door.

*****

Joe slammed to a stop in the McIvey's Café parking lot, leaving the truck door standing wide open as he ran to the door.

"Abby." He yanked on the locked door. "George McIvey. Are you in there?" He yanked on the door, sending the gingham curtains falling to the floor. "Abby, I know you're here. Open this door."

George and Margaret's truck pulled around the side of the cafe. George rolled down the window. "Joe, what are you doing? Trying to break my door?"

Joe ran across the lot to their truck. "Where is she? Is Abby inside?"

"Ain't nobody in there except Rodney." George shrugged. "He came in drunk and is sleeping it off in the backroom."

"Abby left with Winslow about fifteen minutes ago," Margaret said. "What did you do to her? I've never seen her so upset, and believe me, I've seen her in pretty bad shape."

Joe's heart raced. Pain settled in the pit of his stomach. "Where did they go?"

"You tell me what happened first," Margaret yelled at him.

"North, toward the airport," George answered.

Joe ran to his truck, slammed it into gear, and sped down the snowy road.

Joe drove like a NASCAR driver on speed. The pickup blew through snowdrifts, sliding sideways down the narrow road.

He wanted to kill Kelly Childers, to slowly, painfully wring her scrawny neck. He pounded the steering wheel with his fist. The whir of helicopter blades in the airport's runway lights caught his attention. Damn, he was going to be too late.

A long, black limo pulled alongside the helicopter as Joe spotted Winslow and Abby moved across the snowy tarmac.

"No!" he yelled, pushing the accelerator to the floor. The pickup slid hard, nearly crashing into the ditch. He fought to keep control. A tall chain-link fence surrounding the small county airport forced him to drive completely around the complex to the front entrance gate.

The bed of the truck slid off the pavement, slamming hard into one of the entrance gate's steel posts. Joe fought the wheel, swerving hard to get the tires back on solid ground. The tires spun, pawing at the road, spewing gravel.

He raced across the parking lot, dodging parked planes, driving recklessly through the open doors of an airplane hangar. His truck's front fender buckled as he plowed into a bright red toolbox, sending it careening across the hanger. He pushed hard on the brakes, nearly skidding, into the parked limo.

The anti-lock brake system groaned under the sudden pressure, finally coming to a stop just as the helicopter lifted off the ground.

He bolted out of the truck. "Abby!" His voice was silenced by the drone of the helicopter blades.

In just a few seconds, they disappeared into the darkness. Joe stood alone on the runway, the snow falling in heavy flakes around him as he stared into the black sky.

Chapter Nineteen

"No you don't." Matt pulled Kelly away from the door. "Dad might be able to walk out of here, but I'm not letting you." He pushed her back into the room. "You will explain exactly what you meant about me not being Ben Childers's son." He planted himself in front of her.

"Will everyone just stop pushing me?" Kelly screamed, went to the bar and poured a tall brandy.

She downed it in one gulp. Once again, she was in trouble. She didn't plan on making it worse. "You want answers, you see Daddy."

Matt wrapped a bar towel around a handful of ice and pressed it against her face. Damn, why did her dad make her so mad? Her brother was the last person, the *only* person she didn't want to hurt. When he looked at her accusingly like her dad did, her anger unleashed. She took the ice from him and sat on a barstool.

"I'm asking you, Kelly," he pleaded.

She walked to the far end of the bar, putting distance between them, running tap water into her empty glass. "About two years ago, I found a stash of papers. Well, they were actually letters. Love letters." Swirling the water, she stared into its depths. "They were from Joseph Baer, Sr. to our mother, Rebecca." She took another sip of her water.

"Back in high school, Mom, Dad, Big Joe Baer, and Sarah Baer were really good friends. You know, a clique." She snapped her fingers. "Back then, Dad was dating Sarah, and Big Joe, well, he and our mom were quite the couple. I found yearbooks with love notes, and *Mrs. Rebecca Baer* was written all over his yearbook picture. There were dozens of pictures of them together." She slid onto a barstool, swirling the water around in the snifter.

"When Sarah died, our mom became Big Joe's best friend. I think they rekindled their high school fling and Mom got pregnant with you. Apparently, Dad was none the wiser until two years ago when he found the letters."

The color drained from Matt's face. She sat next to him. "I'm sorry. Dad had passed out drunk one night. I was walking down the hall and saw papers scattered across the bed. Well you know me. I just had to read them. I spent the better part of the next hour reading those letters. Daddy woke up, smacked the crap out of me, and said if I opened my mouth, he'd kill me." A sarcastic laugh erupted from her. "Well, I disinherited myself tonight, but at least I'm still alive."

"I'm glad you told me the truth." Matt squeezed her hand. "At least now I understand his hatred of Joe Baer, and why he wants Hidden Rock so bad."

"There are lots of things about Joe Baer to hate, Matt." Kelly snorted. At least getting even with that bastard had worked out. The look on Abby's face was truly inspiring. *Take that, Joe*, she thought. Now he knew what a broken heart felt like.

"Now, tell me about Hidden Rock's mortgage," Matt's face had become a mask. Now that the shock was wearing off, she wasn't sure if he was angry or happy.

Kelly laughed and headed toward the stairs. "That information, big brother, you will have to get from Dad." She yawned. "I'm going to bed now. It will probably be the last night that I have one to sleep in, at least at Childers Ranch."

"Please, I need to fix things." He ran up the stairs after her.

"What are you going to fix? Dad? Joe? Burn the mortgage? Be realistic Matt, there is nothing you can do." She patted his hand. "Dad got his vengeance, he got Hidden Rock." *And I got mine.* "I'm just sorry a guy as good as you is the bastard child who gets screwed."

Matt's eyes were saddest thing she'd ever seen. He pulled his keys from his pants pocket, heading to the front door. "Where are you going?" He didn't stop. "Matt, don't leave like this."

The front door slammed shut. The truck started, the engine revved hard, and then he was gone.

*****

Winslow popped the top on a can of soda and handed it to Abby. She took a long, thirsty drink. Winslow's home, like his office did not match his public image. It was a very modern home, all black, chrome, glass, and austerely Zen.

The house was glass on three sides that gave the illusion that nothing, not even glass, separated you from the outside.

The interior walls were filled with abstract art. He was a fan of form, but not color. Nearly all the artwork was in shades of black, gray, and white. Bronze sculptures were everywhere, and they too were abstract, without form.

The full glass front gave a glorious view of towering Wyoming mountains. There was an ancient, simple beauty about the state. Craggy, old mountains circled by a tapestry of small towns and wide open spaces. The crisp ringlets of snow blew in a million designs across the land in front of her, spinning like a prism in the moonlight.

"He did it, didn't he? The cowboy broke your heart?" Winslow broke the silence.

Abby finished her soda and dropped the can into the trash. She had been willing to borrow a million dollars for Joe. He didn't need her. He had Kelly. All he had to do was trade sexual favors for the deed to his ranch. He was just the latest to break his promise to her, to lie to her.

Winslow took her hand. "Sit down. We need to talk some business."

Abby followed him into a large office off the living room, with a black lacquer desk, pewter walls, and a black marble floor. The walls were filled with gold records, trophies, awards, certificates, and pictures with other celebrities. Grammy awards filled several shelves, and a dozen pictures of his daughter lined the edge of his desk.

"I've hired a stylist and a markup artist for you." He pulled a paper from his drawer. "Jack likes those new electronic things to keep track of me, but I'm old school, I like my paper calendar." He laughed.

"I'm going to wear what I want." Abby sat in a high-backed, black leather chair across from his desk. She still hadn't signed the contract, and she wouldn't if she didn't get her way.

"Sure, darling, the stylist is just to help you learn to dress for the stage and for the camera." He pushed a file folder to her. "In case you didn't realize it, none of those Hollywood ladies wake up looking perfect or knowing how to work a camera angle. In the folder is a list of King Management clients. I told you to contact any of them if you need a reference. All their phone numbers and e-mail addresses are listed."

Abby took the folder, seeing the surprised look on Winslow's face. Obviously, he didn't think she needed any references. No one was going to burn her again. She intended to call all the people on his list, and if just one of them had something negative to say, well, she might look elsewhere for an agent. If they wanted her this bad, so would someone else. She hoped.

One lesson she'd learned very well was to trust no one, and that lesson was going to be applied to everyone she met from now on.

"You'll need to be in Nashville in three weeks. The songwriter we've contracted will have some music ready for you and then we'll be doing a photo session. After your concert debut, we'll be in contact with the usual celebrity magazines for interviews."

An older woman came into the office with a tray, setting it on Winslow's desk. "Thank you. Millie, this is Abby. She'll be staying here."

"Hi, dear. Would you like some breakfast?" The woman looked to be in her late sixties, with gray hair, a gorgeous complexion and was well dressed to be a housekeeper.

"No, thank you," Abby said. Millie softly closed the door as she left.

"She's my housekeeper, secretary, and occasionally my conscience. Millie has been with me since my first record deal," Winslow explained. "Jack may be important, but Millie is indispensible."

Abby headed toward the door. "I won't be staying here."

"Wait."

She stopped, as Winslow came to her.

"I'd like for you to stay."

Abby reached for the door. Winslow gently grabbed her hand. "I don't know what happened, and I don't care. I do care about you. Stay here as long as you need. No one, including me will bother you. I promise."

How many promises had she heard? Every damn one of them had been broken. "I don't much believe in promises anymore, Winslow."

He kissed her forehead. "You can believe mine." Letting go of her hand, he pointed up the stairs. "Second door on the right at the top of the stairs is the guest room." He put both hands on her shoulders. "We've all been hurt by love."

"I need to get some sleep." She took off her orange heels and headed up the stairs. She felt his gaze on her as she walked. She didn't believe him. She didn't believe any one.

Out of sight, she leaned heavily against the wall, staring at the orange high heels.

*****

Joe pulled his chaps, leather glove, and protective vest out of the tack box. Mugs snorted, pacing in his stall.

"Yeah, I know I'm an idiot," he said in answer to the horse's snort.

"I let the best thing that ever happened to me fly off with a man who can give her everything. It was her fault. She wouldn't let me explain. She believed what she saw, not what happened."

He sat on a bale of hay, working mink oil into the leather chaps. It had been over a year since he'd ridden in a rodeo, and that bull had kicked his ass. He'd only lasted four-seconds. In two days he was going to have to last eight, *and* get points from judges.

The barn was his favorite place to think. Mucking a stall or softening leather had a way of making a man face his problems. He had a lot of problems to face -- the ranch, the rodeo, and Abby.

He worked the oil-soaked rag harder into the chaps. Abby wouldn't even stop to listen, wouldn't let him explain anything, she'd just run out. After what they had shared, after making love and confessing their pain, she just left.

He'd understood about the pictures of her and Winslow. Angry as they made him, he'd let her explain.

Shaking out the vest, he straightened the hard inserts. Abby didn't even yell or argue. It seemed pretty damned easy for her to leave. He had been right all along, women weren't worth it. None of them. He was an idiot for letting this particular woman get into his heart.

His glove was stiff. He poured drops of oil on the cloth and worked it into the palm.

This rodeo wasn't going to be easy. Ben would see to that. Joe didn't know what the man had in mind, but he knew Ben wouldn't lose easily. It was a Professional Bull Riders, or PBR sanctioned event so there would be rules. Ben however, was an expert when it came to bending the rules, and he would make money on the event regardless of whether Joe won or not. The million dollars was pocket change compared to what he stood to make.

Ben probably had endorsements and media contracts would be worth multi-millions. He hadn't offered the mortgage to Joe to be gracious. He knew riding that bull for eight-seconds and getting a high score would be almost impossible. Ben was betting Joe would to lose, and then nothing would stand between him and Hidden Rock, and he'd make more millions.

Media crews had been showing up for days, officials from the PBR had booked two hotels in town, and horse trailers, vendors, and rodeo workers had been busy for days getting the Sentinel Arena ready.

Joe leaned back looking at the barn. There were a lot of good memories amid the bales of hay, oak timbers, and horse sweat. If he didn't win this rodeo, there would be no more memories made here. He'd hoped to make memories with Abby, but that wasn't going to happen.

Joe tried on his glove. It fit snugly. He flexed his fingers, and then made a fist. He didn't intend to lose Hidden Rock without one helluva fight.

Chapter Twenty

"The outlook isn't good, Mr. Childers." The doctor read over the medical chart. "Your son had a horrific accident. He has suffered multiple fractures and internal injuries. If we don't find a compatible blood donor within the next twelve hours, there's absolutely no hope."

Ben Childers stared through the glass of the ICU window. Matt lay quiet, plugged in to a dozen different hoses and wires. His leg was plastered from toe to thigh, trussed up in traction. What little of his face was visible under the thick bandages was purple and swollen.

"Why don't you let us test your blood? You're his father."

Childers interrupted. "I'm not compatible. He had his mother's blood type." Or Big Joe's. *He damn sure doesn't have mine.* "Doesn't this hospital carry type O blood? That's a universal donor isn't it?

The doctor closed the cover on the medical chart. "I assumed you would be aware that Matt has a very rare blood type."

"He's never been sick or had an accident. There was never a reason to know his blood type." Damn Big Joe, what kind of shitty DNA did he give this kid?

"Most people are that way. They don't know until they need blood. We have a large Native American population here, and many have a blood antigen known as RZRZ -- very rare. Antigens are proteins found on the red blood cells of every blood type. Some are quite common, others very rare like RZRZ. If I use blood without this antigen, it could kill him. Is there another family member that we could test?

"No. Indian, Indian blood?"

The doctor gave him a quizzical look. "You didn't know?"

Ben didn't answer, pulling a cigar from his breast pocket.

"You can't smoke that in here," the doctor protested.

"I built most of this hospital." Ben glared at the doctor. "I'll do what I damn well please in it."

"Not while I'm working here, you won't. I'll not have you jeopardize my patients." He yanked the cigar from Ben's hand and deposited it in the trashcan at the nurse's station.

"You won't be working here much longer," he threatened. This Podunk town wouldn't even have a hospital if it wasn't for his money.

He'd be damned if this pip-squeak of a doctor was going to get away with treating him like this.

"If he tries to light another one, call security and have him removed. Tell them Doctor Slinkus, S-L-I-N-K-U-S, authorized it." He spelled his last name slowly.

The nurse nodded. "Then, see if you can track down his blood type in Cheyenne, or maybe at the Native American Blood Bank in Oklahoma." He slid the chart into its slot and walked down the hall.

"Ben, how is he?" Margaret stood beside him.

"Not good. The doctor says he needs blood. Seems Matt has a rare type and there isn't any to be had in these parts."

Margaret put her hand on his shoulder. "We both know who shares that blood type."

He pulled hard away. "Never."

"Would you rather see him die, Ben?" Margaret touched his shoulder, but he yanked away.

"Yes, I would." Ben marched down the hall.

*****

Kelly looked through the window of the ICU room, staring at her bandaged brother. If only she hadn't told him. He was so hurt, so angry when he slammed out of the house. She should have stopped him. She didn't care if he wasn't Ben's son, he was still her brother.

"You told him, didn't you?" Margaret asked.

Kelly turned, startled. "Told him what?"

"You know exactly what I'm talking about." Margaret stood inches from her face.

"Actually, I don't." Kelly stepped away. Matt was still. The only sounds were from the equipment. How had she made such a mess of things? Before it was about money and revenge, but Matt could die because of her.

"You might want to say goodbye," Margaret said.

Kelly didn't understand. "What?"

"It seems there isn't any of his blood type available." Margaret looked through the glass, staring in at Matt. "So it's only a matter of time before he dies."

"You're lying."

"No, Kelly, I'm not. Your father even said to let him die." Margaret gave her a long, intense look. "High price to pay for a sin you didn't commit, isn't it?"

Margaret stepped into the elevator. The look she gave Kelly before the doors closed was pure hatred.

Kelly reached into her purse and furiously dialed her cell phone. "Daddy? Daddy, Matt needs blood. You've got money enough to find it somewhere," she screamed at the phone.

The nurses' heads all sprung up at the sudden noise. Kelly lowered her voice, burying her face into the green mortar wall. "Daddy, please don't let him die like this. Daddy, are you there?"

Tears poured down her cheeks as she walked back to the window.

"Oh, Matt, I never meant for this to happen." She whispered, pressing the palm of her hand against the glass.

*****

George's old truck engine had finally given out, so Joe drove him to the hospital. Only after they arrived at the Intensive Care Unit did George tell him who he was coming to see.

"I drove you, but I'm not staying." Joe put his hat back on, heading toward the elevators.

Margaret quietly stepped beside him at the elevator. "Joe, he's had a horrific wreck. Matt has multiple breaks and internal damage. He's lost a lot of blood."

Joe folded his arms across his chest, giving her a long, hard look. "Why is this my problem? I just drove George here."

Margaret wouldn't look him in the eye, a rare thing for her. Joe glanced back at George who instantly looked the other way. What weren't they telling him?

A doctor ran up to them. "You said you might have a donor?"

Margaret put a hand on Joe's arm. "This is Joe Baer. He might be a match."

Joe looked at Margaret. How could he be any kind of blood match for Matt Childers? "What?"

The elevator doors opened. Ben exited in an angry rush, his face was red, his coat flung open, and his temper raging. "You listen to me, Margaret McIvey. I didn't ask for your help and I don't want your help." Ben waved a threatening finger in her face.

Joe walked between them, his voice low and angry. "Get your finger out of the lady's face before I yank it off your hand."

Ben took a step back then shoved his way to the doctor. "I refuse. I won't allow this man to donate blood."

"Mr. Childers, you don't have any choice in the matter. Matt is over eighteen years of age and coherent enough to make his own choices in the matter. If Mr. Baer agrees and is found to be a match, there's not a thing you can do about it."

Ben walked to the registration counter, slamming a fist down hard. "I want the hospital administrator, now."

"Sir, Mr. Clancy isn't available." The receptionist answered, her eyes darting around the hall.

"I didn't ask if he was available. I said I wanted him. Now. Do you understand? I don't care what you have to do to get him here, just do it."

The receptionist nodded and picked up the phone.

Ben turned back to the doctor "I will have your job over this, I promise you that. And Baer, you have a rodeo in less than twelve hours. You'd better save that blood for yourself." He shoved his hat on, returning his attention to the receptionist. "I'm walking to Clancy's office now, he'd better be there by the time I am." Ben stepped into the elevator.

The woman dialed frantically.

"If you will come with me." The doctor motioned to Joe and went into Matt's room.

Joe eased Margaret away from the group. She swallowed hard, staring up at him. "Margaret, what's going on?"

"Joe, this isn't how I'd planned to tell you. I hadn't really even planned on telling you." She wouldn't look at him. "It's a long story, but right now all you need to know is that Matt is your half-brother." The words slammed into his chest like a mule kick. Brother? Half-brother?

The elevator doors slid open and Kelly came out. All he could see was the smug look on her face that night. Her naked body in his bed. Before he knew it, his hands were around Kelly's throat.

Margaret was suddenly beside him, prying his hands off her throat. "Joe, not where there are witnesses."

Kelly grabbed her throat, running back to the elevator, pushing the buttons in a panic. Margaret clung to Joe's hand as the doors slid shut.

"Why am I here?" he asked her. She held his hand and led him to the window that looked into Matt's room.

Joe stared through the glass at the doctor adjusting the IV drip for Matt.

"He's the reason I asked George to bring you."

George rested his hands on her shoulders.

"You didn't have engine problems did you?"

George nodded that he didn't.

Margaret drew a deep breath, staring up at him. "After your mother passed, your father, Big Joe, needed a friend. Back in high school, Big Joe, me, your mom, all of us were friends. You see, Big Joe and Rebecca Childers, well, she wasn't a Childers then."

Joe folded his arms across his chest and frowned. George nodded for him to keep silent.

"Big Joe and Rebecca were a couple in high school. Well, Ben sort of came into the picture and they split."

Joe whipped the hat off his head, running a hand through his hair. "Margaret, what does this have to do with me being here?"

She looked back into Matt's room. "After your mom passed away, Big Joe and Rebecca ended up having an affair. Matt is your half-brother. He has a rare blood type and I think you might be a match."

Tear welled up in her eyes. "Rebecca was my best friend. She told me everything. We never told anyone. It was best no one knew. It would have ruined a marriage and reputations." She turned to look at him.

Joe slowly put his hat on.

"After everything the Childers family has done to me, you expect me to donate my blood to them?" He headed toward the elevator. "Even angels aren't that forgiving, and I'm damn sure not an angel." He walked inside, not bothering to look back

*****

Joe sat alone at a table in the nearly deserted hospital cafeteria. Two nurses sat at a corner table, talking in whispered tones. Two cooks were sharing jokes behind the counter, and annoying music played over the speakers.

Of all the women in Wyoming his dad could have had an affair with, why did he have to pick Childers's wife, the wife of the man who was dealing with the devil to take his ranch? Could Big Joe have damned his family any worse? One brother was missing, Joe was losing the ranch, and now he finds a brother he didn't even know existed an hour ago. "Thanks one hell of a lot, Dad," Joe mumbled, laying his hat on the table. He rubbed the pain between his eyes. It was quickly spreading to his temples.

The chair slid out next to him, and Margaret pushed a cup of coffee in front of him. He started to get up, but she gently pushed on his shoulder.

"All these years and you never told me?"

"I promised Rebecca. I keep my promises." She sat stiff and straight in the chair. "Until this moment, no one needed to know."

Joe slammed his fist against the table and droplets of coffee scattered around the paper cup. "I needed to know. Matt needed to know."

"Why?" Margaret snapped back at him. "I wouldn't have said a word now if there was any other way to save his life."

"I can't do this. I won't do this." Joe stared at the woman he'd called a friend his entire life. A friend he'd trusted. A woman his mother had trusted. She'd kept her promises, but trust?

"That man is your brother, a part of you."

"Not as far as I'm concerned." Joe picked up his hat. "He is the son of the bastard who is stealing my ranch." He put on his hat, sliding away from the table.

"Wait. Listen to me." Margaret begged. "Please."

Joe waited, but there was no argument Margaret was going to make to convince him to change his mind.

"No one, not your dad, not me, ever meant for you or Matt to get hurt." Her voice cracked. "Matt isn't any more to blame for this situation than you are. This was a mistake your parents made." Tears erupted, falling down her face in long streams.

Joe yanked a napkin from the dispenser and handed it to her. How he hated to see a woman cry. Margaret wasn't a woman he'd seen cry very often, and if he'd known she was going to now, he would have run out of that room. "A mistake we are both suffering for," he finished for her.

"You're suffering, but your brother is going to die." The words were cold and harsh and hung in the air like daggers. "You've lost one brother. Don't lose another one." Her eyes were bloodshot. She'd been crying a lot.

"That was unfair." Joe walked out of the cafeteria.

Margaret jogged after him. "Life is unfair, Joe." She ran in front of him. "Damned unfair, but sometimes we're offered a chance to make it just a little more fair."

Joe stopped, his hands filling the pockets of his duster, his heart in splintered pieces. The lump in his throat was the size of boulder, and the only thing his mind could see was Abby's face as she left that night. "Nobody ever made it fair for me."

"I'm trying. Tessa is trying. She's gone after Abby right now. Rodney told us what happened--"

"I don't give a damn. After what Abby and I shared, and she wouldn't even give me a chance to explain--" He was angry and hurt. "She ran. She ran to Winslow. If she has that little faith in me, I sure as hell don't want her." Joe circled around Margaret and down the hall toward the exit.

A sarcastic, loud voice broke the quiet of the hallway. "I can find my own way to his office. I helped build the place. I ought to know where it's at." Ben Childers's shrill voice echoed off the walls.

"Clancy, I want Slinkus fired, and I want treatment withheld to Matt Childers." He slammed the man's office door shut.

Joe stopped, listening to him. Matt was still his son, part of the woman he said he loved. How the hell could Childers just refuse care for him? He had the money to order blood or treatment, everything necessary to save Matt. He had turned on Matt just like he had turned on everyone else.

At that moment, Joe knew exactly what he needed to do.

Chapter Twenty-One

Winslow's fingers tapped an angry beat on the table. "Come on, darling, let's go. The plane is fueled and ready. I'll leave tickets for Jack and Tessa at the window. They can follow us on a commercial flight."

Abby looked out the airport windows, watching for Tessa. "No, Winslow. Tessa was panicked about something. I can't leave without knowing what's wrong."

Winslow slammed back the last of his cocktail. "When your records air and your face is on every magazine around the world, you aren't going to have the luxury of sitting around and waiting on a desperate friend. Time is money, and friends will have to catch up to you and work around your schedule." The vinyl seat creaked as he leaned hard against it.

Winslow's face was red, a temple was bulging on his forehead, he was pissed, and she didn't care. Tessa was her friend, perhaps the best friend she'd ever had. It would be a cold day in hell before she walked away from her. "Then maybe I won't be doing any recording." The color instantly drained from his face. "As much as I want this, all the fame in the world isn't worth deserting my friend."

Winslow cleared his throat and took hold of her hand, leaning in close to her. "You are a talented, beautiful woman, and you will have all the friends you could ever want. Not to mention fame and money."

She squeezed his hand. "Winslow, I don't mean to hurt you, but what kind of price are you paying? How long has it been since you've seen your little girl?" The look on his face sent chills down her neck.

"That was a low blow, Abby." He pulled his hand away and motioned to the waitress for another drink. "I have a great life. I chose it a long time ago and I'd make the same choices again today. I thought you wanted fame, money. Was I wrong?"

Abby stared out the windows, watching a plow scrape snow off the runway. "Winslow, I want fame. I want money. I've been hungry, and I don't ever want to be there again." She met his gaze. "I'm just not sure if I'm ready to pay such a high price for it. If I can't make time for my friends or my family, what good is the money?"

He sat in the back of the booth, his face obscured by shadows, his hat dropped down to cover his face. The waitress brought his drink and nearly knelt beside the table trying to get a look at him. Several heads turned when they entered the airport. Winslow wasn't happy that he couldn't takeoff when they arrived. The airport was now holding flights due to snow.

The snow had stopped, but the crews were cleaning the runway, and the controllers weren't letting any planes leave yet. So far, no one had recognized him, or if they had, they'd kept their distance. His eyes would dart around the room as if ready for an onslaught of mercenaries. The price of fame was obviously very expensive.

Winslow touched his throat and coughed, then clicked on his cell phone. "Loretta, its Winslow." His voice sounded scratchy. "I'm sorry, but I won't be able to perform at the benefit this Saturday. Doctors orders, can't sing. I'll send a check." He clicked the phone off and winked at Abby, dialing again.

"Elaine, I would like to make arrangements to take Lisa to that ice show this Saturday. You know the one with all the cartoon critters. Would you be willing to let me have her for the weekend? Thank you, I'll pick her up at noon." He clicked the phone off.

Abby smiled. "I'm proud of you, Winslow."

He pulled her toward him across the table, and his lips were on hers. His hand squeezed hers, as his other hand grasped the nape of her neck. His lips were warm, tender, and experienced. Slowly he released her neck as she almost fell back into the seat. Pain ratcheted through her heart, remembering Joe and his betrayal. Her hand went to her mouth.

"Just what are you doing?" Tessa smacked Winslow so hard he grunted. "Don't you be hitting on another man's woman." She smacked him again.

"Tessa, what are you doing?" Abby came to her feet.

"Abby, we need to talk." She gave Winslow a hateful glance. "In the ladies' room." She marched toward the bathroom, with Abby on her heels.

"What do you mean it was a setup?" Abby folded her arms across her chest, half-sitting on the bathroom vanity. Tessa was talking in Texas high-speed and Abby was having a hard time understanding her.

"What I mean is Rodney spilled his guts. He drove Kelly to Joe's that night. Kelly sneaked into the house and made it look like she was doing the wild thing with Joe when nothing, I mean nothing, happened." Tessa checked her make-up in the mirror and adjusted her bra. "It was all done to break the two of you up. You could use a little lipstick." She searched through her purse.

"Are you sure? Why would Kelly do that?" Abby's heart soared. Joe hadn't betrayed her. He hadn't lied to her. "Dang, honey, she hates him and she doubly hates you." She handed Abby the lipstick. "Put this on, you'll feel better."

Abby twirled the tube abstractedly between her fingers. "Are you sure?" It was too good to be true. "I mean, you said Rodney was drunk, so maybe..."

"I'm telling you the truth. I tortured Rodney. He told me everything." She adjusted her breasts again, smiling. "Ouch, do you ever get those little hooks just a pinching against your back?" Tessa tried to reach behind herself, but her arms were too short.

Abby lifted the back of the tight spandex blouse. The bra strap had twisted. Abby tried to twist them back into place. The strain was too much and the hooks broke loose. Tessa's bra, spandex top, and a long string of pearls all sprung loose like a tightly wound coil. Her blouse flipped up to her neck, the pearls scattered across the tile floor, and the bra disappeared somewhere into the depths of the spandex.

Tessa's ample breasts sprung free, bursting forth with an energy all their own, as Winslow and Jack burst into the ladies' room.

"Aaagghh," Winslow yelled, his feet slipping on the pearls. He landed with a crash flat on his back at Tessa's feet. Jack struggled to stop his fall, but the pearls skidded under his shoes, his balance failed, and he landed on top of the country superstar.

Tessa let out a yelp, trying to keep Jack upright. She bent down, making a grab for Jack. Her knees crunched into the pearls and she sprawled ungracefully across both men.

Abby reached for Tessa too late. The three made an odd pile of human wreckage. She helped Tessa to her feet. She kicked a dozen pearls out of the way, trying not to fall herself. Then she offered a hand to Jack as two women entered the restroom.

"What the...?" one of them managed to utter.

Tessa rolled over, her breasts following. Jack reached quickly to pull her blouse down over the wayward duo and Winslow moaned as Tessa's cowboy boot scraped a long path up his thigh into his groin.

"Perverts," One woman yelled.

"Get a room," The other added with snarl as they left.

Tessa found the bra and pulled it back in place. Jack snapped the hooks shut like an old pro and helped her get her blouse adjusted.

Winslow slowly sat up.

Abby took his hand and helped him to his feet. She dusted off his jacket and picked up his hat.

His hands clasped hers. "Don't leave me, Abby," Winslow whispered. "Jack told me what happened. Don't go back to that cowboy. Stay with me."

Two more ladies entered and one of them instantly beamed as she recognized the superstar. "Winslow. Winslow Dodge. Oh, my God," she screamed.

Jack sprung into action, closing the ladies' room door behind her. "Please, if you'd like an autograph keep your voice down. If the entire airport ends up in here, you'll never get to talk to Winslow." He pulled the two ladies over and made an introduction. Suddenly arms wrapped around Winslow's neck and red lipstick was plastered on his face.

"I want to have your baby," one screamed.

Abby stood in stunned silence as both women almost tore the clothes off him. He smiled through it all and autographed papers for them. Jack worked his magic and got Winslow and the women safely out of the ladies' room.

"I'll help you pick up the pearls." Abby bent to retrieve some, but Tessa grabbed her by the shoulders, yanking her to her feet.

"We don't have time. I have to get you to Sentinel. Joe has entered the Silver Bullet Rodeo and you have got to stop him."

"Why? Joe told me he's ridden in lots of rodeos."

The look on Tessa's face told her this rodeo was different. "Because." She took Abby's hands in hers. "Because he's riding for Ben Childers, and Ben sponsored this rodeo." Tessa turned serious, holding tight to Abby's arm. "Listen, Abby, Ben Childers does not lose and Joe isn't about to forfeit Hidden Rock Ranch. He'll ride in that rodeo if it kills him."

The pearls fell from Abby's hand as she realized she didn't ever want to be without him. She nodded to Tessa and they bounded out of the ladies' room door.

Winslow stood at the side of the bar waiting for her. "Don't go, Abby."

"I have to, Winslow."

He grabbed her hand as she started to walk away. "I think I love you."

The two women from the bathroom made their way across the lounge in his direction. "I think this is what you love, Winslow."

The ladies giggled and soon, half a dozen other women were gathering to make an approach to their idol.

He let her arm drop. "You did make a commitment to be my opening act this Saturday." He straightened his tie and adjusted his hat. "Business is business, I expect you there."

Abby gave him a hug, whispering, "I don't let my friends down. I'll be there."

*****

Joe took off his cowboy hat as he left the elevator.

"You're a good man, Joe." Margaret smiled at him.

"Good hasn't got anything to do with it." He smacked his hat against his thigh.

"Are you the potential donor?" Doctor Slinkus asked, poking his head out of Matt's room.

Joe nodded.

"Please follow me. We must get you typed. You are a relative, correct?"

"That's what I've been told." Joe followed him into Matt's room.

"You have Native American ancestry, correct?"

"Yeap."

The doctor wrote notes almost as quickly as he talked. "In case you aren't a match, are there any other family members we could test?"

Joe took in a deep breath. Besides his brother, the only other person was Tom. Odds weren't damn likely he'd donate. "None I can think of."

A young nurse followed them inside, pushing a stainless cart with oddly shaped vials, needles, and syringes on it. Joe sat in a chair laying his hat on the table, and rolled up a shirtsleeve. She slid a needle expertly into his vein.

Joe took a long look at his newly discovered brother. Matt's mother's features were most pronounced, but there was a little of Big Joe mixed in. Matt was tall like Joe and Connor. He had their blue eyes and those high, native cheekbones.

Right now, he looked weak, helpless, and alone. The man he thought was his father wanted medical services withheld, his sister had disappeared, and a brother he didn't even know existed was the only person in the room with him, besides doctors and nurses. Joe knew all about being alone and abandoned.

Abby had left him without giving him one chance to explain. He'd never forget the look on her face, and he'd never forgive her for leaving without another word.

*****

Tom unfolded the map. "We've drilled two wells and nothing, not a single drop of water." He added a spoonful of sugar to his coffee. "That's a lot of money and time, and this reservation is running out of both."

Connor Baer looked at the map, his eyes tracing the expansive property lines of Hidden Rock Ranch, which backed up against the reservation. In spite of all the anger between him and his father, he did love that ranch. Mostly, he loved his brother, Joe. All Tom had to do was explain the situation and Connor had headed home. Screw, Ben Childers. He'd find water if he had to dig the damn well by hand.

"I know it's there, I know it." He circled a spot on the worn map. "Satellite images show an eighty-percent chance we'll find a good reserve of water on that ridge."

Tom drew a deep breath. "We have nothing so far and if we don't have water, we won't have a future." Tom exchanged worried looks with his wife. She put on a fresh pot of coffee, set out an extra mug, and left. Right on cue there was a knock on the door.

Tom started toward the door. "There is someone I want you to meet. I'm asking that you keep an open mind."

A man that looked to be as ancient as the granite cliffs surrounding the reservation shuffled inside. Silver hair hung to his waist and a medicine pouch bounced on his chest as he stood straight, staring at Connor.

"This is Dark Water. The tribal elders say he can find water."

The old Indian walked to the table and placed his finger on the map. "There."

Connor rolled his eyes. "Water there?" Dark Water nodded. "No offense, Dark Water, but I've done thousands of satellite images of this reservation. Wolf Ridge is the only spot where there is any trace of water, and there isn't very much of it there." He angrily circled the area on the map where Dark Water had pointed. "This is the most desolate piece of ground on the reservation. There is no water there."

"I told you he would not want my services. He believes in his machines too much." Dark Water shrugged.

"I think he can find water." Tom said.

Connor looked stunned. Tom was well educated, but sometimes he still fell back on tribal superstitions. "He can find water better than my satellite? I don't think so. Thanks anyway, Dark Water." He folded the map and picked up his coat, heading to the door.

"How do you think my people found water before satellites?" Tom asked.

"If he's so good, why haven't they found water before now?" Connor whispered.

"No one asked me to look." Obviously, age had not damaged his hearing.

*****

"I've just received the lab results, it looks like you're match, Mr. Baer." The doctor beamed. "If you'll just lay back and get comfortable, we'll get started."

The nurse fluffed the pillow, pulling the tray of instruments close. "Why don't you pull off those boots. You'd probably be more comfortable."

"I'll keep them on if it's all the same to you."

She smiled, expertly sticking the needle into a vein in his arm. "How long will this take?"

"Not too long. We can't suck you too dry." She smiled again. He watched his blood fill the plastic tube and meander its way into a plastic bag. "I brought you some orange juice," the nurse whispered. "It helps. You know, only bad guys wear black hats." She nodded toward his hat.

His thoughts went to Abby. "Someone else told me that."

"You should listen to her." The nurse started out the door.

"How do you know it was a her?"

The nurse smiled a knowing smile and quietly left the room.

"Security." The doctor's angry voice boomed just outside the door. "I want you out of this hospital now." The door pushed open and Ben Childers stepped inside the room

"I'll kill that bastard." Ben shoved the doctor to one side.

George took two steps in front of him. Joe didn't know Ben was still at the hospital. "Don't." The word was small, quiet, and the most powerful statement Joe had ever heard George make.

The doctor stood beside George. "Mr. Childers, I will have you arrested. I've called security. I suggest you leave now, or I will have you put in jail." The doctor might have been a small-built man, but he had the courage of a lion. Ben Childers was big and threatening, a man who was used to intimidating nearly everyone he encountered.

"I'll leave, but you listen to me" He pointed an angry finger at Joe. "If you aren't at that rodeo on time, in gear and ready to ride, you forfeit our agreement."

"I read the contract I'll be there." Ben's team of lawyers had drawn up the personal agreement for Hidden Rock, and it left Joe no recourse.

Ben laughed. "Your misplaced loyalties make you a weak man. This little blood transfusion, it's going to cost you Hidden Rock. You'll be too damn weak to hold the bull till the bell." He pushed his hat firmly on his head. "That will work out just fine for me."

Chapter Twenty-Two

The huge, four-wheel drive truck covered with large, yellow roses veered in and out of the traffic. Mostly pickup trucks littered the snow-covered lanes of the highway. Tessa drove like a stunt driver at the county fair. Abby tightened her seatbelt, holding on to the grab handle beside the window.

"Joe's only got to stay on the bull for eight seconds and he wins, right?" Abby asked, closing her eyes as they fishtailed.

"Honey, haven't you ever been to a rodeo?"

Abby shook her head no, both hands now on the grab handle.

"There's a little more to it than that." Tessa glanced in the rear view mirror, fluffing a handful of hair. "First, there are the qualifying rounds. He's got to beat out all the competition to get to the final round, the money round."

"How many rounds are there?" Abby pushed her feet hard against the floor.

"Depends." Tessa was either fearless or insane, cruising around other trucks and cars, driving with one hand on the wheel. "Depends on how many entries there are, how many eliminations it takes to get down to the finals. Then there are three judges. Only two actually get to vote, unless of course there's a tie. Then the third judge, who stays at the back of the chute keeping his own score, will get to vote." Her hand went into the huge purse she always carried. "I need some lip gloss."

"I'll get it for you," Abby nearly screamed as the truck swerved into the other lane, where a rather upset driver was blowing his horn. "You just drive, all right?"

"I'm just trying to get us there quick." Both hands went to the wheel. "Anyway, there is a score of one hundred points possible. Each judge has fifty points at his disposal. That's twenty-five points for the bull and twenty-five points for the cowboy."

Abby stopped searching for the lip gloss and looked up at her. "The bull gets points?"

"Oh, yeah, if you don't get a good bull that moves his butt out there, there isn't any way you're gonna win." Tessa waved a hand and the truck fishtailed. Gravel from the shoulder sprayed up the side of the truck. "You want that bull to turn, kick, and buck like an Okie tornado to get some good points. The cowboy, now he holds on to the rope with one hand. It's called a bull rope. If his free hand touches the rope or the bull, he'll lose points. He can spur the bull a bit to make him buck more, which can be good and bad. Good if he just bucks more, bad if it really ticks the bull off."

A turn signal clicked on as she hit the exit ramp, doing about eighty. Abby braced a hand against the dash.

"Did you find that gloss? I can't go into that rodeo with these washed out lips."

Abby found the gloss and handed it to her. "So, they do use spurs?"

"Yep, but they aren't sharp. They got this little blunt end on them so they don't cut the bull, they just aggravate him." She laughed and winked. "Kinda like my long fingernails, if you get my drift. The rodeo is into protecting animals and cowboys. The cowboys wear flak vests anymore to protect them."

"How do they know who gets to ride what bull?"

The traffic was heavy on the road going into the arena. The LED flashing message board announced the one million dollar bull-riding event. Police officers were stationed everywhere, directing traffic.

"Usually, not in all rodeos, but usually they are picked on a computer. It's a random draw." Tessa laid on the horn as another pickup truck cut her off from the side. "That's it. I have had enough of this pokey crap." She flipped the switch on the dash, putting the truck into four-wheel drive, and took off across the field next to the parking lot. Just as several cops were starting to go after her, a dozen more pickups followed.

Tessa came to a sliding stop. "Let's go save your cowboy."

*****

Matt had shown signs of improvement by the time Joe left for the rodeo. In spite of Ben, it looked like he was going to make it.

Now, four elimination rounds were complete and Joe was number one in the standings. Joe's shoulder ached, his back was on fire, and his butt, well, he hoped it went numb soon. It had been over a year since he'd ridden on a bull. After four elimination rounds, his body was telling him exactly how long it had been and how old he was getting.

"Joe, I need to talk to you." Rodney shadowed him along the fence that separated the riders from the audience. "I'm sorry. I'm sorry about Kelly."

Joe refused to look up. He walked into the riders' dressing area.

*****

"Ladies and Cowboys, welcome to the Seventh Annual Silver Bullet Rodeo," the announcer shouted. The crowd cheered. "This year's rodeo is turning out to be one of the best. We've still got more roping, more riding, and more bulls, horses, cowboys, and cowgirls coming up." His voice echoed off the metal walls.

Abby stared into the arena. It was massive, with two huge tractors leveling the dirt in the center, corrals of horses and bulls were on both sides, and cowboys by the dozen. Country music echoed behind the announcer's voice.

"The events tonight are for points, money, and glory!" he announced. "We have the Million Dollar Bull ride coming up. Eight seconds! Yes sir, that's all it'll take to grab that prize. Eight seconds on the bull and the best ride of your life. That event is being sponsored by Ben Childers of Childers Ranch and Childers Farm Implements. Now, everybody get yourselves some fine chow, furnished by Spradling Brothers Restaurant, where the half-pound cow burger is the rule, not the special. Intermission will be over in about five minutes." The microphone clicked off.

"This crowd is awful, Tessa. I feel like a fish swimming upstream." Abby could barely move through the crush of people. Dust filtered through the air and horses snorted. Despite the cold outside, inside the arena was stifling hot thanks to the sold-out crowd that brought in ample body heat.

"I have never seen so many folks at a rodeo." Tessa's voice was difficult to hear above the din. The bleachers were filled to capacity, people were wedged tight and five or six deep along the fences around the main arena. News of this rodeo with its million-dollar purse had traveled fast.

They finally burst through a thick throng of humanity and onto the arena floor. An ear-piercing whistle echoed off the metal walls of the arena. Tessa was making sure everyone moved out of her way.

"Coming through, honey." She smiled at a handsome cowboy and he tipped his hat. "Sweetheart, can you tell me where the riders for this rodeo are corralled?"

"To the left of the north bleachers." He smiled at her breasts. "Ya won't be able to get in there. You'll need passes or a contestant number."

"Don't bet on that, honey. Come on, Abby." The gang of young boys, men, and cowboys parted like the Red Sea as she strutted through. Her hips swung in red, molded spandex, her breasts stood at attention, and a smile worthy of a cover model spread across her face. "Don't you worry, Abby. I'll get you in there."

Abby had no doubt.

*****

Margaret and George fought against the tide of people as they tried to get into the stands. "I want down next to the arena floor, George." Margaret hated going into the upper seats, and she didn't want to be far away when Joe was riding.

The million-dollar purse had brought the worldwide media to the quiet western area of Wyoming. Every major cable sports network, television network, sports magazine, and internet sports outlet was vying for position.

Only three riders had signed up to ride for the million dollars. Without a large corporate sponsor, the substantial entry fee of twenty-five thousand dollars pretty much eliminated most cowboys. Margaret spotted a small opening next to the fence surrounding the floor of the arena. A woman had parked her coat, purse, and large cup there. Margaret smiled, sat down nearly on the drink, and started sliding the stuff toward the woman, making room for her and George.

The woman's face went red. "Excuse me, but that was rude."

"So was taking up four seats in an arena this crowded." Margaret snapped. George smiled and sat down next to her.

"I'm not feeling good about his rodeo." Margaret squeezed his hand. "A million dollar purse sponsored by Childers, this can't be good."

George patted her hand, handing her the rodeo program. "We'll just have to watch and see, honey."

Margaret looked through the program, worried about Joe. After giving blood, losing Abby, and learning about Matt, he was in no shape mentally or physically to ride. She spotted his name in the list of riders, shivering when she saw him listed as a rider for Childers Ranch. "George, oh, heavens, George."

"What?" He learned toward her.

Her breathe left in a gush, her hands suddenly felt like lead weights, and bile rose in her stomach. She pointed to the list giving the names of the bulls in the Million Dollar Round. George turned white as a ghost.

"We've got to get to Joe. He's going to get killed." Margaret yanked George along behind her, running to the rider waiting area.

*****

Ben admired the oversized bull with the bad attitude. Anyone who came near Soul Taker was snorted at, and if one dared to get too close, they got horns through the bars.

He was a mean bull that had killed two cowboys and done severe damage to several more. He'd been yanked from the rodeo circuit before he'd even completed one season. At the local fairs and rodeos, he was good for selling tickets. Everybody who knew his reputation wanted a picture, or at least a little bang on the bars from the beast just to say they had traded dust with him.

For this rodeo, Ben had a very different plan for the bull. In the two stalls beside Soul Taker were Devil's Partner and Dark Shadow. All three bulls had bad reputations and weren't on the current rodeo circuit. His legal team had found a few ways around the PBRs obnoxious rules.

He leaned against the gate at Soul Taker's stall. The bull snorted, pawed the dust, and charged the gate. Ben jumped back, laughing. "I've got a special cowboy just for you."

Charlie Hoffman, owner of Soul Taker rounded the corner. "Hey, Ben." He nodded.

"Charlie." Ben walked toward his private viewing box.

"What's Soul Taker doing over here in the stalls for the rodeo bulls? He should be in a paddock outside, like usual."

"I'm giving him a chance to come out of retirement." Ben went into the viewing box, with Charlie right on his heels.

"You can't do that. That bull could kill someone. I didn't bring him so you could rodeo him. I'm getting the arena manager to see that he's pulled from the program." He headed toward the door.

"You listen to me. I contracted for the bull. You didn't ask what I wanted the bull for. I have a contract and I have your cancelled check. It's a done deal. Now go take your seat and enjoy the rodeo." Childers held open the door for him to leave.

"Everybody, including you, knows that bull's reputation. Why, Ben? Why would you want to jeopardize one of these cowboys like this?"

"There will only be one life at risk. A life that owes me a lot." He shut the door in Charlie's face.

*****

Joe joined several cowboys standing on the corral fence, as angry voices drew their attention. Just over the fence, Charlie Hoffman was in a heated argument with the young cowboy in charge of the bullpen and gates. Charlie had a buckskin cover slung over his shoulder. Was he carrying a rifle?

"The arena manager director wants things ready to go." The cowboy closed the large metal gate.

"My bull is in there. I have to withdraw him from the rodeo," Charlie pleaded.

"Take it up with the director." He was sarcastic, slamming the gate shut.

Charlie un-slung the rifle, sliding the cover off.

"Is that a gun?" The cowboy's eyes grew huge.

"Yes."

The cowboy backed slowly away.

"What are you doing, boy?" The cowboy's hands went into the air.

"It's a hunting rifle, you idiot."

"Sir," a shaky, terrified voice squeaked behind him. "Sir, put the gun down."

Charlie turned around, seeing a pimply-faced security guard of about eighteen, pointing a tiny little pistol at him. "P-P-Put the gun down."

"Charlie, what the hell are you doing?" Joe shouted.

"Hang on Joe, I got a situation to handle here."

The security guard's hands were shaking, Charlie looked pissed, and the cowboy at the gate was about to faint. This situation was going from bad to worse, fast.

Joe started to climb the fence.

"I wouldn't do that buddy," the cowboy on the fence next to him warned. "You leave the riders' staging area, you forfeit."

"What?" Joe had never heard of such a rule.

"In the rules handed out for this rodeo." He grinned. "But if you want, go ahead, that'll mean one less rider I have to whup."

Joe climbed back to his side of the fence.

"Son, you better put that pea-shooter away before you get hurt." Charlie folded his arms across his chest. "This here's my hunting rifle. There's a killer bull in that corral. I didn't enter him in this rodeo, I don't want him in this rodeo, and I sure as hell don't want him to hurt any cowboys. If you'll bring me a rope and give me a hand, we can get him out of there, if not I'm gonna shoot him."

He saw the kid's hands tremble. "Put the gun down."

A woman screamed. "That man's got a gun."

Joe moaned. Could this get any worse? "Officer, he won't hurt anyone. Charlie, put the gun down before someone gets hurt." It was no use. Several more women screamed.

Charlie nodded at him, shook his head, pulled his rifle from his shoulder, and laid it on the ground. "Okay, kid, here's the rifle. But I gotta get to the show manager."

"No way, mister. You kick that rifle over here and you lay down on the ground or I'm going to shoot you."

"What is going on over here?" the Laramie County sheriff asked as he walked up behind the young security officer.

Joe was never so glad to see the county sheriff in his life.

"He's got a gun." The young security guard answered.

"Son, this is Wyoming. Nearly everybody in this whole arena probably has a gun." He touched the kid's arm. The gun went off, shooting straight up into the air.

Charlie and the sheriff sprawled flat on the ground. The pistol recoiled, whipping back, the grip conking the kid square in the middle of the forehead. Joe and the cowboys ducked, and screams echoed through the crowd. "I've been shot." The kids eyes crossed, the gun fell from his limp hands, a huge plume of dust rose as he fell flat of his back, unconscious.

The wayward bullet struck an overhead fire sprinkler, sending a torrent of water over an entire section of arena. Bulls and horses panicked in their corrals, mooing and snorting. People ran for drier ground. The sheriff picked the gun up, sticking it in the waistband of his trousers.

"Did he pass out from the blow on his head or the terror of having fired the thing?" Charlie stood up, looking at the unconscious kid.

The sheriff moaned, pulling his walkie-talkie off his shoulder. "Get me maintenance and tell them shut off this water." He handed the rifle to Charlie. "Take this out to your truck, before another kid in a security guard suit actually shoots you."

Joe and the cowboys jumped off the fence, looking for a place to escape the water.

"Are those Childers ranch colors on your back, Joe Baer?" The smug cowboy gave him a look that needed no explanation. "Things must be pretty bad if you're riding for that blood sucker."

Joe tightened the flak vest around his chest, saying nothing. He pulled several pairs of gloves from a tack box, trying each one on until he found one that was comfortable. The cowboy shook his head and walked on. Joe picked up the leather vest. The tall, red letters of Childers Ranch made him feel vulgar as he pulled it on.

"That money is mine, cowboy." A large man leaned against a post, staring at Joe. "I've got the belt buckle to prove I'm the cowboy to win it."

Joe glanced at him and at the buckle.

"I thought you'd like to know who your competition is before you cowboy up." He spit out a wad of tobacco. "Name's Colton Dean." He extended a hand.

Joe nodded and they shook. "Joe Baer."

"Well, good luck, but not too much." He smiled, leaving silence in the small horse stall Joe was using for a dressing area.

A sudden rush of lightheadedness washed over Joe. His body felt heavy and his heart beat hard and fast. Groping weakly to the back of the stall, he sat cautiously on a rugged tack box, taking deep breaths.

A trickle of sweat dripped down the side of his face. The nurse at the hospital had said he might be a little weak. Maybe he could find some orange juice. She said it would help.

The announcer's voice echoed through the arena. "Next up, the event you've all been waiting for, bull riding. All bull riders to the gate."

*****

The noise of the crowd was deafening, and the surge of bodies bore down on them. "What's going on?" Abby yelled.

"I don't know, but everybody seems to be trying to get away from the south end of the arena." Tessa grabbed her hand and bulldozed through the crowd.

Abby was frantic. "Tessa, we've got to get to him."

"We will." Tessa stopped in her tracks. She bent down and picked up a very muddy, much battered rodeo program. She scanned a few pages, turned and smiled at Abby, and threw the program back down. "I got an idea. Whatever I do, you follow my lead, got it?"

Abby nodded. She didn't care. She just wanted to get to Joe.

Tessa slid under the ropes that went around the contestant area. A large, thick hand clamped down on her arm.

"Where do you think you're going?" A beefy security guard stopped them. "Nobody gets in here without a contestant number." Again, the crowd surged behind them.

"What is going on?" Tessa was shoved into the guard.

"Some idiot on the south end of the arena fired a gun and the sprinklers over there went off," he explained. "No one wants to get wet when it's ten degrees outside."

"A gun?" Abby scanned the mass of people. "Someone fired a gun?" She skirted under the rope, too. She thought about breaking into a hard run. The guard couldn't catch both of them.

"Shh, it ain't no big deal. Now follow my lead." Tessa batted her eyes, looking up at the guard. "You are just the man I was looking for. This is Luann Price. She's in the woman's bronc riding contest and we are having the darndest time finding the lady contestants' dressing area. I'll bet you know where it's at."

He gave the Abby the once over.

"What's your contestant number?" He opened his copy of the rodeo program.

"Its number four hundred and forty three," Tessa answered, smiling up at him.

Where you from Luann?"

"She's from Tulsa, Oklahoma."

"Who are you?" He asked Tessa.

"She's my cousin, Jenny, and my manager," Abby answered, putting her hands in her pockets. She stood with legs spread slightly, head up, staring him in the eye. "I've only got five minutes until my time expires to sign in. I'm counting on this paycheck, if you know what I mean."

He raised his eyebrows. "I do. Follow me. I'll take you over there."

Tessa and Abby exchanged excited glances, trotting after him.

They entered the ladies' dressing area, only to be meet by mean stares and even meaner tempers. "Who the hell are you two?"

"Just two ladies passing through." Tessa didn't miss a step, pushing right through the area with Abby in tow.

"Tessa Marie, is that your voice I hear?" A small built woman appeared from behind a stall door. "I should have known when I heard gunshots and the sprinklers went off that you were here."

"Pam? Pam Bicknell from San Antonio?" They squealed the way only two Texas women can do, hugged, looked at each other, and hugged again. "This is my first cousin, once removed, by marriage." Tessa offered in way of an explanation.

"Pam, ladies, I need your help." In one breath, talking with machine-gun rapidness, Tessa fed them Abby's entire story. Abby was mortified, and tried more than once to shut Tessa up. Only an animal tranquilizer was capable of doing that.

When she stopped, for what Abby thought was a breath, one of the cowgirls walked over and pinned a contestant number to Abby's back. "It belonged to Sara. She had to scratch, so she won't be needing it. It should get you into the area where he's at." She patted Abby on the back.

Pam popped a cowboy hat onto her head. "Makes you look official." She motioned for Tessa and Abby to follow.

Through a dusty maze of stalls, corrals, vending machines, tack boxes, and cowboys, they followed her. The smells of leather, horses, sweat, blood, and hay filled the air.

"He should be somewhere over there." Pam pointed. "They're at the gate and getting ready to load."

Abby spotted him, the unmistakable black hair, the wide shoulders, and the hated Childers Ranch colors on his back.

*****

How could she find the words? How could she make him understand?

"Joe." His name came out a whisper. "Joe." His shoulders went rigid. He stopped working the leather glove on his hand and turned around.

Their eyes met. The noise ceased and the dust blew in slow motion. Neither of them could move. Joe pushed the hat back on his head, going to the fence that separated them.

"You don't have to do this. I've got the money to pay Childers."

He looked at the ground.

"Please, don't do this."

His eyes caught hers. "Winslow's money? I don't think being in debt to him would be a better deal."

There'd be no debt."

His voice was hard, cold. "I'll take my chances with the bull." He started to walk away.

Her eyes stung from the tears. "I know you didn't sleep with Kelly."

"You had to take someone else's word over mine." He kept walking.

"If it had been Winslow in my bed, would you have believed me?"

He stomped back to her. "I did. When those pictures of you two were plastered in every newspaper. I did believe you." He shook his head. "I just wanted you to believe in me." He headed toward the chutes.

"Joe, please don't." Tears gushed down her face. "I don't want to lose you."

He stopped in mid-stride. "I will not lose Hidden Rock without a fight." He turned to look at her. "And I won't be in debt to another soul to keep it."

"Joe!"

He kept moving ignoring her pleas.

Tessa stood behind her, putting a hand on her shoulder.

The announcer's voice sounded suddenly strained. "The sponsor of tonight's bull riding event has asked that we announce a few changes to the event. There will be no flak jackets allowed."

The crowd gave a collective gasp. Murmurs spread through the stands.

"The judges have decided, in light of this change, if any of the riders wish to withdraw, they may do so without a point penalty and they will be reimbursed their entry fee" No one pulled out. "All right, cowboys, good luck to you. This is going to be one fierce bull riding competition folks." He snapped off the microphone.

Abby ran along the fence. She knew at that moment what she wanted. It wasn't fame, it wasn't money, it wasn't the house in Indiana.

It was Joe Baer.

"First rider into the chute." The announcer began the event. "This is Cody Ritter from Colorado Springs, Colorado." The crowd cheered, stomped, clapped, and whistled loudly. "Cody is the young'un of the group. This is only his second year on the rodeo circuit and his first as a bull rider. You must have one good sponsor."

Cody laughed, nodding as he climbed the fence of the bull chute.

"Cody will be riding, who?" The microphone clicked off, abruptly. "Cody will be riding Dark Shadow, owned by--" he hesitated--"Childers Ranch."

Boos and insults came from all corners of the audience.

Abby pushed past cowboys, climbed over tack and gear, and made her way as close as she could get to the bull chutes. She pressed tight against the fence near the chutes, watching the young cowboy wiggle his hand into the cinch around the bull. Joe was nowhere in sight.

"Cowboy up," one of the wranglers shouted.

Cody nodded, the bell rang, and the chute opened. Less than two seconds passed before the young cowboy lay sprawled nearly breathless in the dirt. The bull charged at his limp body with a vengeance.

Two front hooves came down in the middle of his right leg. The crush and crackle of bones could be heard three rows up into the stands. The bullfighters and clowns ran around, frantically trying to get the bulls attention.

"You boys need to be a little faster there. Looks like Cody may have taken a pretty nasty hit." The announcer's voice was surprisingly calm.

The beast snorted, pawed, and trotted proudly around the arena before making his way out the exit chute.

Paramedics checked Cody over. They cut a slit up his jeans and blood spurted. Bile rose in Abby's throat as the jagged edge of the snapped leg bone bursting through the skin. They got his neck and body braced, and moved him out of the arena.

"Let's give it up for a brave cowboy." The crowd cheered. "We hope his injuries are minor."

Tessa pushed her way in beside Abby. "Honey, you could get hurt standing here."

"Tessa, I've got to stop him."

Abby tried to climb over the fence, but was stopped by an arena cowboy. "Whoa, there, get your tail back outside this fence. You want to get stomped to death by a bull?"

Abby reluctantly climbed back over.

"Honey, you've done all you can," Tessa said. "Cody was just a kid. Joe's an experienced bull rider."

"Our next rider will be none other than Colton Dean, the reigning Pro Rodeo bull riding champion. Colton has drawn..." His voice trailed off and the mic clicked off. It was long minutes before he clicked it back on, and his voice was quickly loosing it calmness. "Colton will be riding Devil's Partner."

The crowd came to its collective feet, protesting, booing, and hissing.

Colton smiled with confidence. He tightened up his chaps and pushed his hat down on his head. He climbed the fence, standing on the upper rail, straddling the bull. Devil's Partner didn't like the confined space of the chute. He snorted and kicked the fence, then jumped straight up, high kicking and working up a lather.

Tessa pulled Abby back a few steps. "We really shouldn't be this close."

Abby pulled away. She wanted to be where Joe was. She had to stop this. If she had to climb into that damn chute with him and the bull to stop him, she would.

"This ought to be a ride worthy of your ticket price, ladies and cowboys," the announcer called out. "That bull's not going to give any up anything to this cowboy."

"It's my fault, Tessa. I should have stayed and listened to his side. I shouldn't have let my temper get in the way."

"You listen to me, Abby." Tessa put her hands on Abby's shoulders. "The only person at fault here is Kelly Childers. She is responsible for all this mess. When I find her, I'm going to give her the worst beating she's ever had in her life."

"Cowboy up," a cowboy shouted.

Colton slid his gloved hand under the bull rope, squeezing and adjusting the fit. The bull slammed against the side of the chute. Colton jumped off the bull onto the fence.

Abby didn't need Tessa to pull her away this time. The bull was big, angry, and determined not to let the cowboy on.

"Looks like this bull's not ready for his entrance. He's a chute fighter." The announcer's voice never broke.

Colton nodded and once again eased onto the bull's back.

"Cowboy up." The crowd cheered.

Colton's slid his hand under the bull rope. Pushing his hat tight on his head, he gave a final nod.

The chute opened and the bull slammed against the fence, pounding through the chute. Colton's head snapped back hard and his hat flew across the dirt as his leg bled from the impact against the fence. He held on. The bull raged, kicking high, throwing his head back.

"Ride 'em cowboy." There was genuine concern in the announcer's voice. "That's five seconds. This bull's a head thrower." The words had barely left the announcer's mouth when Colton's face impacted the top of the bull's skull, sending blood pouring from his nose. He lost consciousness. His body flailed down the side of the bull, smacking repeatedly into its side, his gloved hand stuck under the bull rope.

The clowns circled the beast. Hooves went high into the air. The bull snorted, twisted around, and jabbed his head and horns at the limp cowboy.

"Cowboys, them clowns need some help." Two cowboys on horseback entered the arena, whistling and slinging ropes at the bull.

A scream stuck in Abby's throat as the bull pushed the cowboy's body against the fence inches from where she stood.

One clown threw himself onto the opposite side of the bull. Two others scattered around him. The first clown yanked and yanked, but the cowboy's hand wouldn't come free. One of the horseback riders came alongside, pulling the clown onto the horse, racing alongside the bull. Again, the clown yanked Colton's hand, finally pulling it free. "Get that cowboy out of there." The bull sprinted to the far end of the arena and out the gate.

Colton's limp body lay in the dust. The paramedics checked him. The crowd was silent. Long minutes passed.

Abby and Tessa held each other.

There was a nod from one of the paramedics, and then they loaded the cowboy onto the stretcher. The crowd whistled, stomped and cheered.

Joe headed into the chute.

"Joe," she shouted.

He was climbing up the chute fence, giving her an irritated look.

"Joe, please don't do this."

The cowboys who readied the riders pushed her out of the way. The huge bull was loaded into the chute.

*****

"This is going to be a rodeo to remember," the announcer said. "So far, the one million dollar purse is going unclaimed, but we have one last rider willing to go for it. Joe Baer, riding for--" again he hesitated, -- "Childers Ranch."

Half the audience gasped and the other half grew silent. "Joe has drawn..." The microphone clicked off. The announcer's voice didn't hide his feelings this time. "Looks like Joe has been unlucky enough to draw Soul Taker."

The crown went berserk, shouting, screaming, cussing. "This bull is sponsored by Ben Childers. There's still time to withdraw, Joe."

Joe shook his head no, standing on the top rails, straddling the bull. Soul Taker was eerily quiet in the chute. He didn't buck, snort, or fight the confinement. Joe pulled the glove tight on his right hand and pushed his hat snug on his head. His legs felt rubbery. The lightheadedness was back.

"You sure you want to ride this beast, cowboy?" one of the gate helpers asked. "It's going to be a long eight seconds."

"Good luck to you." Several men patted him on the back. He nodded a silent thanks and lowered himself onto the bull.

"Joe." He turned slowly, looking down at her from the top of the chute. "I love you."

The chute opened.

*****

Thick lines of ice formed around the small opening in the ground. The drill bored deep through the Earth's crust, pulling ancient rock from its depths. The hammering and drilling reverberated across the wide valley.

The vibration created small concussion waves in the snow around the drill. Several hours into the process, the well driller shook his head, looking very discouraged.

Tom walked back to the truck, poured two steaming cups of coffee from his thermos, and handed one to Connor. He knocked on the truck window, offering Dark Water some. The Indian just shook his head, leaned his head back against the seat, and closed his eyes. The man running the well drilling equipment walked slowly toward them. "You aren't quitting are you?" Tom asked.

"I think we need to. There's no use charging you more money. I haven't found one sign that water is here at all. Nothing in the dirt, no rocks that usually run where I find water, not even mud, other than what my water going into the hole is making. There just isn't any water here. I'm already down one hundred eighty feet. If I go too much further, I'll have to get a different drill. Frankly, I think you're just wasting your money at this location." He wiped his runny noise on the sleeve of his jacket.

The truck door opened. Dark Water pointed his walking stick at the well driller. "Dig twelve more feet and you will hit water."

"Sorry, chief, but there's no water out here," the driller answered.

"I am not a chief. Water is there. Dig some more." He closed the door, looking very offended.

"Call it a job, Tom," Connor pleaded.

"Dig twelve more feet," Tom instructed

The men turned, staring in disbelief.

"Tom, be realistic." Connor shook his head.

"Twelve more feet," he told the man. "You're already this deep, what's twelve more feet?"

"It's robbing you."

"It's my money."

"Yes, sir." The driller went back to the truck, starting the drill's motor.

They stood beside the pounding drill as it banged hard against something solid. The well driller shut it off.

"What was that?" Connor asked.

"Probably the continental shelf." The man's voice was sarcastic. He adjusted his equipment, sent more water into the drilled hole, and restarted the engine. He reversed the drill then moved it forward, but the drill seemed to be wedged.

He repeated the procedure a few more times, not budging the drill. He turned the engine off and leaned against the truck. A loud clunk boomed from deep within the hole. The drill dropped a bit as the Earth rumbled under their feet.

"Holy shit, I think I hit a natural gas pocket. Run."

They sprinted away from the drill.

They all turned, watching a huge geyser of water burst from the drill hole and shoot nearly sixty-feet into the air. They didn't speak for several minutes as they watched a liquid more precious than gold spray the open rangeland and begin turning to ice.

"Twelve and a *half* feet." Dark Water stood beside the well driller.

*****

Soul Taker thundered out with the speed of a greyhound and the temper of a wolverine. The beast jumped nearly five feet off the ground with all four hooves in the air at the same time. He twisted inward, almost forming a half-circle with his body, pitching, bucking, fighting like a horde of wasps was stinging him.

"Four seconds! Ride 'em cowboy."

Joe felt like his body was splitting open from groin to belly every time the bull's hooves slammed the ground. He doubted his ribs were going to be able to keep his lungs from oozing out, his backbone felt like it was being pop-riveted into his skull, and he knew his wrist had fractured from the yanking against the rope.

"Six seconds! This cowboy might just make it!"

Time stopped.

A lifetime passed in seconds.

The bull twisted hard to the right, ramming his body and Joe's leg into the fence. That just made the bull madder. Hooves clattered as he kicked out, banging the fence in defiance. The slick metal against hoof made the bull's center of weight shift, his hindquarters went down, back legs sprawling. The bull panicked, struggled hard to stand, falling onto his side.

Abby's face, Hidden Rock's grotto, his dad, his mom -- images came into his head, playing like old black and white movies.

His mind was screaming. "Was that a bell? Can't let go yet. Eight seconds, don't let go of the rope. Don't let go."

Two thousand pounds of outraged bull, twisted on its back like a turtle, its four legs thrusting into the air, as Joe fought for life underneath it.

Searing, burning pain, a burst of white light shot through his head. Joe saw the world in slow motion, like an old silent movie. He felt only the crushing weight of the bull and mind-numbing pain. The taste of a sweet liquid ran into his mouth, thick and sticky.

Suddenly air filled his lungs, and he was slung across the arena, slamming into the fence with brutal velocity. He hadn't heard a bell. Soul Taker circled the arena, bulldozing a clown and charging Joe.

Three cowboys on horseback entered the arena, ropes twirling. One rider galloped hard, putting himself between Soul Taker and Joe. The bull didn't slow. He put his head down, charged even faster, and pummeled the horse.

The mare went down hard, her ribs poked through skin and brown fur became instantly covered in blood. The cowboy went airborne, catapulting across the fence into the stands.

Joe pulled himself to his feet. Soul Taker backed up a few steps and charged. The clowns shouted and ran. The other cowboys rode alongside, slapping the bull with ropes. The audience was screaming. The announcer was pleading for help.

*****

Abby screamed as the bull's head rammed into him. A horn caught his shirt. The bull reared his head back, picking Joe up and flinging him nearly thirty feet across the arena. Soul Taker snorted, pawed the dirt, and ran toward the man she loved.

Two cowboys on horses charged in between, making the bull hesitate slightly. It missed most of Joe's body, stomping a leg as he charged away. The bull planted his two front hooves hard into the dirt. He turned on a dime and came for another pass when two gunshots reverberated across the arena.

Absolute silence filled the air. The bull stood in mid-gallop for several seconds, snorted, shook his head, and fell dead.

The man put the safety back on, shoved the rifle into its case, and slung it across his back.

Abby clambered over the fence, sprinted across the dirt, and fell on her knees at Joe's side. "No, no, no, Joe." She tried to turn him over, tried to get him to speak. "Dear God, no."

Hands were pulling her away.

"No!"" She fought them, screaming when they wouldn't release her. "No! Let me go." Her screams echoed across the silent arena.

Paramedics were at his side. Blood covered his face and chest, and his head was lying in an unnatural position.

Abby pulled against the men, unable to get loose.

"No, honey, stay here and let the paramedics do their job." Mike's voice was gentle.

"He'll be all right, Abby." Hal was on the other side.

"Let me go. He needs me," she sobbed. "I need him."

"No, Abby." Mike held tighter.

"How's that cowboy?" The announcer broke the silence.

The paramedics worked for a few more minutes, then lifted him onto the gurney.

"Joe." She searched the paramedic's faces for any sign.

The men looked at each other, and then looked at Abby.

The look said it all. Abby fell to her knees, sobbing uncontrollably.

Chapter Twenty-Three

Tessa held Abby's hand on their way through the hallway, heading toward the hospital waiting room. The last time Abby was in a hospital was the day her grandmother died. She stopped in the hallway. She couldn't do it. She didn't have the guts to walk into that waiting room.

"Abby." Tessa looked at her, waiting.

She leaned against the hard wall, sliding down it and sitting on the floor. Pain slammed her gut, and her head felt like it was about to explode. She kept reliving the bull ride. Over and over again, she watched the bull pummel Joe, charge him, shred his body. Abby could hardly breathe. She couldn't bear it if she walked in that room and they told her he was dead. "I can't do it, Tessa. I can't go in there."

"I can't believe the association allowed those bulls in the competition." Hal's voice seemed loud coming down the hall.

"Ben got the hell out of there in hurry." Mike snorted. "If I could have found Charlie, I'd a borrowed his gun."

"I saw Ben arguing with the judges just after Joe's ride. You know the son-of-a-bitch is gonna say he didn't make the bell." Hal slapped his hat against his thigh.

Abby's legs were rubbery, as Tessa helped her to her feet. She could still smell the dust, bulls, and blood from the arena.

"Soul Taker? Of all the bulls, Soul Taker?" Mike paced across the waiting room. "Ben didn't just want Joe to lose. I think he wanted him dead."

Hal elbowed Mike as Abby walked into the waiting room.

"Is anyone here related by blood to Mr. Baer?" A nurse asked the group, hopeful. They all shook their heads no and she disappeared behind a set of stainless swinging doors.

Connor arrived at the hospital Margaret introduced Abby to him.

She was glad Connor had come home, glad he was there for Joe.

"The nurse was out here awhile ago, looking for someone who was a blood relation to Joe." Margaret nodded toward the woman in scrubs.

Connor went to the reception desk and explained who he was.

A few minutes later the doctor appeared. "Are all of you here for Joseph Baer?"

"Yes," Margaret answered for the group.

"Mr. Baer isn't doing well. He's had massive trauma. He has a broken wrist, a fractured rib, his left lung was punctured and collapsed, he has several deep lacerations on his head, and a possible concussion. There is a severe puncture wound to his side, which fortunately missed all major organs, but did cause a significant loss of blood."

"I'm his brother. Maybe I can supply any blood that he needs," Connor offered.

"That's been taken care of." He opened the chart he'd been holding. "A Kelly Childers supplied us with a donation from the Native American Blood Bank in Oklahoma. From what I understand, she had gotten it for Mr. Baer's other brother. When it wasn't needed for him, she made it available to us."

"What other brother?" Connor interrupted.

"Honey, that's a whole other story." Tessa patted his arm.

"Is he going to make it, Doctor?" Abby's small voice quieted them all.

Closing the chart, he inhaled slowly. "I don't know, especially with the amount of blood he lost. I'm sorry I can't be more positive, but right now based on his injuries and all his vitals, I just don't know."

"Can we see him?" Connor asked.

"Not all of you. I'd prefer just family visit until he's more stable."

Abby wobbled, leaning against Tessa.

Connor grabbed Abby's hand and took her inside the hospital room with him. "The only person that looks as bad as the patient is the person in love with them."

The room was dark. Shards of light from the parking lot filtered through the mini-blinds, adding a gray pallor to the room. Small, dim lights in the corners, the blue LED readout from the machines, and a whir of beeps, pumps and dings made it surreal, as though it were someone else's nightmare and she was just walking through it.

In the center of it all, her large, overbearing cowboy looked small, broken, and fragile. Connor took in a sharp breath. They stood beside the bed, still holding hands.

"Hey, Joe, it's Connor. I got a hold of your girl here. If you don't get your butt up, I'm gonna run away with her. She's pretty hot." He squeezed her hand. She tried hard not to cry.

"Joe." She bent over and kissed his cheek. It seemed to be the only place on him that wasn't bruised, cut, or stitched. "I think you actually had the bull scared for a minute or two." She couldn't hold back any longer. Taking his hand in hers, she laid her head over on the railing and sobbed.

"He's tough. He'll be all right." Connor patted her shoulder. "Hidden Rock has lots of work to be done, little brother, and you know I ain't the ranching type."

Abby stroked his forehead, pushed a stray lock of hair away from his eye. Connor pulled a chair from the wall and motioned for her to sit.

Joe didn't move. His hands didn't jump, his face didn't twitch, his eyes never fluttered. It was as though he was gone, but his body remained.

Connor had the same angled jaw line as his brother, the same deep-set eyes, only his were dark brown instead of blue. Connor had bigger hands and a softer, more refined appearance, but the family resemblance was unmistakable.

She reached for his hand. "Thank you allowing me in."

"He needed you to be here."

A soft knock interrupted them.

"We are all getting a little worried and slap-happy out here." Margaret eased into the room, with Mike, Hal, and Tessa on her heels.

"Oh, heavens. Tears began a slow stream down Tessa's face. She rested a hand on Abby's shoulder. "He's a mess, honey."

"Tessa," Margaret scolded.

"She's right," Abby said. "He looks even worse than I did when I blew up the fireplace." Everyone chuckled. She'd hoped Joe might hear it and move. He didn't.

"Folks, he can't have this many people in here." The nurse sounded tired and irritated.

"Sorry, ma'am." Mike nodded to Hal. "We'll be getting out of your way. Abby, we're heading back to the ranch. You want to come with us?"

"No. I'm staying here."

Each one gave her a hug and made their way out except Margaret. "I can stay in the waiting room."

"Go home. There isn't any sense in all of us staying," Abby said.

"You two call and we'll come."

"Thanks." Connor found another chair and slid it beside Abby. Margaret gave him a long, motherly hug and left.

"Would you like some coffee?" Connor asked.

"Yes, I would."

Abby eased beside Joe on the bed. "Don't you die on me, cowboy," she whispered. "I finally found someone who loves me as much as I love them. Don't you dare leave me." She laid an arm gently across his body afraid she would hurt him. "I want to be with you for the rest of my life."

By the time Connor returned with the coffee, she was sitting calmly in the chair. He'd also picked up two pillows and a blanket on his way back. "I thought we might need these."

"Thank you." The pillow felt good behind her back and the coffee, well it was hospital machine coffee, so it was at least hot.

They sipped their coffee, watching Joe. They looked out the window. They stared at the floor.

"Joe will be glad to have you back." Abby sipped the coffee.

He looked up slowly. "I'm not so sure. I kind of left under bad circumstances."

"I don't know the circumstances, but I do know he missed you a lot. He mentioned more than once how much he wanted to see you."

"Really?"

"He thought you wouldn't want to talk to him, actually."

Connor shook his head. "I hope we have a chance to make up for lost time."

"I hope you do, too."

"Are you two engaged?"

She smiled. "No. I'm his aggravation."

He laughed. "He's needed one of those for a long time." He crushed the coffee cup, tossing it into the wastebasket.

"How did you know Joe was hurt?"

Stretching out his long legs, he leaned heavily into the plastic chair. "Margaret called Tom." Folding his hands behind his head, he stared hard at his brother. "We were up on Standforth Reservation, Tom had asked me to do some surveying up there. I'm a geologist and he needed me to help them find water," he explained. "Damnedest thing is we found it today in the least likely of places. Ben Childers is going to be insane when he finds out."

"Why would he care about water on the reservation?" Abby sipped the last of the wretched coffee.

"You didn't know?"

"Know what?"

"The water that feeds the reservation runs right through Ben Childers's ranch. By law, it's public water. Ben managed to get the rights to it and cut off water to the reservation. I guess with enough money and bull you can get anything." The muscle in his jaw flexed hard. "Water is pretty scarce out here, and when you shut off the only known source to several hundred people, they'll pretty much be at your mercy. When Ben found out Tom held the deed to Hidden Rock, he cut off water to the reservation. In order for his people to have water, Tom handed over the deed."

"Now it makes sense. Joe just could not figure out why Tom would betray him like that."

"Tom tried to hold out. They trucked in water, they drilled in several places, they even tried to negotiate with the Army Corps of Engineers to help them drill or find another source and pipe it in. Tom simply ran out of options." He cracked his knuckles, twisted his neck. "I thought Joe knew."

"He had no idea." Connor had dark circles under his eyes and she thought his jaw might unhinge if he yawned one more time.

"Go to a hotel and get some rest. I'll stay here tonight."

He smiled. "If you don't mind, I'd like to sit here with you tonight."

"I'm glad to have you here."

*****

"I filed a perfectly legal and legitimate protest against the judges." Ben inhaled the cigar smoke deeply. "I will have my day in front of the review board."

"Mr. Childers, I have three judges, two rodeo officials, and the video tape that proves Mr. Baer was on the bull the required eight seconds, scored the highest in points, and is the winner of the bull riding event." The man snapped his pencil in two.

Ben took two steps toward the small man, letting out a long stream of smoke into his face. "I'm telling you, Mr. Hammond, that bell didn't ring."

Mr. Hammond's eyes watered. "I came here to acquire your paperwork, Mr. Childers. Not to listen to your idle rants, be belittled by you, or tolerate your smoke in a non-smoking environment." He put his gloves on. "I will deliver these papers to the review committee, and they will make the final ruling. They will notify you of their decision and it will be the final, and only, decision." He turned, nearly knocking the hotel busboy down on his way out.

"Sir, your breakfast," the busboy said.

Ben grabbed the cart, shoving it against the busboy's stomach. "Get that thing out of here."

"But, you just ordered this."

"Are you deaf? I said get it and you out."

He shrugged, turning the cart around and leaving.

Ben clicked on his cell phone. "Remember that contract I had you look over? Yes, the one with Joe Baer and Hidden Rock Ranch, I need you to go over that thing with a fine-toothed comb. See if you can find me any kind of a loophole."

*****

The shift changed and a new nurse entered the hospital room, checked all the equipment, checked Joe, nodded Abby and Connor, and left.

The morning sky was gray outside the small window. Connor had grown a major field of stubble overnight and Abby felt as though glue had been poured over her tongue.

Connor had dozed on and off several times through the long night. Abby, however, couldn't close her eyes. Every time they shut, she would relive the bull rolling over on Joe, his body lying like a bloody piece of meat in the middle of the arena.

Connor stood, yawned, and stretched. "I need some breakfast. I'll buy," he offered.

"I don't have much of an appetite, but thanks."

"I understand how you feel. But you won't do him any good if you're in a hospital bed too."

"I'll eat, just not right now," she promised.

He nodded and left.

She picked up Joe's hand. It was dry, heavy. Propping a hip on the bed, she stared into his face, talking low. "Joe? Can you hear me, Joe?" There was no response.

"You know they say you can hear people talking about you, even if you can't talk back, so I'm going to trust that and keep talking to you." She watched his face again. "Anytime you feel like moving a finger, a lip, an eyebrow, you go right ahead."

Absentmindedly, she counted the fingers on his hand, noticing scars she'd never seen before, feeling calluses on the palm.

"You wouldn't have been in debt to me you know? I would have given you that money free and clear, even free and clear of me. I probably owed you more than that for all the stuff I broke on the ranch." She laughed. "I don't think I'm cut out for ranch life. There are just way too many things I can break. I can't quite figure out what I am cut out for. But I do know that I want to be with you." She laid her head on his chest. "I miss you so much, please come back."

Another day passed. Everyone offered to take her back to Hidden Rock, or to stay with her, or a million other kindnesses. Connor opted for a hotel by the end of the second day. Abby stayed with Joe.

There would be a change. There would be a movement. She knew it, and she wanted to be there for it.

Forty-nine gray tiles and thirty-eight green tiles covered the floor of Joe's hospital room. Abby knew. She'd counted them at least a dozen times. One of the monitors bleeped every seven minutes and the IV drip sent a drop down the tube every nine seconds but Joe didn't move. She sang to him. He said he liked to hear her sing, but her voice didn't wake him.

"Abby?" Tessa entered the dark room. "Honey, you look like something I've scraped off my boots." She pulled up a chair, sitting beside her. "You need to go to a hotel, get a shower, eat something, and get some sleep."

"I'm not leaving."

"You're going to have to. Look at you." She pulled a mirror out of her big handbag. "Is your face what you'd want to see when you woke up in a hospital room?"

Abby looked at her red, swollen eyes, sunken cheeks, uncombed hair. She really did look awful.

"You're liable to give the man a heart attack."

Abby shot her a look.

"Well nobody else is willing to tell you, so I will. And in case you forgot, you are the opening act for the earl of country music in less than a week. You know the legend who wants to make you a star?" She snapped her fingers. "Sitting here isn't going to save him, Abby."

"I know this. I do." She stared at Joe. "I'm just afraid if I leave I won't ever get to talk to him again."

"If you stay like this, he won't ever get to talk to you again. You can't keep this up." Tessa pulled back, staring into Abby's face.

"Jack is outside with a limo. Let me take you to the hotel, get you rested and cleaned up. Margaret said she'd come sit tonight and Connor is coming back tomorrow. Honey, Joe ain't going to be alone. In fact, he'll probably wake up just to get rid of us." She smiled.

Margaret came into the room carrying a large basket with her. "I brought my knitting and some books to read. I might as well make the most of being able to sit awhile."

Always practical Margaret, Abby thought.

"Come on, Abby." Tessa headed to the door.

"Can I have just one minute, please?" The ladies nodded and left her alone with Joe.

"Hey, Joe. I'm going to leave for a bit, because I smell really bad." She kissed his forehead. "I've got to go and earn that money I promised you. Margaret and Connor will be here." She kissed him again. "Please wake up for me, Joe." She watched his face.

"I love you." She pulled her coat on and walked out the door.

*****

Abby started again. She wasn't singing well at all. Her voice seemed to have lost its edge. She'd been in Winslow's recording studio for hours, and nothing was coming out right. Abby pulled off the headphones, rubbing the throbbing ache between her eyes. She hated being here. Ironic, since this was the place she'd dreamed of being her entire life. Being here meant being away from Joe, away from the man she'd unwittingly fallen in love with.

He'd been so angry with her. What did he expect? She knew he and Kelly had a past, and then there she was, naked in his bed. *Damn, Joe*, she thought, *what did you think I'd do*?

When the pictures of Winslow and her were plastered across every tabloid, he'd been mad, but he had believed her. She rocked her head from side to side, the kink in her neck getting bigger by the minute.

"Let's take it from the top." Winslow's voice sounded irritated as it came across the mic into the recording studio. She glanced up at the glass window that separated the studio from the engineers. Winslow had lost his million-watt smile.

Abby tried some deep breathing. She tried stretching and flexing. She had to do something to calm down and sing. She put the headphones back on, the music started, she sang and her voice sounded as pitiful as she felt.

"What the hell is wrong with you?" Winslow shouted into the mic. Abby ripped the headphones off, throwing them on the floor.

"Do you really need an answer to that?" She shouted back.

"Hey, Abby." Tessa's Texas drawl boomed into the recording studio. "Sounds like you could use a little inspiration. Well, honey I just came from the hospital and Joe is doing better. His blood pressure is up, all those other medical things are up, and the doctor is pretty sure Joe will be up soon."

"Really?"

Tessa's smiling face appeared on the other side of the glass.

"Yes, ma'am, the doctor said he might be upgrading his condition level real soon." She gave Abby a thumbs up.

It was the first bit of good news since the rodeo. A wave a relief washed over her. She fought the urge to do a happy dance in the middle of the studio.

She sailed through the rest of the rehearsal and recording. Her voice melted over the lyrics like butter melting on a hot sidewalk in August.

*****

The next morning Abby and Winslow were at the Cheyenne Civic Center where they would be performing. The lights were tested and retested. The sound tests were the worst. Squeals, squalls, and static echoed across the stage.

Abby stood center stage, looking into the empty audience seats. How many years had she wished to be here, pretending to be a famous singer in front of her bedroom mirror, using a fat marker for a microphone, signing every song that came on the radio? Standing there for one moment she enjoyed her dream, feeling it, letting it invade her being. The smell of the stage, the warmth of the lights, the sounds, the echoes across the auditorium.

But no one she loved was there to share it. There would be no Granny Martin to wave to in the audience, no Mom or Dad to thank, and no Joe to hear her love song to him. The dream didn't suddenly feel so great.

"You'll do fine." Winslow had rolled up his shirtsleeves. Perspiration was moist on his brow. "I'll let you in on a little secret. After all these years, I'm nervous as a virgin at a volcano every time I go on stage."

She laughed. "That's pretty nervous." The spotlight flashed in her eyes. She squinted and lowered her eyes.

"Don't look away from it. Look to the side of it. That way the audience thinks you're looking at them and the light makes your eyes sparkle even in the cheap seats." He squeezed her hand. "Give us a few minutes to get everything finished back here and we'll run through a few sets."

*****

"Testing, one, two, three." Winslow seemed obnoxiously loud to Abby.

She sat in the back row of the Civic Center, waiting on a call from Tessa. She'd been using Jack Spencer's phone, checking it every few minutes, but no calls had come and no messages had appeared.

"Tomorrow, I'm going out and getting you a cell phone." Jack took a seat beside her. "You haven't missed any calls from Tessa, I swear." Abby smiled.

He laughed. "It's a good thing or I'd never hear the end of it."

"You really like her don't you?"

Jack leaned back into the seat. "I guess I do. She's like no one I've ever known. I seem to be drawn to her, much like a moth to a flame."

Abby laughed. She could see that. Jack lingered on Tessa's every word, her every move.

"You know Winslow really has a thing for you?"

"He has a thing for every woman he meets."

"This time it's different," Jack said. "You're different. I've seen him with lots of ladies through the years. I think most of them were publicity dates. With you, he doesn't want to be in front of the press, he just wants to be with you. For a publicity hound like Winslow, that speaks volumes."

Winslow's amazing voice filled the center. The spotlight flashed a soft blue halo around his head. He looked into the audience at her.

No, he didn't. That was his key to being one of the most lusted after men in the business. Every woman in the audience thought he was singing just to her.

Chapter Twenty-Four

Somewhere in the distance, Joe heard Margaret's voice. All he wanted to do was find her, but she seemed so far away. Was that George? Why was it so hard to get to them? Joe fought to move, but his body didn't respond. He swallowed, and swallowed but his voice wouldn't make a sound.

"If that boy don't wake up soon, everyone in the county is going to get a scarf for Christmas." George laughed, looking at all the yarn next to her. "Thought you might be hungry, and I miss having dinner with you." He kissed Margaret on the cheek, unwrapping sandwiches and opening a fresh thermos of coffee. "Any change in Joe?"

"I could have sworn I saw his head move a minute ago, but I guess it was just wishful thinking."

"Got some extra coffee?" Joe's voice was hoarse.

Margaret shouted, "George get the doctor in here. Joe, can you hear me?"

"Yep." Boy could he hear her. Her voice sounded loud and close. His eyes were still closed tight, his eyelids feeling like boulders.

"Boy, you had a heap of folks worried sick about you."

Slowly his eyes opened.

Margaret hugged him. It made every place on his body scream with pain. He moaned.

The doctor and a few nurses burst into the room, checking everything at once. "Mr. Baer can you hear me?" the doctor yelled.

"I'm badly broken, doctor, but not deaf."

The doctor laughed. "Sorry. How do you feel?"

"Like I've been pummeled by a bull,"

George laughed, hugging Margaret.

"Please, I still have evaluations to do. I'm not sure if Mr. Baer is recovering or just awake."

"Quite the optimist aren't you, doc?" Joe's voice was beginning to come back.

"I'll have the nurse get you some juice. That will help." He checked Joe's vitals, ran a light over his eyes, checked his stitches. "We're glad to have you back with us. Of course, this is an early and preliminary prognosis. I'll know more after we've run a few tests." He scribbled notes on a clipboard before leaving.

"I brought someone to see you," Margaret whispered. Connor stood beside his bed.

Joe squinted, staring up at him.

"I've missed you little brother." Connor clasped his hand, then gave him a hug. The two held each other for a long time. They hugged a bit more and stared at each other. Words were useless.

"I've got to call Abby." Margaret pulled out her cell phone.

"No." Joe's voice was cold. "I don't want her called."

"What? Why not?"

"Joe, that girl's been here every day. She's watched over you and prayed over you."

"She's not here now."

"She's with Winslow." Joe's heart slithered into his stomach. First, she walks away without letting him explain anything, then she just slips right onto Winslow's arm. Joe had been right all along about women.

"They've got that concert."

Joe turned his head, not wanting to hear anything else about Abby. "I'm really tired."

"All right, everyone. Let's give the man some peace and quiet so he can rest." Margaret herded them all out and then came back to Joe. "You know, Joseph Baer, for a bright man, sometimes you can be a real idiot."

Joe was silent.

"I'm not sure what's eating at you, but that girl had to be dragged from this room. She was willing to give up the opportunity of a lifetime for you. You might want to give that some thought." She kissed his forehead. "I'm glad you're back, cowboy." She quietly closed the door as she left.

*****

The courtroom was nearly empty. Civil cases didn't attract much attention. Ben Childers walked in with his attorney. He was damned unhappy at having to be in court. He paid a legal team to keep him out of court.

"This isn't going to work, Ben. As your attorney, I'm advising you to drop this litigation, cut your losses, and move on." The man sat his briefcase on the table.

Ben stared at him long and hard. "I pay you good money, Randolph. I expect you to leave a loophole or clause in every contract I make."

Randolph shook his head. "First, that was not made clear, and second, if it had been, I would have declined my services."

"Boy, you are not your daddy's son. He became a rich, rich man, and I believe put you through Harvard Law, by listening to his best client, me. I suggest you find a loophole, or I will call the owner of your law firm, Deidre Randitz, and have your ass fired." Ben smiled at the courtroom crowd and took his seat.

Randolph turned as Tessa strode into the courtroom. She was dressed head-to-toe in a popsicle-orange suit. Her high heels clicked across the marble floor as she made her way to a front row seat next to Jack and Connor.

Ben snapped his fingers. "Would you focus on this case and not an attractive ass?"

Connor stood as his attorney entered. "Jillian, good to see you again."

"Connor." She nodded, opened her briefcase and laid her files on the table. "Can you give me an update on the health of your brother?"

Connor reported the amazing progress since yesterday.

The morning dragged on with several other cases being heard first.

The judge took a few minutes to read over the contract between Joe and Ben. Jillian made him aware of Joe's hospitalization and that Connor was present on his behalf. Ben's attorney made a half-hearted case against the contract, which the judge found no fault with it.

After several pleas, Jillian interrupted and offered the video tape as evidence. The judge chose to watch the tape in his chambers, giving them all a recess.

Barely twenty minutes later, the judge returned to the courtroom. "Mr. Childers, would you please rise?" Ben stood, smiling. "Why are you choosing to waste my time and the taxpayers' money with this frivolous litigation?"

"Sir, Mr. Childers is only trying to uphold his end of the contract," Randolph pleaded. "The bull rider, Joseph Baer, did not ride the bull to the full time limit and therefore has forfeited his--"

"Unless you have a different way of telling time than the rest of the known world, Mr. Baer rode that bull a full three seconds after the bell rang. By my calculations, he more than fulfilled his end of the contract. It is the decision of this court that the deed to Hidden Rock Ranch be remitted to Joseph Bear, without encumbrances. You will instruct your client to give that deed to the county recorder's office within twenty-four hours or he will be held in contempt." He hammered the gavel on his desk. "Case closed."

"Well, that was the easiest case I've ever won." Jillian smiled at Connor. "I'm disappointed. I was prepared for a fight."

"What the hell just happened?" Ben lowered his voice. "I gave you a video for the judge. That was what was supposed to be submitted. Where did he get the original tape? How did he get it?"

Randolph snapped his briefcase shut. "You were right, Mr. Childers, I am not my father's son." He headed toward the door. "Looks like you're going to have make that call to Ms. Randitz," he added and left.

Ben turned to Connor. "Don't look so smug. I guarantee you haven't heard the last from me."

"Is that a threat, Mr. Childers?" Jillian asked. "Right here in the middle of a United States Courtroom, with video cameras in every corner?" She smiled and folded her arms across her chest, standing nearly toe-to-toe with him.

Ben slammed on his cowboy hat and stomped out the door.

*****

Joe struggled to sit upright. There wasn't an inch of him that didn't feel pain. It even hurt when his hair moved.

Somewhere in what felt like a distant memory, he remembered hearing Abby's voice. He remembered her singing. It must have been a dream. She hadn't been there since he woke up. Not that he would have expected her to be. The night she left, his heart froze. Abby was the first women he'd ever really loved, and she wouldn't even stop and listen to him.

Finding the controls to raise the bed, he groaned as his body shifted. He pulled back the sheet, looking at the puncture wound in his side. It wasn't pretty. Yellow drains were sticking out of it, staples were holding his gut together, and an ugly, red, swollen ring circled it.

The left side of his head felt about four times bigger than the right and he kept leaning that way in spite of his best efforts to keep it straight. The left eye was still swollen shut.

Joe strained to read some sort of chart on the far side of the room. A gaudy, green splint circled his right wrist, and someone had drawn a little horse's head on the top of it. He must have been pretty drugged to let someone draw that thing on his arm.

"What do you think you're doing?" A nurse's voice startled him. "Do you know how badly you're hurt?"

"Yes, ma'am, I can feel it."

"You need to be lying down, resting." The nurse went for the bed controls.

He tucked them under the covers.

"Mr. Baer," she scolded, holding her hand out.

"I'd really like to sit up awhile."

"You really shouldn't be." Pulling a few extra pillows from a cabinet, she put them on either side of him. "I'm afraid as weak as you are, you might hurt yourself. Are you able to eat?"

"I'd like a little something."

She smiled. "Let me see what I can find."

She had just left when Tessa, George, and Margaret came in.

"You are one pitiful looking man." Tessa's hands were on her hips, giving him the once over. "Abby is going to have her work cut out, getting you back into shape. I'll bet she was as excited as a kitten on a dairy farm when she found out you were up and kicking."

"He didn't want us to call her," Margaret told her.

There was an instant explosion of anger behind Tessa's eyes.

"Abby doesn't know you're awake and getting better?" Her big green eyes bore down on him like a missile loaded fighter jet. "Why not?"

"She's the one who stormed out. I don't need her and I don't want her."

"You chauvinistic, self-centered, egotistical, brainless jerk. She stormed out because there was a naked woman in your bed. She was just too nice." She wielded her orange acrylic fingernails like talons, arcing way too close to his face for comfort. "If it had been me that walked in on that little show, you'd be in a heap more pain that you are right now. Compared to what I would have done to you, that bull was a gentle soul."

He didn't want to listen. He was too hurt. "Nothing happened."

"We all know that. But it sure didn't look good, and if Rodney hadn't confessed, I'm not sure any of us would have believed you, especially considering your less than stellar history with Kelly Childers."

"Tessa, that's enough." Joe didn't need advice from her or anyone else.

"I am far from done, cowboy. Abby spent days here, not eating, not sleeping, and barely walking. She only left because she made a promise to Winslow and because she thought her singing would get you enough money to buy your ranch back." Her hands went her hips. "After all that and you think she done you wrong by leaving. Maybe walking out was the smartest thing she could have done."

She pulled a cell phone from her purse. "I don't care what you want, Joe Baer. That girl deserves to know that your sorry butt is alive and getting well." George touched her shoulder. "Hang up the phone, Tessa."

"I will not." Her Texas drawl grew thicker.

"Listen, he knows what he wants, and it isn't your place to call her. It's his." George turned his back to Joe, talking to Tessa, his voice going all soft and sweet. The rest of group seemed intent on George, and a weird smile crossed Margaret's face.

"George," Joe called.

"Please." George patted Tessa's hand.

"Oh, all right, but I sure hope Abby never finds out." She clicked off the phone, looking over George's shoulder and pointing at Joe. "If I lose my friend because of this, I'll never forgive you." She stormed out of the room.

"Heaven help the man that marries that girl." Margaret laughed.

Connor was nearly plowed over by Tessa as he came into Joe's hospital room. "Afternoon." He closed the door behind him. "Sorry I wasn't here this morning but," Connor cleared his throat. "I was in court with Ben Childers."

Joe gripped the metal bed rail. In court? He was laid up in bed and Childers was vicious enough to take his family to court. He was going to kill the bastard when he got out of this hospital.

George leaned against a cabinet, and Margaret wrapped an arm through his. "Connor," she said, "it might help if you told him you beat the pants off the old fart."

"Since you were in the hospital, Ben subpoenaed me to court in your place." A big smile crossed Connor's face. "The details don't really matter, but the court ruled in your favor. Hidden Rock's deed is being recorded back in your name as we speak."

"The bastard contested the contract and whether I rode the bull to the bell, didn't he?" Joe's eye twitched behind the gauze that covered it. "I have things to do. I should have been there." He flung off the covers. "I won't have another man fight my battles." The pain enveloped him.

"I'm not another man, I'm your brother."

Joe couldn't make his legs work, he felt the wound on his side rip open, pain ripped up his torso. His body fell limp on the bed.

The nurse rushed into the room as the call button sounded. Joe felt the flurry around him, felt the needles in his arm being touched, heard the monitors beeping. He opened his eyes and saw the nurse standing over him.

"The next time you try to get up, I'm ordering restraints. He needs some rest, folks," she suggested and left the room.

Margaret and Connor gathered their coats and headed for the door.

"If you don't mind, I think I'll sit a spell with Joe." George slid a chair next to Joe's bed. Joe coughed, grabbing his ribs It hurt like hell to breathe, and it hurt even worse to cough.

Margaret gave George a suspicious look.

"I won't let him do anything stupid." He held up a hand like he was taking an oath.

George sat in the hard plastic chair after they left.

Joe's breaths were quick and shallow. "Is there some reason you're sitting over there staring at me?" He couldn't take George's quiet looks any longer. "Did you get stuck with babysitting detail today?" Joe loosened up the sheet around his legs.

"Yep, I drew the short straw." George smiled, leaning back, pouring coffee from his thermos. "How are you feeling? I mean really feeling, none of that sugary stuff you think everybody wants to hear."

Joe sighed, staring for long time at the ceiling. "I hurt worse than I can ever remember." He gazed at George with his one good eye.

"I was more scared than I've ever been in my life. I figured I'd lost it all in those eight seconds, my ranch, my life." He stopped abruptly.

"And Abby?"

"Can't lose what I didn't have."

George shook his head. "I don't usually like to admit this, but in this case my wife was right. You are an idiot." He sat forward, resting his elbows on his knees.

Joe looked back at the ceiling. He didn't want to listen, and he was stuck.

"That's the only reason she skedaddled out of your house the way she did that night. Boy, you are seriously undereducated in the ways of women."

"I suppose you're an expert?"

"On women? There ain't no such thing, but there are things you can understand. Abby came into your bedroom where a pretty, naked woman was laying. It doesn't take an expert to see the problem there."

"The problem was she didn't give me a chance to explain. Me. She took someone else's word, not mine."

George stood up, putting the chair back near the wall. "So, you're willing to throw away the best thing that ever happened to you because she didn't hang around while you stood there naked, or so I hear, with a naked woman in your bed and let you explain?"

He put his hat on, tightening the lid on his thermos. "Abby was here for days. She washed you, combed your hair, massaged you, and she prayed one heck of a lot. You know why she left, Joe? You."

George pulled on his coat, snapping the buttons. "In a couple of days, Abby is going to be singing on a stage. Pretty soon the world is going to know about her. She is going to be famous and rich." He searched his pocket for his gloves. "Tessa found out she asked for a loan from Winslow, a one million dollar loan, that she was going to use to save a certain ranch.

Joe turned toward him. When did all this happen? How long had he been unconscious? Abby that he was so mad at had done all this for him, for Hidden Rock?

George pulled his gloves on and tucked the thermos under his arm. "When Abby finds out you didn't want her called do you know what's going to happen?"

Joe's heart sank. He was going to lose her, the only woman he'd ever loved. She was the woman he wanted to be with, to spend his life with, and in an instant of egotistical anger, he'd lost her.

George leaned close to the bed. "If I know her, and I think I do, she'll never speak to you again, you'll never see her again, except on magazine covers. Abby will be the newest singing sensation to hit the air since Elvis. She'll be on the arm of Winslow Dodge. And you? You're going to be a proud man bumbling around your great big ranch, all alone."

George stared at him a few seconds and left.

*****

"I'm sorry, ma'am, but the only information we can give you over the telephone is that Mr. Baer is in stable condition." The receptionist sounded annoyed.

Abby hung up the phone and curled up with a pillow on the bed. The hotel was sterile, cold, and lonely. It was the best hotel in town, and by any standards it was elegant, richly decorated, and had plenty of amenities.

Is this what her world would be like as a famous singer, staying in hotel after hotel in a string of nameless cities, playing dark concert halls amid an endless sea of flashbulbs, and never seeing the light of day or having someone to share the adventure with?

She'd lived this kind of existence for a while with Billy and his band. Numbed by grief after losing Granny Martin and their home, she hadn't really thought much about her life. She did a gig and moved on. When had things changed? She was still in pain over Granny Martin and there was the horrible, gut-wrenching pain over Joe, but she didn't feel numb anymore.

It was as though all of her emotions had been laid bare, feeling everything without reserve. It was terrifying. She wanted to feel and experience everything, but she didn't want to do it alone. She'd wanted to share it with Joe.

The phone rang. Abby looked at the clock, it was nearly seven in the morning. She answered. "Jack here. The boss wants you at the Civic Center in half an hour. He's got international press, MTV, CMT, and a dozen other news outlets of various alphabets. You're on."

*****

The staples pinched as the doctor snipped them out rather abruptly. "This has healed nicely and quicker than I'd anticipated."

The staple remover clanked against the stainless steel tray. "I'm impressed, Mr. Baer. You've come a long way very fast. When you were first brought in, I wasn't certain you'd even make it through the night." He checked the medical chart on the computer screen, and did a quick run through of Joe's blood pressure and other vitals. "Your wife was sure convinced you'd make it, though."

Joe's head shot up.

"If there is anything to prayer, or positive thinking, or just plain steadfast determination, she pretty much kept you alive single handedly." He smiled. "Pretty voice, too. The nurses and I would hear her singing to you nearly all night."

He logged out of the computer, securing the medical chart. "Well, Mr. Baer, if you have someone to look after you for a few weeks, you can probably go home early next week." He breezed out the door.

Joe stared out the window. Snow was blowing past and the sky was an ugly gray. George's words were still ringing in his head. He remembered Abby's eyes, staring up at him through a soot-streaked face. It brought a smile to him. He thought about the little bull, and the way she'd found him and nursed him back to health.

The ranch was like an alien planet to her, but she'd jumped in with gusto and determination. Hell, she'd made a crew of beef-ranching cowboys eat tofu. He laughed aloud, then groaned from the pain.

He could still smell her perfume and taste the essence of her. He remembered every curve of her naked body next to his, the way she gave herself to him, they way they shared each other.

The night she left was the first time in years Hidden Rock had felt like a home. The kitchen was warm, treasured dishes lay on the table, and wonderful smells came from the oven. It was happy. He wanted to feel that way again, and she was the only one who could do that. Damn, he loved her and he didn't want to spend his life without her.

Joe tried to turn, but his side hurt like hell. The bandage was off his head so he didn't look so much like a bad movie mummy anymore, and he could almost inhale without feeling as if someone had dropped a lit kerosene lantern into his lungs.

This wasn't Abby's fault. It was Kelly Childers and her manipulating and scheming. No, it wasn't. It was his fault, his ego and his temper that had caused him to lose her.

If only she'd waited, he would have explained. He'd fought and nearly died for Hidden Rock. Would he do less for the only woman he'd ever really loved?

He picked up the phone and called George McIvey. "I need a favor."

Chapter Twenty-Five

It was a sellout show. The Civic Center was overflowing with screaming fans. T-shirts, pictures, and books, water bottles, key chains, CDs, DVDs, and a hundred other items with Winslow's name and likeness being sold at the entrance.

Several radio stations were broadcasting outside and winners of their ticket giveaways were anxiously waiting to be sent backstage to have their picture taken with Winslow.

Abby looked in the mirror. Her butt looked big, her boobs looked small, and the cowboy boots she was wearing hurt to walk in. She'd tried it Winslow's way, after all he was a star, but she just couldn't do it.

She kicked off the boots, and stripped out of the cowgirl get up. She slid on her favorite second-hand sweater, a pair of tight-fitting jeans, and held up her orange stilettos. With a little cleaning and buffing, they still looked brand new. They had walked her into her future, just as Granny had told her they would, and tonight she was going to wear them onstage. "I hope you're onstage with me tonight, Granny. I'm terrified." She looked at the ceiling, talking toward heaven.

Tessa burst into her dressing room. "How are you doing, honey?" She squeezed Abby's hands, bouncing on her toes.

"I'm scared to death. Do you hear all those people?" She stared at her reflection again. "What if they don't like me? What if I forget the words?" She turned to Tessa, utter panic in her voice. "What if I can't sing? Maybe I sang it all out in rehearsal and I've got no voice left."

"Get a hold of yourself. I'd hate to have to slap you before you go on stage." Tessa led her to the makeup chair. "Take deep breaths." She started fluffing Abby's hair, then opened the makeup tray and began applying it as she talked. "This is what you want, and you're an amazing singer."

"I'm not sure that it is what I want anymore." Abby thought of Joe, of Hidden Rock, of the McIveys.

"Well, for the moment it is. You'll never know what might have been unless you go out there. I know you're thinking about Joe. He is going to be fine. I promise you."

Abby wasn't so sure.

"I'm not so sure I'll be fine without him." She missed him so much, and she'd wanted to share this moment with him so badly.

Tessa pulled back, holding a mascara wand. "He will be fine, and you two will work it out." She stabbed the wand into the mascara. "You want to spend the rest of your life with the likes of Billy Butcher, or broke and living in that cottage on the ranch? No, you don't." Tessa answered for her. "The good Lord gave you the voice of an angel for a reason. Now you're going to go out there and sing." She leaned in close to Abby a gorgeous smile covering her face. "Honey, life will take care of the rest." She dabbed gloss on Abby's lips.

Abby took in a deep breath and harshly rubbed her forehead.

Tessa nearly screamed, yanking Abby's hand away from her face. "Don't go rubbing any part of your face. That stage makeup is like putty." She poured a glass of water, handing it to Abby. "When you get done, we'll go to the hospital and you can argue with Joe."

A knock on the door ended their conversation. "It's Winslow."

"Come in."

Winslow burst into her dressing room, carrying a huge armful of bright red roses. "Whoa, don't you look gorgeous?"

He didn't look so bad himself. Dressed entirely in black and smelling wonderful, he planted a kiss on her cheek. "Don't look so worried. You are going to do great." He handed her the roses. "Just wanted to say break a leg."

"Do you really think that is such a smart thing to say to her?" Tessa's eyebrows went up.

Winslow laughed. "Probably not, but I am a man of tradition."

"Thank you."

"The Swinging Huskers are going on first. Then you'll be up." He looked at his watch and grabbed her hand. "I know what kind of talent is inside you, Abby. It's time you showed the world." He kissed her hand and left.

Tessa watched his butt as he left the dressing room. "He is a delicious man. I will regret not sleeping with him."

"Jack got in the way, huh?" Abby set the flowers on the dressing table.

Tessa grinned, not answering. Her cell phone rang.

"What? Jack, you are not making one whit of sense." Tessa rolled her eyes, looking at Abby as though Jack had been suddenly dumbstruck. "Honey, I'll be right there." She clicked the phone off. "I think I need to rescue Jack. Will you be all right?"

"I'm as good as I'm going to get."

Tessa gave her a long hug and left.

Abby stood in front of the mirror again. She straightened her sweater, smoothed her jeans, and posed with the cowboy hat propped on her head. Ugh, it looked dreadful. No matter how good they looked on Joe, Tessa, and Winslow, they looked ridiculous on her. She threw it onto a chair, and squeezed her toes tight inside the stilettos.

"Ms. Clark, time to go," the stage manager called through her door.

"Ladies and gentleman, King Management is proud to introduce a new talent who will be performing for the first time on our stage tonight. Please give a grand Wyoming round of applause to Abby Clark." The audience applauded.

The band played an intro as she started to walk on stage. Her legs stopped. They just freakin' stopped. She shook them out and just as they started to move, the spotlight flashed bright and warm in her face. Claps and whistles echoed and flashbulbs exploded. Her heartbeat was probably registering about a nine on the Richter scale.

"Thank you." She nodded to band and the melody began. The audience settled down.

The Swinging Huskers had been awesome, and coming on stage after them, this audience was going to expect a great performance. She prayed she could deliver.

Inhaling deeply, she closed her eyes, clasped her shaking hand around the microphone, and began the haunting lyrics of a song Winslow's music director had written for her.

"Thank you," she said to the crowd after finishing. Abby bowed several times to the never-ending applause. Flashbulbs lit up the auditorium and the band kept playing a small drumbeat, keeping time with the audience's applause.

"If Winslow doesn't mind, I'd like to do another song." The audience cheered long and loud. Abby glanced backstage at Winslow. Held up a hand and nodded for her to go right ahead.

"I'd like to sing it for someone," her voice broke. For long minutes, she couldn't speak. The audience became eerily quiet. This wasn't in her plan. She hadn't intended to do anything except sing her two songs and then run off the damn stage. Then her mouth opened.

"I'd like to sing it for someone who'll never hear it. It says things that, well, sometimes a song can say the things we can't. The song is my favorite country song, Tears."

She turned, seeing Winslow laugh backstage and giving her a thumbs up. The audience howled with approval, and the band kicked into the song. She squeezed her toes inside the orange stilettos, memories of Granny Martin sailed through her heart. The pain of losing Joe gripped her voice and the emotion covered the audience.

*****

In the back of the Civic Center, a pair of blue eyes watched her. The song ripped through his layers of pain, leaving only raw emotion. The song was for him, and at that moment, no one else except Abby existed in the world.

For all that had happened between him and Abby, he had no idea what the outcome of what he was about to do might be. It was either going to be the best or the worst day of his life.

The pain in his side was excruciating. He prayed the wound wouldn't start bleeding. A slow, swirling dizziness invaded his brain. He shrugged it away.

Mugs pawed at the carpet under his hooves and he didn't seem too happy to be wearing all the gaudy tack. If the horse decided to throw a fit, he wasn't physically well enough to control him.

George tugged on the horse's reins, leading the horse into the auditorium. If ever there was a time in Joe's life when he hoped the universe was going to treat him kindly, this was it.

Abby finished the song to a standing ovation. The stage lights went down. Jack and Tessa had helped him arrange this moment. A spotlight burst out on Abby's face. She looked totally confused, like a panicked filly in a thunderstorm. The horse's shoes echoed a rhythmic clip-clop as he slowly walked down the center aisle of the auditorium. George had brought Mugs, helped him on the horse, and now turned the reins over to Joe and stepped aside.

He sat astride the huge stallion. The horse glowed from his shiny fur to the high polish on his hooves. The delicately hand-tooled leather halter, reins, and bit were polished to a high sheen. Mug's saddle was pure old West, exquisitely tooled leather with inlaid silver and Mother-of-Pearl.

The microphone dropped from her hands. The audience was nearly silent with only a few whispers filling the darkened auditorium.

"Abby Clark." He had a small microphone pinned to his shirt. The little thing sure did amplify. He swallowed hard. He patted the horse's neck. "Help me out here buddy."

Mugs snorted, his magnificent head bouncing high.

"Abby, it's almost sunset." He rode to the front of the stage. Mugs pawed the ground and snorted. "I want to know if you'll marry me and ride off into that sunset with me and the nag here?" The audience was completely silent as they held their collective breath.

Tears streamed down her face. Her hands went to her mouth.

"Yes." Abby rushed to the edge of the stage and slid into the saddle behind him.

The audience came to their feet. Whistles, cheers, applause, and flashbulbs erupted across the auditorium. Mugs snorted, head held high, his long black mane shining in the spotlight.

"I love you, Joe Baer." She whispered in his ear, planting a kiss on his cheek.

"I love you." He tucked her arms around his waist. Nudging the horse gently, they rode outside the auditorium just in time for a dazzling Wyoming sunset.

Chapter Twenty-Six

Winter had given way to spring. The fields surrounding Hidden Rock were a vibrant green with ankle-high sprouts of wheat, corn, and hay. Across the valley, large masses of delicate, early spring wildflowers were in full bloom. Dozens of birds had returned, and their chatter vibrated across the canyons.

Hidden Rock Ranch was warm, busy, and full of life, more life than usual. The ranch was about to host a wedding.

The rock grotto was brimming with small strings of lights, white, billowy bunting, and vases of lavender tucked into small crevices. The lavender was Abby's wedding present. Joe had planted nearly five acres of it for her.

Dozens of folding chairs lined each side of the middle aisle and candles sparkled within the crevices of the grotto.

"Oh, Abby, you look really beautiful." Margaret nearly cried when she saw her.

"It was Joe's mother's dress. Do you like it?" The wedding dress was ivory, lace and struck her just below the knees, with a scoop neckline, long lace sleeves, and a fitted bodice that fell gently into a full skirt. A short veil with a hand-tatted edge fell in soft folds around her face.

Tessa fastened a strand of pearls around Abby's neck. "These were my momma's. That should cover the part about having something borrowed."

Margaret took Abby's hands. "I know you don't have family, so George wanted to know if you would like for him to walk you down the aisle."

Abby sat slowly on the edge of the bed, trying hard not to cry. These people whose lives she'd fallen into had become her family. They cared about her. They wanted her to be a part of their lives.

"Margaret, tell George I would be honored to have him walk me down the aisle."

Margaret kissed her forehead. "You've got a good man there, Abby. I know he'll make you happy."

"On the days he don't drive you nuts." Tessa's voice of reality made them laugh.

*****

Joe fidgeted as Connor tried to fix his tie.

"Hold still. You're worse than a two-year-old."

Joe sighed, standing still.

"There, all fixed. Now, I have to pin these flowers onto you."

"Need some help?" Matt limped into the room.

"No crutches?" Joe leaned his head around Connor to get a look.

"The doctor put a walking splint on just in time for the wedding." Matt pulled up the leg of his suit so they could see.

"How'd Ben take you coming to this wedding?" Joe finally took the boutonniere from Connor and pinned it on himself.

"He pretty much wrote me off at the hospital, and I think he's a little too busy with some of Kelly's creditors to have much to do with me. It seems she did rack up hefty debts and most of it wasn't from banks." They both smiled and nodded. "In fact, he may have to mortgage his ranch to get them off her back."

"This day just keeps getting better." Connor slapped him on the shoulder.

Joe saw Mike usher in Tom and Naomi. Abby must have invited them. She was intent on having all the family together.

Naomi made her way to Joe. "I'm very glad you invited us. I know things have been difficult between you and Tom." She kissed him on the cheek. "I hope you find as much love with Abby as I have with Tom."

"Thank you. I just wish Tom had told me the truth from the beginning." He'd learned of the whole water fiasco just after he'd asked Abby to marry him. If only Tom had come to him, things might have worked out better. He looked over at Connor with Mike and George and thought about Abby who would soon be his wife. No, things had worked out just fine. He extended a hand to Tom. "I'm glad you're here today."

Tom bypassed his hand, giving him a bear hug. "I'm honored to be part of your day."

"Folks, if you'd all take your places, we need to get started." The minister ushered them into the grotto. Nearly the entire town sat in chairs facing the old stone. "Looks like you got the girl, cowboy." Winslow extended his hand. "You take damn good care of her."

"You can count on it." Joe nervously made his way to the front of the room joining Connor, and Matt. They wore black western suits, dove grey shirts, and bolero ties. Joe smiled at how they looked like uncomfortable ten-year-old boys with their perfectly combed hair, and the hands neatly folded in front of them.

Winslow took a seat beside Jack Spencer. Rodney sat on the far side of the room sending looks of death to Jack. Tessa had dumped him. No matter how much he begged or blamed it on the booze, she was done with him.

The minister nodded to the back of the room as the wedding march began, played solo on a single wooden flute by a member of the Shoshone tribe.

Tessa entered the grotto first, sending Jack a wink as she walked past, standing across from Connor at the front.

*****

George stood with Abby for a minute before rounding the corner into the grotto. "Look at that, Goldie Locks." He peeked into the grotto. "It's the three Baer's waiting on you." Abby laughed a little too loud and the room turned to stare.

"And one of them is just right." She kissed his cheek.

The guests stood. The cowboys from the ranch all pulled at their ties, pulled at their jackets, and didn't know what to do with their hands. They folded them, stuck them in pockets pulled them out, folded their arms across their chest. Abby wondered how quickly after the ceremony they'd all be back in jeans. Margaret had sneaked to her seat beside Naomi Talking Horse.

At the front of the room was Joe.

His suit jacket fit snug over his shoulders, his dark hair was perfectly combed, and his blue eyes were inviting. Right here, right now her world was absolutely perfect.

Abby smiled at him as George led her into the room.

*****

"Breathe, Joe." Connor whispered.

Joe took in a deep gulp of air. Everyone else in the room disappeared as she walked down the aisle. Her smile rocked his world. He never expected to feel the way he did at this moment. He'd made fun of friends when they talked about seeing their wife in that gown. She looked like an angel. Her hair was down, curled softly, her face was radiant, and those large, sexy eyes were fixed on him.

George slipped her hand into Joe's, then slid into a seat next to Margaret.

The minister smiled at them, opened the Bible, cleared his throat and just as he started to speak, he stopped. His eyes went to the back of the crowd. All heads turned as Dark Water entered the grotto.

Tom left his seat to help the elder member of his tribe. Dark Water nodded and continued without assistance. In his hands, he carried a tribal wedding vase, an urn with two spouts made from dark clay, ornately decorated with tribal designs in ochre, turquoise, and burnt orange. Slowly and with determined effort, he walked to Joe and Abby.

"The water freely given from Hidden Rock Ranch has given my people renewed lifeblood." He held the urn high in the air. "I have blessed the water in this wedding urn. Water is a gift from the Great Spirit. Love is a gift from the Great Spirit. Drink the water from Earth Mother as she blesses your union." His head lowered and in whispered native dialect, he offered a prayer and a blessing.

Joe accepted the urn. "Thank you, Dark Water. I am honored at your blessing." Tom escorted him to a seat of honor in the front row.

Each one took a drink. Matt took the urn and they faced the minister once again.

"Do you, Joseph Larsen Baer, take Abby Lee Clark to be your lawfully wedded wife? To have and to--"

Screams erupted from the back of the room, chairs collapsed, and the sound of ripping bunting echoed off the rock.

"Mooooooo."

Joe's shoulders sank. Abby moaned, afraid to turn around.

"Moooo."

She looked up at Joe, "Its Frosty isn't it?"

"Yeap."

The wedding guests were fleeing in terror as the huge Black Angus bull charged through the crowd.

"Reverend?" Joe said.

The man stood with his mouth hanging open and the Bible very nearly ready to fall from his hands.

The huge bull stopped just inches from Abby.

"Moooooo." It nudged her on the butt.

"Stop it Frosty."

"Moooooo."

She patted his head.

"Reverend?" Joe snapped his fingers. "Reverend, can you just get to the I do's?"

The reverend nodded. "Do you, Joe?"

"I do."

"Do you, Abby?"

"I do." She smiled.

Frosty began to eat Abby's bouquet.

"I now pronounce you man and wife." The reverend took two steps back as Frosty nudged forward, chomping down a vase of flowers.

"Uh, kiss."

"I love you, Abby Baer." He whispered against her lips.

"I love you, too."

"MOOOOO!"

The End

Connect with Jocie McKade

WEBSITE
www.jociemckade.com

EMAIL
jcmckade@gmail.com

FACEBOOK
http://www.facebook.com/jocie.mckade.9

PINTEREST
http://www.pinterest.com/jociemckade9/

GOODREADS
https://www.goodreads.com/goodreadscomjociemckade

TWITTER
https://twitter.com/JocieMcKade

About Jocie McKade

Jocie McKade is an Amazon bestselling author, a freelance writer whose work has appeared in numerous publications and she is the editor of several online sites.

She lives on what she affectionately (most days it's affectionate, some days, not so much) calls Dust Bunny Farm. Knocking back a water-tower sized coffee, and with Diesel the Wonder Dog she crafts stories while watching ArnoldSwartzaweeds grow with impunity in her garden.

You can give Jocie a holler at her website. She loves to hear from readers.

53839864R00132

Made in the USA
Charleston, SC
19 March 2016